PRAISE FOR ROBERT PACILIO

Praise for *Whitewash*

Whitewash is a slow-burn kind of novel, one that allows the reader to take in and really consider the issues at hand. With all the controversy and outbursts one expects in a courtroom drama, we follow the case through the eyes of Tony Rossi, a former high-school teacher, and we meet his fellow jurors and get to understand how they will eventually decide the fate of the defendant. I was very much a thirteenth juror as I read this book, struggling between my own ideals and the need to make a fair and just decision. A thought-provoking and enjoyable read.

— MICHELLE LOVI, ODYSSEY PUBLISHING

D1601517

Praise for *Meet Me at Moonlight Beach*

Robert Pacilio's *Meet Me at Moonlight Beach* is not a romance novel, but there is a lot of love in it. *Meet Me at Moonlight Beach* is about finding the love story you deserve long after you have given up on happy endings. It has been almost a decade since he retired from teaching, but Pacilio's second chapter has an awful lot in common with his first. He still believes in the power of words. He still loves a good redemption arc. And once he's said his piece, he hopes his audience understands a little bit more about themselves and the world around them, and that they will learn to love what they see.

— KARLA PETERSON, COLUMNIST, *SAN DIEGO UNION TRIBUNE*

Praise for *The Restoration*

Robert Pacilio's aptly named third book, *The Restoration*, does as it says. Set in the romance of the Art Deco styled Village Theater on historical Coronado Island, its characters emerge from the devastation of loss and the hopelessness left by the Vietnam War to new beginnings, unexpectedly. The warmth of the Southern California sun and the strength of the human spirit make it a nourishing and satisfying read.

— SANDRA GONNERMAN, SAN DIEGO COUNTY/HUMBOLDT COUNTY SCHOOLS LIBRARIAN, RETIRED

Praise for *Meetings at the Metaphor Cafe*

Oft-quoted American scholar and eternal optimist, William Arthur Ward once said, 'The mediocre teacher tells. The good teacher explains. The superior teacher demonstrates. The great teacher inspires.' We have found in *Meetings at the Metaphor Café* a great teacher, Mr. Buscotti. The descriptions of Mr. B's and Ms. Anderson's curriculum is enough to make anyone want to go back to school, re-read old favorites like *To Kill A Mockingbird* or at the very least, listen to some Bruce Springsteen! Every student deserves at least one teacher like this; a teacher who is passionate about the world we live in and determined to light a fire in each child. This debut novel rings with authenticity. This book is a must for anyone looking for a little meaning and a lot of inspiration, whether you are a new teacher or a lifelong student.

— BaBette Davidson, CEO of Programming for
Public Television – PBS

If you are an English teacher—particularly American literature—you would want to read this novel right along with your students. *Meetings at the Metaphor Café* *will* challenge the minds and hearts of teenagers everywhere.

— Bruce Gevirtzman, author of *An Intimate Understanding of America's Teenagers*

Meetings at the Metaphor Cafe reads like an invitation ... an invitation to sit down amongst its characters and relive your youth. With the turn of every page, you are transported back to a time when the world was new to you, sitting among friends, sipping a latte, discussing love and the meaning of things, and discovering life all over again like it was the first time. Along with the characters, the readers are sent on a journey toward rediscovering themselves and reconnecting with what really matters at the heart of who they are. All the while, the book reads like a who's who and what's what of the 20th century. As a teacher, I can say that this book is a MUST read for any high school English or history class. *Meetings at the Metaphor Cafe* should be in the hands of every teenager in America, and those of anyone who once was one!

— DANIELLE GALLUCCIO, TRINITY MONTESSORI
SCHOOL, ADOLESCENT ACADEMY DIRECTOR

I thoroughly enjoyed this book. Mr. Pacilio inspires the reader to be a better person and gives us faith in our new generation of youth. The take-home messages, however, engage a much wider audience and offer life lessons that build resilience and encourage a positive outlook on life, encouraging both youth and adults to make a difference in our society. This book is a must read for students, educators, and all the people who believe in positive change.

— MICHELE EINSPAR, DIRECTOR, TRANSFORMATIVE
INQUIRY DESIGN FOR EFFECTIVE SCHOOLS

Praise for *Midnight Comes to the Metaphor Café*

Wonderful! "Midnight Comes to the Metaphor Café" was every bit as enjoyable as the Robert Pacilio's first work, "Meetings at the Metaphor Café." Robert Pacilio further develops his characters as Maddie, Mickey, Rhia and Pari prepare to face life after high school. It is a sensitive account of the issues, hopes, and fears of young adults preparing to enter the world.

— Debbie Szamus, Class of '85

The way the book immerses you into the minds of students about to make a tough decision as to what path they will take that will lead them to their future as they make the first decision that is really on their own in terms of going to college.

— Zack Markowitz, Class of '09, Serving in the Coast Guard

I read, and re-read, Mr. Pacilio's *Meetings at the Metaphor*, so I was ecstatic when I discovered that he had written a sequel. I see so much of myself in each of the main characters in the story that, in a way, their story has become my own. As Mr. Buscotti encouraged our quartet of protagonists to find and follow their North Star, he encouraged me to do the same.

— Caela Provost, University of Limerick, Ireland

Midnight Comes to the Metaphor Cafe is a testament to the possibilities of great teaching and the bounty in mind and spirit it can generate in young people. It is chicken soup for the teacher's soul.

— Mark McWilliams, Michigan Special Needs Advocate and Law Professor

To Laura

WHITEWASH

ROBERT PACILIO

*Thank you
for your support.

Robert Pacilio*

Whitewash

Robert Pacilio

Editing, cover design, and pre-publishing assistance by Michelle Lovi of Odyssey Publishing.

Cover photography by Wesley Tingey via Upsplash.

Author photo by Robert Bjorkquist.

ISBN: 979-8-541668-98-8 (paperback)

ALSO BY ROBERT PACILIO

<u>Novels</u>

Meetings at the Metaphor Café

Midnight Comes to the Metaphor Café

The Restoration

Meet Me at Moonlight Beach

———

"The Secrets of Generation NeXt": *Listen Magazine*

Whitewash, a readers theater

Seventeen, a play

"La Petite Café at Midnight New Years Eve": *Creative Communications*
Top Ten Poems by American Teachers

Dedicated to my students at Mount Carmel High School who trusted in me and brought to life these characters in the Readers Theater version of Whitewash.

WHITEWASH

BLACK'S LAW DICTIONARY

Inciting a riot: In criminal law. A tumultuous disturbance of the peace by three persons or more, assembling together of their own authority with an intent mutually to assist each other against any who shall oppose.

1

THE SUMMONS

He stepped off the train gingerly holding on to the steel handrail for support. His knees were still stiff from the forty-minute ride. His summons was the most recent bookmark for the novel he was reading. He checked to see if his cell phone remained in his jacket pocket. His wallet in his left trouser pocket. His ball cap and sunglasses snuggled under his arm pit. He buttoned his blue sports coat. This morning was unlike any one in the last three decades.

He stopped at the entrance of the Santa Fe Train Depot and pulled out his phone which had a post-it stuck to it. The directions. He scrolled to his favorites. The short list made clear his priorities. Top of the list: Deborah. He messaged her: *Downtown. All good. I'll text when I know something.* He then glanced at the post-it and oriented himself. The sun was east. Broadway was to his left. Head straight down there for four blocks.

The Southern District Federal Courthouse will be on the right. Anthony Rossi didn't need to Google it on his phone like his daughter had advised when she called yesterday. Pencil and paper. Old School.

He heard the protesters before he saw the building. He

expected this, although the group seemed larger, around twenty-five people were milling about. The signs were a hodge-podge of proclamations: BLACK LIVES MATTER; PROTECT THE FIRST AMENDMENT; FREE SPEECH / NOT HATE SPEECH.

There were flags, as well. Versions of the American flag. Some were upside-down. Rossi noticed some of them had a blue stripe rather than a red one in the middle. He wondered what that was about. Some flags were black and white. There were more than a few yellow 'Don't tread on me' Tea Party flags. By and large, the groups kept to their own side of the street and acted docile, even sleepy. Rossi wondered when had they first arrived.

He strode to the entrance where a security line formed. Just like at the airport. He removed the usual suspects. Jacket. Shoes. Belt. He emptied his pockets. The armed policewoman asked for his ID and his summons. The tension was palpable. Rossi figured the protesters had to have put the officers on guard, or perhaps this was standard operating procedure in a Federal building. He thanked the officer and managed to get a polite smile from her in return.

He knew exactly what would happen next. The moment he stepped through the metal detector, the red lights overhead would illuminate. Two male officers gave him the freeze signal. Rossi had already stopped.

"It's my knees, Officers. Knee replacement." Rossi said calmly.

"Step aside, sir, and follow me."

Rossi complied. The one officer used his wand and also patted him down. The wand clicked loudly at his kneecaps. The other officer again asked for ID and his summons. Rossi could not tell if they were going to let him through or not. It must be the beard.

"Officer, my driver's license is rather old. I had a beard then ..." He was cut off.

"We know. You can proceed." No hint of smile this time.

He headed up to the second floor like the summons instructed. Room 210. The room was not nearly as large as rooms that he had previously entered when his jury summons was for the California state court. The chairs looked as if they were fairly new, plush. The room had a ceremonial feel as if perhaps the Mayor or some such official would be making an appearance. Instead, the clerk, a woman in her forties, in an understated beige dress with a light blue scarf was at the front waiting for the last of the jurors to be seated. There was a screen that quietly lowered behind her.

The other jurors sat at attention—the atmosphere of the proceedings demanded a seriousness Rossi had not experienced in all his years coming to jury duty. No one was reading a newspaper or a book. All eyes were on the clerk. The room filled up quickly. Rossi tried to estimate how many were there. Maybe one hundred.

The clerk began. "I am Susan Dorsey. I want to thank you for your willingness to serve our nation here in the Southern District of California. My staff and I will do all we can to accommodate you. We hope that you will find this experience rewarding. I can see some of you have cell phones and there are a few laptops. These are permitted; however, prior to entering a courtroom you must turn OFF your cell phone, laptop, and all electronic devices. You may bring a laptop computer but keep in mind there are no internet connections available in the courthouse or in this jury assembly room."

Rossi saw a few eyebrows raised. He assumed that those people had not carefully read their summons that made it clear that attention would be paid to the proceedings. Susan Dorsey continued. "In a moment I will begin a short video that explains, from the viewpoint of previous jurors, how important your service is. It will also go into the step-by-step functions of a federal criminal jury trial. After which I will call the first pool of jurors for today's trial. It will consist of 40 of you. It is quite likely that a second pool of 40 ... even a third pool may be required. If the judge instructs us that the jury has been seated, you will be excused from duty. This video is approximately twenty minutes long. We very much value your time and your effort at insuring justice be served. Thank you for your attention." She gave a polite, practiced smile. With that, the room darkened and the video began.

———

Deborah Rossi was preparing to leave for the YMCA's yoga class when she received her husband's text. She closed her eyes and took a deep breath. She walked back to the kitchen table and washed out her coffee pot, but her mind was occupied with the first column of the front page of the newspaper. She sat down and read, for the third time, the article that appeared above the fold.

"*The* San Diego Union-Tribune: *October 2, 2017: The Associated Press reports that the trial of George 'Duke' Ellis on the charge of 'inciting a riot' has been moved from Riverside, California to the County of San Diego. The trial will proceed at the Federal Courthouse of the Southern District of California in the County of San Diego. This was a mutual agreement reached by both the defense and prosecution.*

"*Mr. Ellis's lawyer, James Devlin, has reiterated that his client is innocent of the charge and will be fully exonerated by the court. The prosecution of the case has been handed off to Jean Peters, the United States Attorney for the Southern District. Mr. Ellis faces up to five years in prison if convicted.*

"*Early indications point to a 'show trial' according to legal experts from the American Civil Liberties Union, claiming that the trial will be a test case for the application of the First Amendment as it pertains to 'racially charged language' and 'election campaigns.'*

"Already media frenzy has developed over the fact that Mr. Ellis lost his bid for the United States Congressional seat in November of 2016. Ellis contends that his campaign faced racial bias and left-wing media attacks that may have influenced the results of the election. Mr. Ellis, who is white, lost the Congressional election to the African American incumbent Congressman James Curtis by a mere two percentage points. Mr. Ellis intends to run again in 2018 if he is acquitted.

"The jury selection is set to begin today."

Deborah Rossi tapped her fingernails on the table and tried to shake off her feeling of apprehension. When the summons arrived a month ago, they had discussed delaying his service. She knew her husband would insist on serving. But postponing jury duty would likely complicate their travel plans to finally visit Italy. It would be their first vacation since retiring. His parting words to her before he left that morning to take the southbound train from Encinitas were, "What are the chances?"

Indeed.

———

Susan Dorsey took to the podium and read the forty names alphabetically. She skipped over Rossi. She asked those jurors to follow her assistant out the main doors. Rossi noticed that some who stood to leave seemed eager, others pensive. Those seated generally looked relieved. Rossi was not sure how he felt. He had never served on a jury, never even had he stepped into a courtroom before. He had pretended to for decades as he reenacted various scenes from the books he taught his students—primarily Atticus Finch, the icon of attorneys, that Harper Lee created in 1960 when she penned *To Kill a Mockingbird*.

Rossi had always been an avid reader of John Grisham
novels and courtroom dramas of his youth on television like
Perry Mason. It always seemed so thrilling to seek 'justice for
all.' But truth be told, Rossi knew that justice is often both blind
and bland. Tedious. Bogged down in legal rigmarole. His attention snapped back to Susan Dorsey.

Ms. Dorsey continued. "I will likely be back within the hour
or so to call for another pool of jurors. Please remain close to
this room. There is a coffee cart located out the main doors. You
may have noticed it as you entered." Dorsey paused and for the
first time she warmed to her task. "I must say that the coffee is
quite good and the pastry compliments it well ... for those
inclined." A flash of lightness. "Thank you for your attention ...
please secure your juror badges, Security here at the courthouse is rather heightened as you likely were aware when you
entered."

A juror raised his hand. Dorsey acknowledged him. "Yes. A
question?"

"Are we being considered for the trial I've read about? The
Duke Ellis trial?"

She stiffened. "I am never at the liberty to reveal such
information."

Rossi knew that the question was inappropriate.

He also knew that it touched a nerve.

2

THE JURY POOL

Susan Dorsey was true to her word on several counts. The coffee excellent. The Danish delicious. In exactly an hour she was back at the podium reading another list of jurors. The last name called was Anthony Rossi.

The group followed her assistant out the main entrance and through a long corridor, then left to another shorter hallway until they reached the paneled doors of Department 2. The bailiff stood guard and the assistant took her cue from him.

"Please enter quietly and take seats on your right," he instructed them. He entered with them solemnly as each juror took their seats. Rossi took in the scene. There were five rows of seats that could hold perhaps seventy people. He assumed it was for the observers. To his far left up front was the jury box. In it, he counted seven people. There were two seats adjacent to the jury. Directly in front of him were the lawyers, he assumed. They stood for the entire time it took for the pool of jurors to gain their seats. They were all smiles.

Rossi quickly surveyed the apparent line up of attorneys. On the left, closer to the jury box, stood a tall, elegant woman. Her light gray business suit shimmered. Her jewelry was subtle.

Pearl necklace. Silk white blouse. She was nearest to the center aisle of the courtroom. At her table to her left, another attorney with a reddish beard faced them. He did not make consistent eye contact with the jury pool. He glanced down at his legal pad and then back up again at the new potential jurors.

To their right and closest to the center aisle was a dapper, handsome attorney. He wore a three-piece gray suit adorned with a burgundy tie. Rossi couldn't help but think that this attorney struck a pose worthy of being on the cover of GQ. He tugged his sleeves so that each was perfectly distanced from his suit coat. At the end of the table stood a man whom Rossi could best describe as 'beefy.' He seemed to barely fit in his black suit —all muscle and ready to burst the seams. His smile was forced.

There was a podium in the center that was tilted so it faced the jury but within the range of what appeared to be the witness stand nearby. The judge's bench was empty. A door on the far upper right opened and a different, younger male bailiff entered, followed swiftly by another man wearing a dark blue suit and a bold red tie. His hair was pitch black, obviously dyed, presumably to make him seem younger. Like all the others he smiled and appeared at ease—almost cocky. Rossi's eyes were not deceived by his colored hair—the man's complexion was that of someone closer to Rossi's age—sixty-five, at least. He took his place with the twosome, edging his way between the attorney closest to the podium and the man standing beside him.

Then the bailiff who had met the pool of jurors at the door walked to the front of the courtroom, stepped up to the side of the judge's raised dais and bellowed, "All rise. This court is now in session. The Honorable Judge Paul Lewis presiding."

Through the door nearest to the jury appeared a diminutive man. He was completely bald and wore thick glasses that brought attention to his eyes. Despite the lack of hair on the top of his head, he wore a salt and pepper beard in the shape made famous by Lincoln, with sideburns coming down to a pointy tip at his chin; no mustache ala the legendary president, and the glasses disguised the fact that his eyebrows were also non-existent. He seemed to be at least fifty years old. He didn't smile until he reached the zenith of his climb to the judge's bench.

Judge Lewis did not need his microphone. His voice boomed off the walls. "Jurors, this trial will likely take two weeks to complete." He thanked the potential jurors for their willingness to serve and told them that he would be asking them a few preliminary questions before either set of attorneys would question each juror.

He got right to business. "I want each of you to consider if you have had a negative view or experience with officers of the law, including the FBI, or if any family members were employed with the police force."

Judge Lewis was calm and he chose his words carefully. "The first and foremost issue each of you must consider is if you can commit to a trial that could last several weeks. I know that the jury questionnaire has already touched on this point; however, in my experience, when a person is put in the position of a formal and firm commitment of time, second thoughts may arise. Please consider what this court is asking of you. Please raise your hands if this commitment of two weeks will pose a difficulty for you or if you feel compromised due to a relationship with law enforcement."

Rossi wondered how many in his pool would try to avoid serving. Surprisingly, only eight hands in his pool were raised. The judge asked each person why they could not make a commitment. A couple said that they had family members who were associated with the police and that they weren't comfortable being on this jury. Another told the judge, "Sir, two weeks is a long commitment for a self-employed person like me."

Eventually, the eight were dismissed, leaving thirty-two of

them in the pool. Then the judge called out several names and those people sat in the jury box. Rossi remained in the gallery.

Judge Lewis spoke to each newly seated juror, all seven. He explained that the last two called could be alternates. He wanted to be sure they understood the responsibilities of being on a jury—being impartial, open-minded and such.

Then the lawyers got involved. Both sides questioned each person regarding their views concerning issues that seemed applicable, like trusting the police. They excused jurors if they implied that they might not be able to put aside feelings on the subject of race. Did they ever feel threatened by people of color? Had they felt any hostility toward people with different religious views from their own?

One juror naively asked one of the attorneys, "You mean like if I think the Muslim ban is a good thing? Because I do. I mean, I just can't forget 9-11." He was excused as were all but one of the seven who were first called. Rossi noticed that the jurors who had been seated in the box before they entered seemed bored and antsy.

Rossi heard seven more names called, and seven more. To him, jurors were dropping like flies. Each lawyer seemed to want just the right person sitting in that box. The lawyers, who were very polite, used their challenge for cause over and over. If Judge Lewis had an issue with a juror who seemed to be getting cold feet, he would excuse them, as well.

After an hour and a half, there were only ten left in the pool of forty; however, there remained three seats left to fill. Judge Lewis called both sets of lawyers to his bench and then explained to all that it was time to break for lunch. He understood how patient everyone was and commended all. He reminded all jurors and those in the jury pool to not discuss the proceedings with each other. They would reconvene in an hour and a half. He told the group of jurors, including Rossi's pool to follow the directions of his bailiff, whom the Judge called Henry, who would give everyone special instructions.

All rose as the judge left the bench. The jurors gathered at the jury box and followed the bailiff out the same door that the judge had used. The lawyers all remained standing ... and smiling.

Bailiff Henry Lamont was a stout black man whose hair had begun to transition from black to white. His goatee, however, was pearl white. Juxtaposed to his skin, he was striking and perhaps fierce looking. Rossi felt that he had to be the senior-most officer of the court. He carried himself accordingly, with an air that implied *Listen to me, People. Don't screw up.* Visually, he personified authority: however, his voice belied that. Rather, his tone carried the utmost concern for the jurors, as if they were his charges. And they were.

"Folks, I'd like you to remove your badges if, I say if, you are planning on leaving this building. When returning, use the main entrance. Eating establishments will be around the corner down Broadway. You might not want to wander too far, folks. Time flies when you are having fun." This was Henry's attempt at humor. Rossi appreciated it. It had been hours of tension and tedium. "Some of you may choose to stay here. That's fine. The coffee cart 'becomes' a lunch cart about now. It's not bad. I have a count of you all, and we will take roll here at exactly 1 pm. Any questions? No. All right." And that was that.

The first thing Anthony Rossi did was call Deborah.

"What's happening? Are you on a jury? Is it the Duke Ellis case, Anthony?" Deborah's voice hinted a note of trepidation.

"Well, I don't know."

"What? Don't know what?"

"All I know is that I have an hour or so to eat lunch and there are three seats left to fill on the jury ... and there are eleven of us to fill it." Rossi tried to be calm and collected, but

the excitement in his voice did not mirror his wife's tone of
trepidation.

"Is it the Duke Ellis case?"

"I don't know that ... but I assume so by the questions."
Rossi hesitated to say more. Was it allowed?

"Oh, great! Anthony, please let me know as soon as you
know something." She decided not to tell him about what she
was watching on the midday local news.

"I will. Don't worry."

"Okay. Fine. Go eat. Remember call me, don't just text." She
ended the call and grabbed the remote. She changed the
channel to CNN.

They were 'LIVE' covering the protest on Broadway.

3

CNN

D eborah stared at the screen. The morning anchor had asked the local reporter for the background behind the protests outside the Southern District of California's Federal Courthouse. "Well, the protest here in San Diego deals with the trial of George Ellis, often referred to as 'Duke.' He was arrested on the evening of September 17th ... four days after what Riverside County police described as a 'riot' that Duke Ellis arguably incited. That so-called riot in question occurred on September 13th at the home of incumbent Congressman James Curtis, who is part of the House of Representatives Black caucus. That night several men were arrested at the scene. They were charged with various accounts of vandalism, disturbing the peace, and hate crimes."

Deborah reached for her phone to send a group text to her three children: *I don't know if Dad is on the jury yet. He might be. He thinks it might be the Duke Ellis trial. I'll let you know when I know. I'm watching CNN bc there are protests in front of the courthouse.*

The CNN reporter was now standing among the protesters. "Mr. Ellis has been charged as the instigator of the demonstration based on a 'rally' he held hours before. Ellis had been released on bail, and at the time, he continued campaigning for a Congressional seat in the Riverside district northeast of San Diego."

CNN had already begun another interview with a DC lawyer who was explaining. "According to the ACLU's website, 'In 1978, the ACLU took a controversial stand for free speech by defending a neo-Nazi group that wanted to march through the Chicago suburb of Skokie, where many Holocaust survivors lived.' So, the ACLU, along with right-wing news organizations, is believed to be financing the legal defense of Mr. Ellis. I read a quote from the United States Attorney for the Southern District, Jean Peters, who told the *Los Angeles Times*, 'It seems that politics makes for strange bedfellows.'"

Deborah Rossi decided she had heard enough. She knew two things were certain. Her husband would want to be on that jury. She also knew that made her very nervous.

4

INTERROGATION

There were three jury seats and two alternate seats left when Rossi was brought back to the courtroom. Judge Lewis seemed a little perturbed that this was going on for so long and apologized to everyone.

Perhaps due to the judge's tone, both sets of lawyers huddled, and when the next six jurors were called, the pace of questions turned brisk. Three of them were dismissed for cause. Three of them filled the final seats in the jury box.

Rossi was conflicted. At this point he wanted to serve, but then again, he was relieved.

Then Judge Lewis made Rossi's stomach flip. "Would Anthony Rossi come to the alternate seat for questioning?"

Rossi rose and followed the bailiff's directions. Judge Lewis explained the role of the two alternates. They must be here for the entire trial; however, they would not participate in the deliberations. This would change if any of the jurors could not continue to serve. "Can you fulfill that commitment, Mr. Rossi?" Judge Lewis asked.

"Yes, Your Honor."

"Fine. The attorneys will ask you the same questions they

have asked the previous jurors. You are required to answer honestly as I am sure you will. The defense will question you first. Mr. Devlin, you may proceed." Judge Lewis fiddled with his paperwork and nodded to the table that Rossi assumed was the defense team.

Devlin smiled and asked for Rossi's occupation. "I am a retired history and English teacher. I taught high school. I taught for thirty-three years and just recently retired with my wife ... who was also a teacher."

"Happy to hear it, Mr. Rossi. And congratulations on your long career. I am sure your students enjoyed your lessons." He smiled and added, "I assume a two-week stint in a Federal courtroom was not in your retirement plans."

For the first time there was a ripple of laughter.

Rossi let the laughter settle. "No, sir. But I am honored to serve."

"I see." A pause. "Mr. Rossi, you taught history. American history?"

"Yes, sir."

"Then you taught your students about the First Amendment ... the freedom to speak one's mind. Correct?

"Yes. I did. It is one of the Four Freedoms."

The attorney spun around to the judge and then back to Rossi. He seemed to feign surprise. Rossi thought he was being dramatic.

"You must realize how constitutionally vital freedom of speech is."

"I do."

"Did you feel as a teacher that you had the right, the duty, to explain both sides of issues that make up the history of this nation?"

"Yes, sir." Rossi cleared his throat. "When there are two sides."

"What do you mean, Mr. Rossi?"

"Well, there are certain facts that require the truth be told. For example, the Holocaust occurred. And so did discrimination toward African Americans during the Jim Crow era." Rossi knew the moment he said it that he was probably going to be dismissed. *They probably will think I'm too biased.*

The defense lawyer merely smiled. He took a moment to ponder his next question and stopped himself. "Absolutely, Mr. Rossi." Then he turned to Judge Lewis.

Rossi sat impassive.

Devlin again addressed Rossi. "I can tell your students must have had great respect for you." He pivoted and as he walked back to his table, he again regarded Judge Lewis, who was no longer fishing through his notes, but rather eyeing Rossi with a singular focus.

Devlin nodded towards the other table of lawyers and announced, "No further questions."

Rossi was not sure what that meant. However, he had no time to ponder his situation.

The judge pointed over to the table closer to Rossi. "Counselor Peters."

The prosecutor slowly strode to the podium. She asked, "Mr. Rossi, I share your views and also wish to commend your service to our school system. May I ask you your view of the Civil Rights Act?"

Rossi cocked his head. "Which one? Are you asking about both? The 1964 and 1968 Civil Rights Acts, I assume."

"Of course," she corrected herself and then grinned. "I was not trying to trick the teacher."

Again, a short burst of laughter. Rossi took a few seconds. "Both the Civil Rights Acts were necessary to ensure that all people are given equal treatment under the law ... of course, they were preceded by the 1866 landmark Civil Rights Act after the Civil War." Rossi figured he may as well go out in a blaze of historical glory.

"Yes, indeed. Mr. Rossi. I am sure your knowledge of this legislation is ... quite thorough, sir." She turned to the other lawyer at her table and walked over to him. He whispered to her. It was clear both were good poker players. In less than a minute, she turned to the judge. "This juror is acceptable to the prosecution, you honor. No further questions."

Judge Lewis nodded and looked again at the defense. The lawyer acquiesced with a nod in the affirmative. "Thank you, Mr. Rossi. Please take the first alternate seat."

Rossi was not sure if this was the best of times or the worst. He would have to be here, but he would be precluded from deliberating. *Well, I guess that is the best I can hope for.*

The second alternate came from one of the handful of members left from the jury pool. She sat next to Rossi and had a half-hearted smile. He understood.

As Judge Lewis huddled with the lawyers, a juror from the very first pool raised her hand to get the bailiff's attention.

Henry, the bailiff, leaned over the rail. The juror whispered something that Rossi could not understand, but it got the other juror's attention. Henry nodded and made a bee line to Judge Lewis.

The bailiff had the judge's full attention, as well as the two lawyers. Judge Lewis had never used his microphone. But after conferring with the others he announced, "Can I have your attention. I would ask each of the jury members, the alternates and the remaining members of the jury pool to step out of the courtroom and follow the bailiff. This will be a short break. I will need to speak with one of the jurors. Thank you all for your cooperation."

———

Deborah picked up the phone on the first set of chimes. "What's up, Anthony?"

"I really thought I would get excused, Deborah, but I wasn't even sure I wanted to be an alternate. It is nerve-racking, to tell you the truth."

"Wait. Are you on the jury? Where are you now ... you sound like you're walking." Deborah stood from the couch and began pacing. Times like these she never could sit. Energy took over and her body had to move.

"This is the first chance I had to call. Long story." Rossi caught his breath. His pace slowed as he came to his first intersection. "I am on the jury. And I am pretty sure that it is the Duke Ellis case."

"What do you mean, pretty sure?"

"Well, the judge told us it had been a long day and that tomorrow he would begin the trial and make all the introductions of the defendant and the lawyers ... wait ... I'm crossing the street now ... I'm going to catch the train so I have to hustle."

Deborah tried to settle him down. "Don't walk and talk, Anthony. At least I know you are on the jury. You can call me when you are on the train. Watch what you are doing." Then she hesitated but added, "Do you see the protesters?"

"That's another long story. But no. We were led out from an exit a block south of Broadway ... anyway, do you want me to call you when I am on the train or would you rather wait until you meet me at the train station?"

Deborah knew then that her husband would need to settle himself and so would she. She knew what she had to know for now. "Let's wait. I'll come get you and we'll discuss everything then. I'm sure you are tired and you seem frazzled. So slow down and I'll see you about what time?"

"Around 4:45 is when the train gets in. I'll text if the train is late. I'm doing fine. Just a little hyper from sitting all day. Okay?" Rossi had three long blocks to go before he reached the train station and hopped on the northbound train heading up the coast.

"Okay. Just relax. We can talk then ... I love you. Be careful. All right?"

"Love you, too. Bye."

Deborah clicked off the phone. She slumped on to the bar stool in the kitchen. She looked out her window to the west. It was an hour before sunset. If he had not been chosen, she would suggest going out for dinner. But now, she figured it was best to be home with him.

———

"Here's the crazy part. The other alternate and I were seated ... and all seemed to be good. The jury was set. But then the bailiff came over to speak with a juror ... I have no idea what that was about and before I knew it, the judge was emptying the courtroom ... except for the one juror who seemed to have a problem."

Deborah leaned closer on the kitchen's island as her husband sat on the bar stool facing her. Rossi inhaled as the day's drama passed between them. "Meanwhile, I'm thinking that this is the worst spot. I'd have to be there for two weeks and then not even be on the jury."

Deborah stopped tossing the salad. "Wait. What?

Rossi explained, "What I heard later as I was leaving was that a juror who was sitting in the box before we came into the courtroom asked the judge if he could say something in private to the court. So, as we left with the bailiff, we all looked around wondering, what is this about? We all went into the hallway and waited for about ten minutes. I looked at the bailiff. He had a look like I know what's going down. Then that juror comes out of the courtroom, goes past us in the hallway and he has a big smile on his face like he's so happy to be out of there."

"Shut up! So he talked his way off the jury?"

"It seems so. We went back into the courtroom and that's when the judge told me to sit in the last seat. I'm the 12th juror."

She dropped down to her bar stool, raised her eyebrows, and let out, "Stop it! Are you kidding me?"

"No, I'm not. Then both lawyers asked me questions again! I couldn't tell what they were thinking. But this time they seemed more interested in whether I had any reservations about a two-week commitment. Maybe that was the problem with that other juror. Who knows? I told them no. The defense attorney asked me if I understood the presumption of innocence. Of course, I told them I did. To tell you the truth, he asked that almost as if he knew it was something that I was more than familiar with ... you know, after what I said about the Civil Rights Acts. Anyway, that's when I think both sides, the lawyers I mean, seemed to be mulling me over because they both went to their tables and talked to their partners. I really thought I would get excused, Deborah."

"Well, they may have thought that you were too opinionated maybe." Deborah got out the salad bowls and stirred the hot water for the pasta. She was trying to balance between concerns about what her husband had committed to but also protective of him since she knew how the news had covered the protests that day. Not to mention what reporters were saying about the days to come.

"Anyway, the judge seemed impatient. I think the lawyers felt that if either kicked me off, they might just tick off the judge and maybe the other jurors. I mean, it was nearing four o'clock. Everyone was really getting anxious. Finally, the attorneys' whispering was interrupted when the judge cleared his throat and said, 'Counselors, if you are not going to object to this juror, then can we move on to name the second alternate ... please?'"

Rossi nibbled at his salad. "So the lawyers nodded. I

breathed a sigh of relief ... sort of. And in the next twenty minutes, they had the last alternate. The next thing I know, I'm on the train heading home."

Deborah shook her head and sighed. "Well, you did the right thing. I mean, I'm sure you are just the kind of person who should be on a jury." Then she poured red wine into their glasses and offered a toast. "Anyway, I guess our retirement will have to wait at least a few weeks. Cheers."

Their glasses touched as they took two sips of irony.

5

THE JURORS

The twelve jurors gathered at the door of Department 2 with the stoic bailiff Henry Lamont standing, arms behind his back, scrupulously overseeing the gaggle of reporters and photographers located down the corridor from the courtroom. It was now, it seemed to Anthony Rossi, that some of his fellow jurors realized the magnitude of this trial. He also noticed a second female bailiff at the other end of the hall, who was checking the credentials of the media. One burly man carried a shoulder-harnessed camera. He acted frustrated, perhaps bored as he grabbed one of the few benches; his chin had dropped to a depth that gave every indication of a lack of a good night's sleep.

Suddenly, the door was opened by the bailiff, and he gestured for the jury to enter the courtroom. Rossi was one of the last to enter. He first looked at the prosecutor and her male colleague, and further from the jury box, the three-member defense. All rose to greet them. Again, all smiles, like salespersons eyeing potential new car buyers stepping on to their lot. They remained standing until each of the jurors sat.

On the defense team's table, left of Devlin, was the portly

man, obviously dying his hair from a Just-for-Men box, his pale skin a sharp contrast to his hairline. Rossi thought that he was desperately trying to look younger than his early sixties. He wore what appeared to be the same dark blue suit and red tie, wide and exceedingly long. But this time a large American flag pin hoisted on to his lapel. Rossi assumed this was the defendant—Duke Ellis.

At the far end of the defense table, farthest away from the jury, was the younger man with a bodyguard's build. He gave the impression he'd rather be anywhere else but here, and he reminded Rossi that lawyers often have investigators working on the case seated with them. At least Perry Mason did, he thought, then he immediately scolded himself for this dated television cliché.

Placed on Rossi's seat, at the edge of the jury box closest to the lawyers, was a notebook labeled JUROR 12. He draped his blue sports coat over the back of his chair. If he was here to administer a fair, impartial verdict, Rossi assumed he would need to take notes and keep his thoughts and observations organized. To his surprise, he would soon find out that his notebook was never to leave the courtroom until deliberations.

While they had waited outside the courtroom, the jurors mostly seemed to avoid eye contact with each other. They each had the look of someone tensing up for confrontation. However, once seated, they warmed to their neighbors on their left and right. At least that was how Rossi perceived their behavior, which he thought odd in a way because some of them had sat most of the previous day in the same seats. He wondered if the fact that people were so often dismissed from the jury that maybe each person did not want to make any connection until the trial had started once and for all.

As he glanced over to the others and smiled, he took inventory of the eleven: he'd only witnessed the responses of the last four jurors since the first seven had been seated in the earlier pool during the morning session. He counted five women and seven men, including him. He considered that since the challenges for cause kept eliminating more and more jurors, maybe both attorneys were forced to accept the last seated jurors.

For example, Juror #11 was a black woman—the only African American on the jury. He guessed she was in her forties. When questioned the day before, she mentioned that she was a realtor, and she was dressed quite professionally, perhaps because it was the first day. He suspected that it may also be because she wanted to convey that serving on a jury was not just an obligation, but a duty she took seriously. Her burgundy pantsuit contrasted with some of the other jurors' outfits.

Next to her was another woman, Juror #10, a county librarian who appeared to be ready to take notes since her pen was already poised. Her short gray hair was cut in a manner that reminded him of the hairstyle Senator Elizabeth Warren wore. Like Rossi, she was dressed casually and comfortably, slacks, knit top and light sweater, ready for a long day of sitting. She was the first to smile and reach over to shake hands with both Rossi and the black juror, who introduced herself as Regina. The librarian reminded them her name was Jane. Jane explained that this was not her first time serving on a jury.

Regina quickly whispered, "I see we all have a notepad. I came prepared myself, but I guess they think we might not take notes, so this is a good reminder."

Rossi quipped, "Well, sometimes I doodle, too." And all three smiled.

Next to Jane was Juror #9, a stout Latino man with a mop of silver hair closely cropped. He seemed anxious to get the proceedings going. Dressed in a dark green polo and khaki pleated trousers, Rossi recalled from the previous day that he was the owner of his company. It was apparent as he took off his jacket with the logo Garcia Brothers Landscaping—since

1977. He had mentioned he had a contractor's license upon the
defense attorney's questioning, and he seemed hesitant to the
commitment of time this trial may require. Nevertheless, he
also insisted that it was a civic duty so he could make arrangements since he was the owner. Rossi figured that this was a self-
made man who knew that time and money are intractably
linked.

Next to him was Juror #8, the first juror that Rossi had
heard questioned when his pool of jurors came into the courtroom. This gentleman seemed to be at least in his mid-seven-
ties. He had removed his cap once he entered the courtroom,
revealing his bald head. What hair he had on the sides was
closely buzzed. He was trim and sat ramrod straight. He had
mentioned that as a retired Navy officer, he had served on many
juries. He spoke as though he had something he wanted to
make certain: just because he was "of a certain age"—that's how
he put it—he felt dead confident he could be fair and open-
minded. Rossi couldn't help but think that he was one of those
retired military for whom jury service was just an extension of
national duty. His eagerness to serve was evident. He sat still,
arms crossed, and unlike Garcia, he gave off the vibe that he
had all the time in the world.

As for the other seven, Rossi could not easily see the row
behind him and could only make superficial observations. The
first, third, and sixth jurors were women. The man at the far
end of his row, Juror #7, was Asian. Rossi noted that the first six
jurors were all white. Only two were seemingly under forty,
perhaps as young as twenty-five.

Juror 1 held her cell phone in her left hand above her lap,
looking around to see if anyone noticed. She appeared to be
scrolling; however, Rossi was not the only person to notice. The
bailiff came over and reminded all the jurors that cell phones
must be turned off or silenced. This was the third time he had
told them, and Juror #1 seemed to blush as the bailiff glanced

her way. She was quite tanned; Rossi assumed her profession put her outdoors quite a bit.

The two alternates, sitting outside the box, seemed bored and could not stop yawning. One woman was, he recalled, a retired secretary and the other was a male nurse, whose leg was bouncing up and down like a piston, but that was his only feature that seemed alive to Rossi. He could not help but wonder what kind of long shifts the nurse had at his job. He'd mentioned he would still work shifts outside the trial sessions. He seemed safe enough as the second alternate.

Behind the lawyers, people were settling in and scampering for the last few seats. It looked as though it was going to be a packed house. Then the bailiff stepped up to the side of the judge's raised dais and bellowed, "All rise. This court is now in session. The Honorable Judge Paul Lewis presiding."

Rossi remembered how taken aback he was when he first saw Judge Lewis. Movies had so ingrained into his psyche that a judge should look like a graying wise owl. He chided himself at his bias. After all, there were plenty of women sitting behind the bench, not to mention in the highest court in the land. Why did he have this prejudice? Rossi shook his head at his foolishness.

Judge Lewis motioned for all to be seated and cleared his throat. He surveyed the landscape of his domain. The gallery could hold up to seventy-five people and there were a few empty seats. He nodded at his bailiff to approach the bench and, pushing the microphone away, he indicated something about the people standing in the back as he pointed with his hand. Henry set off to deliver a message to those people. They scurried to the few remaining seats. Message delivered.

Judge Lewis didn't use his microphone. He swatted it away like it was an annoyance. He had a commanding voice when he wanted to use it, but when speaking to the jury, his tone was warm and welcoming. He quickly looked up from some paperwork and a slight smile formed, almost as if it was part of the protocol. He asked all to be seated. The judge inhaled deeply and his shoulders rose accordingly. He did not seem nearly as relaxed as the day previous.

Rossi thought that it seemed as if he knew, right then, what they were in for. Judge Lewis was in this pressure cooker, too.

6

INSTRUCTIONS

"Hello and good morning, everyone. I'm Judge Lewis, and I welcome you to my courtroom. I want to thank each member of the jury for dedicating their time and effort at seeing to it that justice is rendered in this case. I know it is not an easy thing—to judge someone's actions. But I am certain that as you follow the law and its boundaries, you will be confident in your decision. So again, I am most grateful for your attention to the matter at hand."

Rossi noticed that his confidence came across without any braggadocio, without a touch of arrogance. He personified justice itself.

"Before we begin the proceedings, let me tell you something about this case." Now Judge Lewis transitioned to a more formal tone. "This is a criminal trial, and I am going to be clear about one thing: this has already attracted a great deal of publicity locally, and the national media has already been paying close attention." He stared toward the back of the room, paused, and, returning his focus on the jury, added this: "I'm quite sure that is the last thing you wish to hear."

Rossi inhaled, held his breath, and then released a nervous

exhale. He glanced across the row of jurors, who all seemed to be equally on edge.

After the appropriate pause, the judge continued. "This trial will not require an extensive amount of time, perhaps a week, maybe longer ..." He looked down at his papers and shuffled some. "Naturally that will depend on your deliberations. The facts, you will discover, are not entirely in dispute; however, the interpretation of these events and the intent of the defendant Mr. George Ellis, also referred to as 'Duke' Ellis, will be the source of serious debate. That is the challenge to this jury." He took a moment to make eye contact with each of the jurors seated to his left. "I know you will be up to the task. I thank you for your willingness to serve the American justice system."

He asked the counsel for defense to rise and introduce himself to the jury along with the defendant. On cue, James Devlin stood and stepped forward to the jury. He smiled. "I also wish to sincerely thank each of you, as does my client. Motioning with his left hand, he introduced the defendant as George "Duke" Ellis.

Ellis popped up from his seat and could not have had a more buoyant, confident demeanor. It appeared to Rossi that his reaction was more like a person selected to "come on down" to a game show event. Ellis appeared to be every bit the celebrity. Rossi wondered how Ellis could be so pleased with himself and so oblivious that he was on trial in a criminal court, not making an appearance on a late-night television show.

Judge Lewis then spoke to those at the table where United States Attorney Jean Peters was seated. After she introduced herself, Peters quickly asked her co-counsel to stand. "I am assisted by Patrick Rosen, who is the United States Attorney for the Eastern Division of California which covers Riverside County and has been involved with this case from the very beginning." Rosen nodded. Today his attention was on the jury and not his legal pad. His reddish-gray hair and a closely cropped beard made him appear older than Rossi had surmised. Nevertheless, his demeanor came off as stern contrasting with the warm and welcoming Jean Peters.

At this point, Judge Lewis decided it was time to get down to business. His instructions were given in a succinct, terse manner with his hands placed on his bench and his black robes making him seem like a billowing specter. "Ladies and gentlemen of the jury, you are charged with determining the guilt or innocence of the accused, George 'Duke' Ellis. On September 13, 2016, George Ellis gave a speech to an audience at his campaign rally, just before Election Day. Mr. Ellis has admitted to being a former member of the Ku Klux Klan. His opponent in the congressional race was Mr. James Curtis, the incumbent Congressman. Mr. James Curtis is African American."

Judge Lewis paused for a moment, considering how he wished to convey the nature of the incident in question. "You will hear testimony in this courtroom that will explain what George 'Duke' Ellis said that night, and what happened later that evening when a violent disturbance, which the prosecution has characterized as a riot, transpired at the home of Congressman Curtis. What you must decide is this: did Mr. Ellis incite that riot? What does that mean?" Again, he looked to some papers on his desk. "Incitement is defined as 'the negligent irresponsible action of one person which, done purposefully, causes physical harm.'" The witnesses will tell you what was said, who were present that night, some will tell you what occurred at the Curtis home. From this information, you must decide if the defendant is responsible or not."

Judge Lewis scanned the jury deliberately. "So, you will be making a judgment about the defendant's actions, an interpretation of the intent of George 'Duke' Ellis's speech on

September 13, 2016. For the defendant to be guilty of this crime, the jury must reach a unanimous decision."

Judge Lewis shuffled a few papers before him, and Rossi reasoned that he knew his jury needed some time for the gravity of his last remarks to settle. He then proceeded to caution against distraction. "Some people may cloud the real issues by dealing with the motives behind this alleged action, or the election results, but do not be led astray by this. The election is over and Congressman Curtis has been re-elected. That is established fact.

"Some may say that the First Amendment, protecting one's freedom of speech, is at issue here today. This matter you must consider with the utmost scrutiny. When necessary, I will give you further guidance." The judge stopped, as if he were looking both ways crossing a dangerous intersection and allowed his eyes to fall to the two attorneys' tables before him. Then his full attention returned to his jury. "In this courtroom, emotions may rise—so be careful and thoughtful. And in the end, the question will remain: is the defendant guilty of inciting a riot?"

Judge Lewis let the final question settle over the jury in a dramatic fashion, like a fog so dense that it would take a clear eye to peer through the distance to know, for certain, in which direction to travel. Up until now, Rossi felt that the theatrics of courtroom drama were just for Hollywood. But Lewis's admonition was the signal that this courtroom battle that the media had sniffed out was likely to become, as television news anchors often proclaimed, "Breaking news."

7

OPENING STATEMENTS

Attorney Jean Peters knew her role. She stood and slowly, brushed her copper hair off her left shoulder, and deliberately paced herself toward the podium. Without notes, she glanced toward the judge, nodded, and zeroed in on the jury. She summed up her intent: "Your Honor, distinguished jurors, the prosecution will not beat around the bush in this trial. We are here to prove one simple fact: that George 'Duke' Ellis did, in fact, and with malice and purpose, incite a riot on September 13, 2016. How do we know this? Because in his speech to his 'following'—we all know who they are—he literally told them to kick Congressman Curtis out of office, kick the blacks out of his town. Naturally, he used language that this court and Judge Lewis would find reprehensible; however, exactly what he said is the basis for the charge of incitement. According to witnesses, Duke Ellis said, "We gotta kick the niggers out of this county, this state and let's do it now!" He went on to disparage African Americans and, I might add, other races. You will hear the witnesses tell you in graphic detail what he said and what he wanted his followers to do. And they so acted—on his orders ... on that night."

Peters retreated slightly from the jury box. "Now, why would Duke Ellis want to incite a riot? A reasonable question, but one that raises even more questions. As Judge Lewis has already explained to you, Duke Ellis is a former Klan member. So why did he join the Klan in the first place? Why did he claim to leave that organization? Did he really? What do the Klan and other white separatist organizations like the Aryan Nation, some of his strongest 'political' backers, stand for? More importantly, what do they stand against? Has the Ku Klux Klan ever done such a thing as use violent threats, and, in this case, actions, to intimidate others from voting or running for elected office?"

Then she deliberately slowed her pace. She pointed to the defense table, and in a hushed voice said, "The evidence will show that Duke Ellis and his followers believe that the white race is a superior race, and that only the white race should be in political office in the United States of America. So, members of the jury, this trial is about race and power: the unrelenting racism that Congressman James Curtis must endure and the actions of Duke Ellis to install white political power at any cost."

Jean Peters turned her back to the jury and faced Judge Lewis. Her voice rose for the first time. "Frankly, the evidence will show Ellis and his political organization are guilty of more than simply inciting a riot and attacking the Curtis house." She looked directly at the defense table and pointed at Duke Ellis. "It will show they are purveyors of hatred, prejudice, and violence ... and how do they do it? How? They do it with words. That's right, members of the jury. They have made their words, his words, become the instrument used to attack."

She softened for a moment and looked directly at the American flag located next to Judge Lewis's bench. "When we were children, we would recite that sticks and stones could break bones, but words could never harm us. How naïve we were. It is the specific intent of Duke Ellis's words that are at the heart of this trial."

She pivoted to the jury. "One plus one equals two, ladies and gentlemen. The intent of words and the direct connection to actions are the crime that occurred on that hot September evening at the Curtis home." She concluded, "The government will prove that this man, George 'Duke' Ellis, is guilty and deserves the full punishment of the law. He and his ilk need to face the consequences of his words as well as his actions." She thanked the jury and settled into her chair.

Paul Rosen glanced at her, nodded, and then lowered his head as he took some notes.

Judge Lewis cleared his throat to gain attention. "Mr. Devlin, the defense's opening statement."

"Thank you, Your Honor," Devlin began. He remained standing behind the table, his coat buttoned and his right hand casually placed in his pocket. He picked up his glasses, heretofore not used. It was a prop, in the form of a wand, as he circled his wrist and said, "Well, well, well. I'm certainly glad Attorney Peters didn't talk about all those things Judge Lewis mentioned that might confuse the jury—things that were irrelevant to the case like the election and such."

Now he stepped out and forward, making a calculated stroll toward the podium. Rossi noticed his unruffled approach, as if the speech made by Peters should be considered melodramatic, while he was here to calmly ground the case into simple, irrefutable facts.

"Members of the jury, I am counsel for George Ellis. I am here because I sincerely believe that a guilty verdict in this trial would be a gross miscarriage of American justice. Why? Because the evidence will show Ellis is not guilty of any crime. What he is guilty of is something we all do every day: we use our Constitutional right to free speech. That is all. What the prosecution is suggesting is that you throw away your right to say what you please in this nation. Words, let me remind you, are not actions. But you already know that very important distinction. The government would have you cancel the First Amendment's provision of free speech."

Devlin was now bearing down on the side of the jury box immediate to Rossi. "Oh, you can have the freedom to speak sometimes, just don't say this or don't say that—and who is to say what we can or can't say? What is politically correct? How is a mere offensive remark compared to a criminal act? The government gets to decide. The defendant has a right to his opinion. He has a right to speak it, as do each of you. You may not agree. You may find some of the words repugnant ... offensive. But that is an opinion. There are many words, phrases, that society once held as 'unspeakable,' but today they are part of what is accepted free speech. I prefer to not use those words in court, but I am sure, members of the jury, you know of those words to which I refer."

Devlin decided to let this point sink in. He pointed his glasses at the District Attorney. "Most importantly, the prosecution will not establish that my client George Ellis was even at the scene of the so-called riot. Why not? Because he wasn't there!"

Devlin swung around to Peters and Rosen and spoke directly to them. Rossi felt he was challenging them—reprimanding in tone. "Now, Counselor Peters will say that the defendant incited a riot, but she can never tell you what that is. Even Judge Lewis told you that the media was claiming it was a riot. The media. Since when do the media define what is and is not a crime?" Devlin's glasses waved back to his defense table. "Is getting the Congressman removed from office incitement? Doesn't every Democrat want the Republican out of office?" Devlin was building to a climax as he returned his focus to the jury. "And does incitement justify amending our Constitutional right to free speech?" He lifted his arms and then dropped them down in mock frustration.

He sauntered back to his table. "Finally," he let the word last long enough to get him halfway back to the defendant, "the government may offer evidence that my client George Ellis is a white supremacist. So? Is that grounds, in and of itself, to disregard the First Amendment? The issues are clear—and we are confident of acquittal—but being a racist is not on trial."

Devlin pulled back his chair and slowly relaxed into it. Ellis only showed the slightest hint of a smile as he nodded his head.

Rossi reached for his pen to jot down his thoughts just as Judge Lewis announced, "I will ask both attorneys to meet me in my chambers, and since we are nearing the two-hour mark, I would like the jury to have an opportunity to take a much-deserved break. I thank you for your attention. Now remember, jurors, that you are sworn to not discuss this case outside of court. Your notebooks are to remain here at all times. We will recess until 1 p.m., so that gives you ample time for lunch. This court is adjourned."

Rossi realized that the others were rising as the judge left the courtroom. He quickly jotted down two points in his notebook and was the last to leave his seat. That's when he saw that both sets of lawyers were still standing. Apparently, they would remain so until he left. He placed his notebook on his seat and closed it so none of the jurors could see that he had written: Are words on trial?

8

CAROL COMBS

"Your Honor, my name is C-Carol C-Combs." Mrs. Carol Combs had the look of a grandmother, dressed as if she were attending a church service ... in the 1970s. She was not trying to hide her age, and her floral dress, a white sweater draped over her shoulders, and her oversized eyeglasses gave her a matronly appearance. Rossi could not help but think of Betty White on *The Golden Girls*. She was already prepared for tears, with a pink tissue or two balled up in the hand that she placed on The Bible.

Judge Lewis quickly realized just how nervous the prosecution's first witness was and tried to calm her. "Now, Mrs. Combs, just relax and tell the court what you know." Then he gave her a broad smile.

Combs looked up at him. "I'm-m sorry, Your Honor. It's j-just I've never been in court before and this is all very upsetting."

"We completely understand, Mrs. Combs," said Peters. She was trying her best to quell her first witness's anxiety. "Please tell the court what you saw and heard on the night of September 13, 2016."

Combs took a breath. Her eyes were focused on Jean Peters. Rossi wondered if she would look at the defendant.

"Yes. Well, I live across the street ... that's where I was ... a-and it was about 10 p.m. when I saw those men ..."

"Could you tell us how many men?"

"Oh, um. Five or six at first. But then more started coming ... so I guess fifteen or twenty."

Carol Combs seemed so nervous that she did not understand that she could just continue with what she saw. Apparently, she needed prompting.

"Yes. Thank you. Now, where did these men go, Mrs. Combs?"

"To the Curtis home."

"And ..."

"And they were there."

A beat.

Then it dawned on her to continue. "Oh. They were standing around s-shouting things."

"What were they shouting?"

"Well, it w-was hard to make out e-exactly. I could hear words like *nigger* ... Oh, should I say that h-here?"

"Yes. We understand you are quoting the men. Go on. What else did you hear?"

"Oh. Well, they cussed a lot and said Mr. Curtis's name. They marched around for about half an hour with some signs that r-read 'White Power'—I think. Yes. Some of them were s-shouting 'Niggers go home!' Oh, some of them had shaved heads, too. Then this one man jumped over the hedges and planted a cross on the lawn—and they set it on f-f-fire." She swallowed and tried to compose herself. She wanted to look down, but Peters moved closer to her so that she had to lift her face.

Rossi realized that her face told the story of that evening

much better than she could speak it. Terrified—that was the message.

"Then ... then ... a c-couple of people started throwing rocks at the house—and then—well, about then I called the police. I told them to hurry."

Peters pushed her to keep the narrative going.

Combs was tearing up, her voice shaking. "Well, just b-before the police came, a couple of the younger ones, I think, broke the windows of the Curtises's car that sat out front. Then two men r-ran up to the front door and threw something or did something to the front window ... it w-was hard to see what it was. I heard screaming from inside. It must have been p-poor Mrs. Curtis or her children. There were a lot of men out there ... I mean, more than at first, but when the police c-came tearing up the street, they took off ... fast. Some jumped in cars but some just r-ran. I think they, the police, I mean, caught some of them."

Peters said, "Yes, we will cover that a bit later, Mrs. Combs. But if the police hadn't come, what do you think could have happened?"

"Objection. Speculation." Devlin didn't bother to rise from his chair or even look up from polishing his glasses.

"Sustained. You do not have to answer that question, Mrs. Combs."

"Oh, y-yes, Your Honor."

"Thank you very much, Mrs. Combs. I am sure the event was frightening. I have no other questions." Peters made sure the jury heard the word *frightening*.

Combs might have thought she was finished because she leaned forward as if she were about to rise from the witness stand. When she heard Devlin's voice, she was physically startled.

"I'm sorry to keep you, Mrs. Combs, but I have a few questions, okay?" Devlin's tenor was friendly. "Did you see the defendant here—Mr. George Ellis—in the crowd attacking the Curtis home?"

"I'm not sure. I mean, it was dark."

"Yes. Very dark. Past 10 p.m., I believe you said."

"Yes. I was about to go to bed. Yes."

"But, Mrs. Combs, I'll ask again. Did you see Mr. George Ellis among the men you say were causing this disturbance?" Devlin was not looking at her. He was focused on the jury.

"Well, the men had hoods on ... or those th-things you pull over your face when it's cold, and s-some seemed to be hiding behind signs ... a-and I w-was across the s-street ... s-so they w-weren't facing me."

"So that's fair, Mrs. Combs. Thank you for your honesty. Mrs. Combs, you're wearing glasses now. Were you wearing glasses then ... right before you were ready to retire for bed?"

Combs, taken off guard, placed both hands on the frame of her glasses, as if she were trying to envision the memory of that evening. "Um. Oh. W-well. I think so."

"Hmm. All right. We can leave it at that." Devlin smiled at her. "I sometimes can't remember if my glasses are on my face or not. Funny how that is." Devlin started to turn back to the defense table but acted as if he had just remembered something. "Now, did you hear George Ellis spoken of, perhaps?

"Well, I'm not sure. I-I mean, there was so much yelling." Then, as if she felt compelled to make her point about how scary these men were, she said, "But I do k-know what a s-skinhead is and what a Nazi is, s-sir ... and I saw a few with those Nazi swastikas on their s-sleeves ..."

"Hmm. You could see that, but you cannot place Mr. Ellis there, nor did you hear his name shouted, correct?"

Mrs. Combs admitted she could not.

Rossi noted that, but also observed how impassive Devlin acted, as if this entire episode had nothing to do with the defendant.

Devlin supplied one last question that came off as an afterthought; however, Rossi later figured it was probably planned well in advance. "Mrs. Combs, you said it was 10 p.m. That's pretty late. You said you were getting ready for bed, correct?"

"Well, yes, I was ... but who could sleep with all that ... that, I mean, all those people yelling and screaming?"

"No. Of course not. But when you opened the front door to see what was going on ... it was your front door, correct?"

"Yes. I a-already said so ... didn't I?" Combs's confusion was evident.

"No. Not exactly, but that's fine." Devlin's next question came so diplomatically that he winced as he said to her. "I don't mean to be asking something so personal, but I believe your birthday is next month, and you will be turning eighty-four years old. Correct?

"Um. Y-yes."

Rossi thought that Mrs. Combs seemed flushed by the fact her age was now a public matter.

Devlin nodded to her respectfully. "Let me thank you for your time and service to this court, Mrs. Combs." As Devlin reached for the back of his chair, he announced that he had no further questions.

Combs grabbed her white purse and climbed out of the witness stand. She wobbled down the main aisle. Her eyes were cast down and her body language gave Rossi the impression that she was a wounded soul forced to confront the events of over a year ago and verbalizing it in a courtroom had shaken her to the core.

9

ROBERTA CURTIS

Attorney Peters announced the next witness, Mrs. Roberta Curtis, the Congressman's wife. As she approached the witness stand, her poise contrasted sharply with Carol Combs's nervousness. Here was a woman who, Rossi noted, had been in the public eye before, and her glare—the type that often makes one wilt under pressure—merely made her shine brightly. Attired in a striking black pantsuit, a white blouse, and very little jewelry, she sat erect—head high. Proud. Defiant.

Jean Peters asked, "Mrs. Roberta Curtis, you are the wife of Congressman Curtis and you were in your home on the night of September 13, 2016. Correct?"

"That is correct." Her diction was perfect.

"Would you tell the court what you saw and heard that night?"

"Well, to begin with, my husband was not home. He was out campaigning."

"Were you alone?" Peters asked.

"No," she began, "my eleven-year-old daughter and my nine-year-old son were with me. A few friends called me and told me that that man,"—she pointed directly at Ellis and stared at him—"I use the term loosely—was planning a *rally* near my home that evening." Now she returned her gaze to Peters. "Of course, I am referring to George Ellis. It was close to 10:00 pm when I looked out the window to hear what all the noise was outside. When I first looked, I saw about ten men walking around with their racist signs."

"Was this the first time they had, for the lack of a better word, *appeared* at your home?"

"No, it was not. Some skinheads have walked past several times, using vulgar slurs, calling my husband a *nigger*. Then, two weeks before that night, one of our car windows was shattered and a tire was punctured. We filed a report with the police, but nothing came of it. I suppose someone was testing our resolve." She pulled her shoulders and tilted her head as if to say, *That was not going to intimidate her or her husband.* "Anyway, this was the third time they showed up at our residence. And this one wasn't peaceful." Mrs. Curtis spotted Carol Combs in the back of the courtroom and nodded.

Mrs. Curtis delivered the remainder of her testimony directly to the jury. Rossi felt that she knew whom she needed to persuade.

"As soon as they leaped over my hedges and lit the cross I became very frightened—not for myself, because I know those men are cowards, that's why their kind usually wear hoods— but I did not want to expose my children to any more hatred or fear. When we moved here, Ms. Peters, we thought this *overt* racism and hatred had ended decades ago. I guess we were wrong." Mrs. Curtis then stopped to see the impact on the jury.

"And when, exactly, did you call the police?"

"Right before I saw them smash the car windows *again.* I was calling 911 the second they stuck a cross in my yard and try to light it. So I had called both the police and 911. They said they would be here as soon as they could ... and really, they were, thank goodness. And I want to thank Ms. Combs, who also called the police."

"Did you or your two children incur any physical ..." Peters paused and rephrased the question. "Were you hurt, Mrs. Curtis?"

Mrs. Curtis was her most defiant. "No, not really—although we were almost hit with rocks that they threw through our front window, and we had to put out a small fire in the living room—because those scum threw in a miniature fire-cross. I swear—how could the cross of Jesus be used for such an unholy act!"

Rossi did not need to be a psychologist to feel the tension and disgust emanating from Juror 11, Regina, sitting next to him. It appeared that she and Mrs. Curtis had locked eyes. He knew this was a pivotal point of the day. He also knew that James Devlin was going to be challenged. He wondered what approach the lawyer would take. He was not surprised.

"Mrs. Curtis, I have a few questions—and believe me, neither I nor my client intend to justify the incident—but did you see my client, George Ellis, that night outside your house?" Devlin began. He was seated and remained so for the entire cross-examination.

Mrs. Curtis spat out, "No. But how could I? Many of the men hid their faces as most *cowards* do, Mr. Devlin."

Devlin, in a gentler tone, said, "Did you ever hear him speak, or was he even spoken of?"

Mrs. Curtis leaned into that question. "I'm sorry, Mr. Devlin, but that's a difficult question to answer. Those crazy people were standing outside my home, screaming, 'Go back where you belong, *nigger!*' and throwing things at my home. I didn't realize I needed to be listening for one specific voice. I was just trying not to panic." Her eyes were locked on Devlin.

He apologetically countered, "I am sorry for asking. I understand."

"I don't think you do, sir. And I know your client has no idea what it feels like to be attacked as we have. No idea. None. So don't tell me you understand ... sir." Roberta Curtis was not to be patronized.

"Yes. I'm sure you are correct, Mrs. Curtis. I must ask you ... you said this wasn't the first time?"

"That's right. But I still can't seem to get used to it—this isn't 'politics-as-usual,' you know. In all the other campaigns my husband was a part of, never were there such acts of racism, nor was race brought up by the other candidate."

"Yes, I see." Devlin tapped his pen on the legal pad in front of him. "But, I am curious, when your friend phoned and said there was to be a speech that night, why didn't you phone for police protection then?"

Rossi had leaned forward. Jean Peters noticed. Devlin did what few lawyers of his pedigree do. He asked a question of which he did not know the answer. Had Devlin intentionally underestimated the Congressman's wife?

Mrs. Curtis uncoiled. "Many reasons, sir. First, I believe that in this country, when a man gives a speech you shouldn't need to call in the police to protect yourself from an angry mob that might be *incited* to attack. But apparently I was wrong, sir. You see, with your client, Duke Ellis, free to espouse his hatred, it seems we *all* need police protection."

With that, it was James Devlin who lowered his head as he said, "Mrs. Curtis, thank you for your ... testimony. I have no further questions."

Rossi leaned back. Regina, on the contrary, was still focused on Mrs. Curtis as she stepped from the witness stand, every bit the warrior, and strode through the heart of the courtroom.

The sound of papers shuffling and lawyers mumbling to each other dominated the hushed courtroom. That stopped when Judge Lewis's gavel rapped. He thanked the jury for their attention, reminded them to be back tomorrow morning at 9 o'clock, and dismissed them. The lawyers stood and the members of the jury filed toward an exit the bailiff motioned to. Apparently, it was reserved for only them.

10

DEBORAH'S DILEMMA

Rossi realized that he was far more tired than he thought. The walk from the courthouse was invigorating, especially after sitting for hours. The train was fairly empty so he could stretch out his legs and just settle into the rocking and the clack-clack-clacking of the train's perpetual motion. *I'll just close my eyes for a minute.*

That minute passed, and so did three other stops, and the conductor was leaning on the seat across the aisle and nudging Rossi. "Next stop's Encinitas, sir." He had the smile of a man who had seen this movie many times over.

Rossi's eyes popped open, and the surprise caught him as though he was reading in bed and his book bumped him on the nose. "Oh. We are here already?"

"Yes, you are, sir. Figured I might have to toss you off the train if you didn't come around." The jovial conductor snickered and winked.

Rossi rose and noticed he was the only one nearby. The rows were empty. "Well, thank you. Did I scare off the rest of the passengers?"

"Well, I think they just needed some peace and quiet ... considering the snoring." Another laugh.

Rossi flushed a bit. "Man, that bad?"

"I've heard worse. Take care now." As he walked off, the brakes began their long screech, and Rossi spotted the station sign that let him know he was back in his town.

———

Deborah was fixing his plate while he washed up. She knew he was uncharacteristically quiet on the ten-minute ride back from the train station. He feigned a jump-in-his-step as he strode into their kitchen, but the sigh that came from him as he slumped on to the wooden bar stool, along with the dark circles under his eyes were a signature of a difficult day for him.

Her own nerves were strained as well but for different reasons. It was one thing to be involved in an intense situation and quite another to be seeing it in all its forms on the media.

They sat on the barstools where they usually had their casual dinners. Tonight, it was one of his favorites: baked salmon drizzled with honey and a side dish of pasta salad. She knew how much joy came from her husband's love of her excellent Italian dishes.

Deborah smiled at him. "The merlot is breathing, Tony."

"I'm glad I am, too," he kidded.

Deborah also knew his sense of humor hid his nervousness. Her response was one eyebrow raised and a long "Hmmmm."

A beat.

"What a day," he said, yawning, as Deborah sat down across from him.

"I'd say 'Tell me about it,' but I know you can't say much." She started the day hoping he was excused from jury duty. Now she felt there was no excuse for him to not be on this jury despite what she spent a good part of the day learning.

"No. I guess not. It ... the trial ... has finally got going and there were witnesses and such ... and I guess I just was so focused on everything that was going on. There's a lot of drama —that much I can say." He saluted the chef with his wine and she nodded appreciatively.

"I suppose the judge told you not to watch the news about the trial, huh? They always say that in the movies." Deborah treaded carefully. She didn't want to pry. She didn't want to show him that she was worried about the protesters and all the media attention it was attracting. She certainly didn't want him to hear some of the crazy things being said by the Tea Party folks who spoke to CNN. And last but not least, she didn't want him to worry about her.

"Well, I can say that it's not like an episode of Law and Order, but I must say that the attorneys are very ... um, convincing. Both sides. They really gave me something to think about."

"I bet they did. I won't say much," she hesitated, "but I watched the news and it was one of the first stories on local channels."

"Figures. I saw them as I left even though we exited behind the building. When I got to Broadway there were a lot more of them than in the morning."

"Oh, is that right? Hmm. Well, I paused the TV so we could watch the CBS Evening News." She looked at him for guidance. "I wasn't sure if you wanted to, or are allowed to watch it." Then she lied, "They probably wouldn't bother to cover it ... or if they did a story on your trial. Well, I could hit the mute button."

"Oh. I um ... I don't know. I think if you want to watch the news, that's fine with me. I'm not sure that my trial will be covered, really." Deborah looked at him and thought that he had probably heard enough of the Ellis case for a day. But she already knew they had done a piece on the Duke Ellis trial. Her son Pete had called from D.C. earlier to ask if that was the case his father was on the jury for. She told him that it was. His reaction: "Dad is gonna be in for some very heavy stuff, Mom. It's all over social media."

Heavy, indeed. That started Deborah's journey down the rabbit hole. She had to tell him. She reached across the table and touched his left hand. "I have news, Tony. The Ellis case is making headlines because the President is tweeting about it."

"What?" He dropped his knife.

"He tweeted about it, I'm serious! He's all pissed off that Duke Ellis is being called a criminal ... Wait. Maybe I shouldn't have told you that."

"Of course you can tell me. It's fine. Well, no, it's not fine. I mean ... I don't know yet what I mean. It just seems ridiculous for the President to be commenting on a case that is ongoing, right?"

"Yeah, well, consider the source." Deborah was relieved that she had not said too much.

"I know. Anyway, you're right. No more news of any kind about the trial—okay?"

"Yes, I agree totally. It's just that that's probably why the protests are growing. That's what the local news seems to be implying. I guess, it was already a national story, but now that the President has weighed in ... it's gone viral."

Deborah's wine glass was near empty. She saw him reach for the bottle, look at her glass, and she said, "Just a splash, honey."

Rossi topped his wine glass and looked at the TV screen. Tornado in Oklahoma tearing through a town. Forty-eight car pileup on Florida's interstate. And then the news anchor introduced their political correspondent, who was reporting from San Diego. Deborah quickly hit the mute button; however, the pictures alone captured the gravity of the story: a gaggle of reporters in front of the courthouse and a crowd of protesters outside, an artist rendering of Duke Ellis, attorney Devlin sitting at the defense table, Judge Lewis peering over the

proceedings with a grumpy look on his face. The artist had
captured a moment, but only a moment in the six-hour saga.
Then the picture returned to the reporter and some statistics
appeared. Rossi immediately turned away.

"Sorry, Tony. I guess we shouldn't watch this." Her eyes were
still glued to the news report. "I'll tell you when the warm-fuzzy
human interest story comes on." Human interest. People always
want a happy ending ...

———

Anthony Rossi finished off what was left of his salmon. As he
swirled the last of his wine around and around, he couldn't
help but think about Roberta Curtis's testimony. "We thought
this overt racism and hatred ended decades ago. I guess we
were wrong."

For some people, the happy ending never comes.

11

FRANK STAPLETON

The jury sat outside of Department #2 for forty minutes. The nine o'clock start time had been pushed back, the bailiff explained, because the judge had to confer with the attorneys. He apologized.

Rossi's coffee was now cold. They were all sitting in a side corridor due to all the media attention at the main door to the courtroom. The women in the jury made small talk, sitting or standing in an oval, except for Juror #1. She was, again, on her cell phone at the end of the hall. Rossi noticed she was flustered with whoever was on the receiving end.

The two men, Mr. Garcia and Juror #2, were chatting about business. Mr. Garcia was talking about how he was entrusting his son to run the landscaping business for the next two weeks. He was clearly proud of him, but Rossi overheard him express some concern because this would be a "real test of whether he was cut out for the management of the business. Young people, you know, have little patience." Garcia gave Rossi the impression that he was a self-made man who had success because of his strict work ethic.

The Juror #2 responded with his view of working with

young people. "Twenty years at Sears and I've seen it all. Yeah, the kids come and go ... not saying your son won't do a good job but, you know, so many are flakes ..." His dour expression gave the impression to Rossi that he may have a chip on his shoulder.

Another juror—Juror #4—was pacing back and forth and kept glancing at his watch. He looked like an athlete, trim and fit, and moved like one. Rossi figured he was in his early forties.

Just when Rossi was about to ask if anyone wanted a refill of their coffee, the female bailiff opened the door from the inside and announced that the jury should head to the jury box. As they did, the lawyers again stood, and so did Duke Ellis, although he seemed upset. His face reddened, his smile had vanished and was replaced with a tight thin line.

Rossi opened his notebook, but before he could jot down day two, Judge Lewis entered. He quickly sat and turned to the jury, apologizing for their wait and that it was "unavoidable." He thanked them for their patience, and with that, he asked the prosecution to call its next witness. The witness came in from an entrance the far side of the courtroom where Duke Ellis had appeared from during jury selection. An officer stood next to the witness who wore an orange jumpsuit and was handcuffed. Rossi guessed this must have been the cause of the delay.

"Your honor," Peters began, "Frank Stapleton has already been sworn in and he is a hostile witness, subpoenaed to testify."

"Yes. Begin your cross-examination, Counselor."

"Mr. Stapleton, you were arrested on the night of September 13, 2016, at the home of Congressman James Curtis, correct?"

"Yeah. That's why I'm wearing this orange get-up," he snarled. His head was shaved and his face was unshaven. Rossi could spot a black mark on his left cheek.

"The prisoner will speak in a respectful manner to the officers of this court," Judge Lewis admonished. He addressed Stapleton directly. "If you fail to do so, I will make sure it is noted in your file and it will affect decisions about your sentencing. Is that understood, Mr. Stapleton." This was not a question despite the manner in which it was phrased—it was a threat.

A beat.

Stapleton pursed his lips then slowly nodded.

Peters continued. "You were arrested, tried, and convicted of one count of disturbing the peace, two counts of violent endangerment, two counts of destruction of personal property—the vandalism of the Curtis's automobile and breaking a window to their house—and finally you were one of the men who stuck a cross on their lawn and lit it on fire, thus leading to your conviction for a hate crime. Is that correct?"

"I did some of that, but I didn't light the cross ... some other guy did. I just hammered it into the grass."

"Whatever you say." Peters now turned to make eye contact with the jury. "Let's get to know you, Mr. Stapleton. You are a member of an American Nazi organization and that very organization is part of the 'Unite the Right' group that planned the protests conducted in Charlottesville, Virginia from August 11th to 12th of this year ..."

Devlin was objecting as Peters was finishing her question. "That event has no bearing on this case, Your Honor. It is guilt by association."

"Your Honor, I am not implying Mr. Stapleton was involved in that protest. I am trying to make the mission of this Nazi organization clear to this jury."

Judge Lewis said, "I will overrule the objection; however, let's make sure you link the witness's actions to what we are trying Mr. Ellis with, Counselor."

"Yes. I will, Your Honor. Mr. Stapleton, what would you say is the purpose of this Nazi organization you belong to?"

Stapleton emphatically replied, "We believe there is a war being fought in this country—a race war. The only way we are gonna win is if we fight. We believe it's gotta be an all-white America or else a dead America."

"Why is that?"

"Because we don't wanna have anything to do with the blacks ... and they don't wanna have anything to do with us. That's the way a majority of people feel if you wanna know the truth."

"I'll let that last remark pass, but what is your problem with black people?" Peters egged him on.

"Isn't it obvious? Their culture is a jungle. They dance around like monkeys. They are violent ... with all their gang crap and the men ... the men all get their women pregnant and split. They got no morals. We don't want them around our women. They should just go back to the jungles in Africa and leave us alone." Stapleton sat back.

"But the Nazis have problems with other races, as well. Correct?"

"You mean the Jews. Yeah, right. They horde all the money and they are dangerous. They control the fake news, the newspapers and TV. They watch out for their own. They closed down a Nazi bookstore in New York. They oppressed us!"

"What does your organization make of the Nazi Holocaust?"

"What about it?"

"The murder of millions of Jews by the Nazi leader Adolf Hitler. I'm sure you have read about it." Peters' sarcasm was evident.

Devlin did not stand but he made his objection loud and clear. "Judge Lewis, this has nothing to do with the events in question or with my client, who is not a Nazi."

"I am getting there, Your Honor. Please give me the latitude to examine one witness who participated in the riot at the

Curtis's home. His actions are a reflection of the mindset that Mr. Ellis was appealing to."

"I'll overrule for now. Please connect the dots, Counselor, or I will have to curtail this line of questioning."

The judge gave Peters a look that implied better make it soon.

"Let me repeat the question: how do you and the American Nazi organization respond to the fact that Nazis are responsible for the Holocaust?"

"Let me tell you something ... and all the Jews and the gays and the rest of the degenerates out there. We are the oppressed! That's right. The Aryan race is suffering. But we will rise up ... rise up and take what is rightfully ours. This swastika ..." he turned his cheek to the jury so that the tattooed symbol of the Nazis was clear to all, "this represents the truth. Hitler was right! Hitler died for the white race—he was the greatest white man to ever have lived. George Washington. Jefferson Davis. And Adolf Hitler!"

A beat.

Peters wanted to let the full impact of this outburst wash over the jury. Rossi was taken aback. *My God! Can we allow this man the absolute right to "free speech" even when the words he utters are a direct threat to human life?*

But James Devlin would have none of this. "Your Honor, this is exactly what I was concerned with. The prosecution is associating my client with this monster—who is justifiably locked up. Frank Stapleton is not on trial—he is a convicted criminal. My client George Ellis is not a Nazi ... and even if he was, that in and of itself is not a crime ..."

"And if his former organization, the Klan, aligns itself with the Nazis who supported the murdering of ten million people, you figure that is constitutionally protected advocacy!" rebutted Peters.

"My client has a right to his opinion. Actions, not words, are the issue before the court."

Judge Lewis silenced them both. "I do not need to be told what is on trial here, Mr. Devlin. And I do not appreciate all the grandstanding by either of you. I want this witness to be questioned about the events that are related to the charges Mr. Ellis is facing. I will not entertain any questions other than those. Do you follow me, Ms. Peters?"

"Yes, Your Honor."

"Good. If you have another question, then ask it now."

"Mr. Stapleton. You heard Duke Ellis's speech that night ... you were there, correct?"

"Yeah."

"And then you went to the Curtis home, correct?"

"Sure."

"To do what?"

"It was ... well, we were there to scare him. We don't want none of his kind in our country ... in our government." He shrugged his shoulders.

"So, you hammered in a cross and damaged his car and tossed rocks in his window ... all to scare him?" She was trying not to be too incredulous.

"Well, we weren't gonna kill anybody." Stapleton's expression implied that no one was that stupid.

"That's thoughtful, Mr. Stapleton. And fortunate. So, Mr. Ellis's speech really motivated you, I assume. In other words, sir, if he had not spoken, you wouldn't have acted in such a manner?"

"Objection. Speculation. The witness can't know what would have happened."

"Sustained. You've made your point, Counselor. The witness heard the speech. He went to the Curtis home and he committed several crimes."

"Fine. Mr. Stapleton, was this the first time you heard Mr. Ellis speak?"

"Yeah."

"And, naturally, you agreed with his words that 'we should kick the niggers out of the county'—correct?"

"At least that far."

"No further questions. Your witness." Peters walked to her table, and her co-counsel Mr. Rosen pointed to his legal pad and nodded an affirmation.

James Devlin again did not rise. He merely dropped his pen and, in a matter-of-fact manner, looked up at Judge Lewis and explained, "Your Honor, I am aware that we have been in session for quite a while, so I'll take very little time. This witness demands little of our attention." He looked at Stapleton. "Did you personally speak with Mr. George Ellis?"

"No."

"Did Mr. George Ellis tell you to do any of the specific things that you have been convicted of?"

"No."

"Did you see Mr. George Ellis there at the scene of your crimes?"

"No."

"Is he responsible for you being behind bars?"

Peters interrupted. "Objection. Speculation."

"Sustained."

"Fine." Devlin closed with this: "You are here because of what you did. Isn't that right, Mr. Stapleton?"

"Yeah. And I would do it again if I could," he sneered.

Rossi leaned forward and thought, And that's the point of this trial. Isn't it?

12

ROSSI AND HENRY

"Deborah, I have an hour and a half ... for lunch."

"Really? What are you going to do all that time?" They both laughed because Rossi held a sack lunch in his hand as he sat in a small alcove in the Federal courthouse. Deborah kidded him, "No more wandering the streets getting a two martini lunch, huh, Tony." She had two names for her husband: Anthony the default, Tony for affection.

"This kinda reminds me of our old school days." Rossi sat his phone on the table while he unwrapped his peanut butter sandwich.

"The difference is we had, what, twenty minutes, to eat and run to the bathroom before the bell would ring."

Rossi concurred, "You got that right. You still make the best PB and J sandwiches."

""It's the least I could do. I slipped in a treat by the way."

"I see. Cookies! Now I'm really spoiled."

"Well, we can't have you walking down Broadway in the middle of that fracas today. It's gotten bigger." The Federal Courthouse sat squarely on Broadway and Union in the heart of the downtown, south of Little Italy but north of the Gaslamp District.

"Really? This morning I saw the usual suspects—I guess protesting isn't a morning thing."

They are warmed up now, for sure ... Let's talk about something else. So ... do you think you'll make the same train around four o'clock?" Deborah moved to the office where her laptop revealed the most recent ABC news report entitled 'The Aftermath of Charlottesville.' She had spent much of the morning wading into stories that involved racism.

Rossi sipped his coffee which he snagged from the cart down the hall. "I don't know. I hope so."

A beat.

Rossi leaned into the only available topic other than the weather. "What have you been up to?"

Deborah's tried to sound as matter of fact as possible. Teachers, after all, could be good actors. "Oh, the usual. Bought a dress at Saks, lounged at the beach reading Vogue, then drinks with the girls at the country club." Meanwhile her eyes scanned the article on the riots in Virginia back in August.

"Oh, good. Make sure the cooks have our dinner ready, too. Don't forget to ask the butler to prepare my tuxedo."

Both smiled into their phones.

"No. I'm just sitting here at home ... and watching the news." As she uttered the last four words, Deborah's tone sounded as if they had just received an electric bill for twice what it usually was.

"Don't tell me about the news. I'm getting all I can handle straight from the horse's mouth ... if you know what I mean."

Deborah regretted mentioning it. "Sorry. Just be careful, Tony, especially when you leave. I just don't like the looks of things. Pretty rowdy bunch out there on Broadway."

Rossi took a bite of the first cookie. "Don't worry. Our bailiff,

Henry has us exiting away from everything and he keeps an eye on us. He's a pretty imposing guy."

"Well, good. Call me or text when you are on the train, okay? I'll be ready ... I mean I'll send the chauffer to scoop you up."

"Will do. I'm gonna hang up. Speaking of the bailiff he is heading down here now. I might ask him a question. Okay. Love you."

"Bye, Tony." Deborah's hand slowly deposited her phone on the desk as she read the ABC report: On Aug. 12, 2017, a "Unite the Right" rally in Charlottesville turned deadly when a 20-year-old Ohio man allegedly accelerated his car into a crowd of counter-protesters, killing 32-year-old Heather Heyer and leaving 19 others injured, five critically.

She continued scrolling.

———

Officer Henry Lamont stopped his stroll to the coffee cart to nod at juror Rossi, who in turn looked up at him, "When I was teaching, Officer, I used to wolf down my lunch. Now, I'm still eating a sandwich but I have time to kill."

Henry stopped and smiled. "I know what you're talking about. I've had a few thousand sack lunches in my time ... still do." Henry chuckled. "Guess you didn't want to head out there with the other jurors, huh?"

Rossi didn't particularly enjoy eating alone. He did notice several jurors walking together, and it appeared they were lunching as a small group. He replied offhandedly to the bailiff, "Well, I just didn't feel comfortable doing that. Hard to sit with folks and not discuss the trial. Besides, my wife makes a mean sandwich ... and cookies. Please indulge, Officer." He held up the napkin with several cookies.

"That's very tempting, Juror #12, but I am watching my

petite waistline." His smile cracked open that 'Mean Joe Green' persona.

"Henry, you can call me Tony. Tony Rossi. Okay?"

"And you can call me Officer, okay?" Both men got a kick out of that.

As Henry continued his stroll down the hallway, Rossi took out his personal moleskin notebook and thought about several questions he had so far. He found it necessary to organize his thoughts. He often noted things that a faulty memory would too often lead him to say, what was it I wanted to remember?

When he began his teaching career in 1984, he marveled at how much of his energy a day would consume. During the last ten years of his career, the four hours of being on his feet teaching with only a fifteen-minute break would often leave him exhausted. He would at times drag himself over to the faculty lounge to eat with his colleagues. More often than he would like to admit, he resigned to plop down on a small love seat in his classroom. The love seat was so worn that the stuffing was bursting through the armrests. Several times he was so tired he nodded off while sitting straight up.

Rossi laughed at the memory, and yet those days, years really, seemed like yesterday. He still had dreams about it all. He loved the joyful vibe his students carried into his classroom. People used to tell him that teaching kept him young. And now, he was retired. Retirement for him had one central, looming concern: could I still be relevant?

Rossi caught himself lost in the past as he stared into his notebook. He shook it off and reminded himself of the task at hand. It seemed to him that the prosecution was trying to place Duke Ellis at the scene of the riot. So far there was no proof of that—although it was noted many were covering their faces. He understood that this was a criminal trial, not a civil one, but probably there would be a civil trial, demanding that someone pay for the damages to the Curtis property. That was neither here nor there in this trial.

Then there was the question of guilt by association. A tricky proposition. Frank Stapleton's testimony was appalling, yet how would they know if his actions were the direct result of Ellis's speech? Stapleton heard Ellis. He was brought to a boil ... presumably because of Ellis, but did that mean Ellis was responsible?

Then he underlined the last thought: *are words on trial?*

———

Deborah's eyes scanned down to the final paragraph that explained why the riot had originated on the University of Virginia. It had been there that the Robert E. Lee statue had been the subject of controversy. Along with other Confederate statues, the community had debated tearing Lee's statue down. Next to photos of hundreds of torches and people clashing, she read the article's conclusion:

"The 'Unite the Right' rally consisted of many neo-Nazi followers and other white nationalists holding lit tiki torches as they marched, some chanting the Nazi-associated phrase 'blood and soil.'"

Deborah closed her laptop. She had read enough for now.

13

WAYNE SIMS

"Mr. Wayne Sims, you were a member of the KKK, isn't that correct?" Peters commenced her questioning of the afternoon's witness.

He had a slight Southern drawl and despite his large stature, or perhaps because of it, he was so soft-spoken that she asked him to repeat what he said so the jury could hear.

"I'm sorry. Yes, ma'am." He wore an ill-fitting blue sports coat and an unflattering orange shirt that claimed a collar far too wide to have any sense of current fashion. His hair was buzzed with a military cut that emphasized this was a man who longed for the 1960s.

"You were a member of the same organization that included Duke Ellis, correct?

"Yes, ma'am."

"When was that?"

"Well, I came out to California ten years ago from Virginia. Duke, I mean Mr. Ellis and I met then and I knew him off and on for 'bout five years. I left the Klan back in 2013 or so."

"Why did you leave the Klan?'

"Me and my wife decided that the Klan was too dangerous

—and one of the people that made her ... and me worried was Duke Ellis."

"Now, this was five, six years ago. And you say the Klan was 'too dangerous'—I'm sorry, Mr. Sims, but you didn't already know that?" Peters leaned back against her table.

"Well, ma'am, yeah, of course, but we figured that was the old Klan. The way it was presented to us was like ... well, it was more like the people were just trying to make sure that white folks didn't lose rights, you know what I mean?" He had a look on his face that gave the impression that he was talking to someone who did not speak his language.

"Actually, no, I don't understand why anyone would join an organization that claimed that one race is superior to another. But that's not why you are here today. Please tell us who, as you say, presented the Klan as a seemingly political organization."

"Duke Ellis. He talked me into joining. Honestly, I am a gentle man. I don't believe in violence."

"Good to know," Peters replied sarcastically. "What about all the racial attacks on blacks, Mr. Sims? Was that all right with you?"

"No, ma'am. You know, I was just a dumb redneck. My wife, well, she thought what I was doing was crazy, and I told her that I was just a fool for going along with the other guys. It was all dumb, really." He seemed to Rossi to be resigned to being beaten down by his own actions.

"Tell the jury about the night George—Duke Ellis—spoke to your 'guys' five years ago, the very night you quit the Klan and you and your wife subsequently moved to another city."

"Yeah. Okay. That was when Duke was running for some other local office—I dunno, assemblyman or something. And he had a meetin' and he was all ticked off because the guy he was running against said he was unqualified for the position because of his military record and other stuff. Duke was mad as hell. And he got us all mad, too. So the boys, we figured, we'd go down to that fella's campaign office and mess it up. He was an Or-re-ental guy ..."

"I'm sorry, a what?" Peters seemed genuinely surprised.

"Oh, well, he was a Chinaman. Sorry. Did I say something wrong?" Sims flushed.

"Never mind, Mr. Sims. What happened next?"

"Okay. So, we show up and the other guys start spray painting stuff—race stuff, you know. But before we could do other things," he considered how he was going to say his next confession, "like, um, break the front window, then the cops showed up. One of the guys was getting into it with the cops and, well, he got arrested. But I didn't 'cause I was not really doing much. And Duke, he was there, but when the cops came, he acted all innocent and said he told the guys to knock it off."

"So he did not, as you say, 'do much'?" Peters leaned into the question.

"Oh, he did, ma'am. Sure did. He was the main reason we was there and he was the guy who brought the spray paint ..."

"Objection, Your Honor." Devlin's anger was evident. "This is character evidence and it's not admissible. This incident is prejudicial to my client. The jurors need to know this event has no bearing on the current charge."

Peters responded, "Your Honor, the prosecution is not implying that this prior event caused the current charge. However, it indicates that Duke Ellis had a history of inciting followers to do damage that was racially motivated in a previous election. It speaks to motive, Your Honor, which is an exception to the inadmissibility of character evidence."

Judge Lewis took a breath. "I am aware of the exceptions, Counselor. And I am inclined to overrule the objection, Mr. Devlin. However, the jury is to understand that this event, five years prior to the current charge, cannot, I repeat cannot, prove that Mr. Ellis is guilty of the current charge."

Rossi watched Devlin's reaction to the judge's decision. Devlin was despondent and frustrated.

"Thank you, Your Honor. One last thing, Mr. Sims, please tell the jury why you are here today five years after all this happened."

"My wife read about Duke Ellis over by where we used to live, and she made me promise to tell about what he really was like. She said that that's what Jesus would do and I am not any way like I used to be. The Lord has helped me to see the error of my ... my thinking."

"I am glad you listened to your wife. No further questions." Peters took a seat.

Devlin was rapier quick. "How come you didn't go to the police with this five years ago and tell them it was all George Ellis's fault?"

"Well, I didn't think of that. And some of them was my friends. And well ... I guess I was a coward, sir." He looked down at his hands.

"And all this happened because my client told you directly to do it?"

"Not ex-exactly directly. We just sorta did it. Talkin' with the guys we figured it was what Duke would want."

"I see, you assumed it was what he wanted. Do you have proof that he purchased the paint?"

"What kinda proof?"

"Mr. Sims, you said he 'bought the spray paint.' How do you know that?" Devlin was leaning over the podium.

"Well, no. But he had a can and ..."

"Didn't other men have cans of spray paint? How do you know Mr. Ellis intended for this to happen?" Devlin held the question like a singer would hold a note.

"I-I just assumed."

Devlin pivoted. "Well, that's not too Christian to assume the worst, is it? By the way, you have not seen my client for over five years, correct?"

"Yes ... I mean no."

"And you were not there on the evening of this disturbance that he has been charged with, correct?"

"Um, no." Sims was shrinking as if the air had been let out and his confidence punctured.

"The truth is you know nothing about what he is being charged with, sir."

Peters objected. "Badgering the witness, Your Honor."

"Sustained. Mr. Devlin, I think you've made your point." Judge Lewis wanted to end the torture, Rossi figured.

14

SUSIE HALL

"I call Miss Susie Hall to the stand, Your Honor."

Susie Hall was a study in contrast to Wayne Sims. Rossi placed her as a college student, maybe twenty years old. She would not have weighed more than 100 pounds after eating a full Thanksgiving meal. She wore dress jeans and a blazer with a mock turtleneck top. Her wavy brown hair was shoulder-length, parted in the middle. Her body language gave the impression that she was not nervous; rather she almost jogged up to the witness stand, eager to say what she had to say.

Patrick Rosen, the co-counsel with Peters, did the questioning. "Thank you for driving down to San Diego, Miss Hall. You and I spoke in Riverside County months ago, and I would like you to tell the court what you told me then." His demeanor reminded Rossi of himself when he spoke to students about their troubles.

"Miss Hall, please tell the court how the defendant Duke Ellis accosted you," Rosen began.

"I will. My boyfriend and I were canvassing for Congressman Curtis ..."

"Please explain the term canvassing."

"Oh, sure. My boyfriend Jacob and I were going door to door asking people to support Congressman Curtis."

"Thank you. Jacob is not here today, however. Please explain."

"Right. He is in D.C. ... Washington, D.C., working for the Congressman. He is Mr. Curtis's press secretary. He could not be here because of conflicting engagements. I decided that what happened needs to be told. I mean, I felt strongly that people needed to know what Duke Ellis and his campaign workers were really all about."

"I see. Go on." Rosen was far less loquacious than Peters. His "just the facts" style kept things to the bare bones.

"Jacob's last name just happens to be Rosen—no relation to you, Mr. Rosen. But like you, sir, Jacob is Jewish. This is important because three weeks before the election, while we were in a particular neighborhood close to the Ellis headquarters, Duke Ellis's men came up to us and asked us what we were doing there. We told them what was obvious; after all, we had signs and posters for Curtis. They then grabbed the posters from my hands and Jacob's flyers and told us to leave."

"Leave?"

"Leave. We were like, 'What are you doing? Are you guys goons or something?' Then Jacob tried to grab the posters back and one guy shoved him and called him a Jew boy."

Rosen paused before asking the next question to make sure her last words landed. "How did these 'guys,' as you referred to them, know this?"

"Because Duke Ellis told them." She looked directly at Ellis.

"Objection." Devlin stood. "This witness has no proof of this charge, Your Honor. It is hearsay at best, and a fabrication at worst."

Ms. Hall spoke up before the judge could rule. "Judge, let me explain."

Judge Lewis seemed as if he had a second thought on the

objection. "Overruled. Explain how you knew this. I do not want to hear what you think your associate believed."

So Hall continued, "So, just as Jacob was about to get into a real fight with the two guys if they didn't give our stuff back, around the corner comes Duke Ellis—he just happened to be there. He asked what was going on and one of the guys, his name I didn't know then, but I do now ... his name was Bud Temple. Anyway, he said he was an assistant to Ellis and he said something like, 'These two are bothering people in our town.' He pointed at Jacob and said, 'This Jew is telling lies about you.'"

It appeared to Rossi that the defense and both sets of lawyers just froze like mannequins—all hanging on Hall's next words.

"That's when Ellis acted shocked, like he was not happy with his men, and said that we could be there, as if we needed his permission, and then looked at this Bud Temple moron and said so sarcastically, 'We don't want any trouble with their kind.'"

"What did he mean by that?" Rosen pushed for closure.

"Jews. Obviously. I mean, how did he know Jacob was Jewish, huh? He knew ... because he knew. He knew who worked for Congressman Curtis and he knew Jacob. And that buddy of his had to be told by Ellis because how else would he know? Seriously?"

"I see. You deduced Ellis had told him. Just a few more questions: you said he took your voter information and posters. Did you get them back?"

"Sort of. They tossed them on the ground when Ellis told them to return our stuff, but only after Ellis told us—tried to intimidate us—to not bother people or tell lies about him. He was so sarcastic, Mr. Rosen. He was saying one thing and pretending to be all above board, but you could tell it was all ... fake."

"Were you harmed physically?"

"Not me. Jacob was pushed around, but no. It could have gotten really bad—of course, there was Duke Ellis so conveniently around the corner, ready to be Mr. Peacekeeper. Look, the message was clear: get out of here. We felt threatened. We called the Congressman, Mr. Curtis, and he told us we should leave. He did not want anything to happen to us. So we left. That's the way Ellis operates ... and he thinks he should sit in the United States House of Representatives. He makes me sick." Rossi thought Susie Hall wasn't pulling any punches.

Rosen turned to Judge Lewis. "Jacob Rosen's sworn testimony was deposed in Washington, D.C. It corroborates Miss Hall's testimony."

Judge Lewis looked at Devlin. "You have read this, I presume."

"Yes, Your Honor. May I question the witness?"

Rosen waved his arm toward Miss Hall. "I have no further questions."

Rossi glanced at Regina next to him. Her face wasn't meant for poker. It was clear she was worried about how Miss Hall was going to handle cross-examination. So was Rossi.

Devlin buttoned his coat and slid out from behind the defense's table. "Miss Hall, I am sorry about the incident that occurred to you that you just described, as I am sure my client is, too." Devlin was trying to appear warm as opposed to confrontational.

"I do want to get some clarification, however. You said you were not harmed physically, and Mr. Jacob Rosen's letter indicated that he was not harmed in that manner either, correct?"

"That depends on your definition of harmed, sir." She did not back down.

"No broken bones or cuts or any reason to seek care from a doctor. That is what I mean by physical harm."

"No. But I was scared out of my mind. I think that counts."

"Yes. I imagine those two men you say accosted you were more than a little frightening, and I agree you had every right to be 'canvassing' for Mr. Curtis. But my question is that, in your own words, you deduced that Mr. Ellis had told them that Jacob Rosen was Jewish. You have no knowledge that that happened. No direct knowledge."

She leaned into the question. "Like I said, how else would they have known?"

Devlin turned and looked at the jury. "Well, Mr. Rosen was a well-known adviser—he is presently in D.C. working for the Congressman, so one could also surmise that his background was public knowledge just as easily as deducing that Mr. Ellis told the men he was Jewish. Isn't that also another reasonable assumption?"

"I don't know. That isn't really the point." Hall stiffened.

"Perhaps, but let's get to the point. Didn't Mr. George Ellis order his workers to stop harassing you? He reprimanded them, and then told them to return your materials, correct?" Devlin stayed focused on the jury.

"Reprimand is too strong a word, sir. And by return, I didn't appreciate them tossing our campaign posters on the ground."

"Didn't Mr. Ellis caution you to not fabricate lies about him to the people you were speaking with?"

"We weren't doing that; we were just informing people about Congressman Curtis."

"But do you admit that both campaigns complained about exaggerations or misinformation that was being publicized? Isn't that something that seems to happen far too often in politics, Miss Hall?"

"I agree. But Duke Ellis was trying to intimidate us."

"How?"

"What? Are you asking me? I've already told you how. They took our stuff. Threatened us. Knocked Jacob to the ground ... what do you want?"

Devlin remained cool. "I agree with you that Mr. Bud Temple and the other man with him physically accosted you, but you have no proof that Mr. Ellis ordered them to." He turned to her, "Do you?"

"Some things are obvious, sir."

"Perhaps to you ... especially in a very competitive political race. But I ask you again, with what did Mr. George Ellis use to intimidate you?"

A beat.

Susan Hall searched for the right words. Then she acknowledged the obvious. "With words. That's how he operates, sir. That's what he used in his rallies—words—and he used ... uses them to strike fear into people and make them angry. Don't you see?" She had her wits about her to realize it was the jury that she needed to convince, and her eyes moved from Devlin to the jury box.

"I see." Devlin smiled. "Politicians do that. They use words, as do teachers and doctors and lawyers, Miss Hall. Mr. Ellis was promoting himself and what he believes in. Isn't that what the First Amendment is all about?"

"Duke Ellis was promoting racism, sir."

"That is not what he is charged with. Were you at the rally that occurred before the crisis at the Curtis home?"

"No. Of course not. Why would I be?" She crossed her arms.

"You wouldn't. And you can't possibly tell this jury if he incited a riot. That is all I have for this witness, Judge."

15

FAMILY MATTERS

"Tony, you look like you've had a long day."

"I did." Rossi was sinking like quicksand into the recliner. It was his go-to place to watch TV, but it doubled as his favorite place to doze off.

"I'm heating some rotisserie chicken and we are having a salad with it. I'd offer you some wine, but I am not sure you'll stay awake." She knew her husband better than he knew himself. When he was quiet as he was on the trip back from the train station, Deborah knew that he was rummaging through his thoughts. How each of them handled the day's tribulations was a sharp contrast. Deborah would generally want to talk about her students or the inter-actions with her colleagues, but her husband often mulled things over before eventually articulating his latest news. But this evening, she was not sure he would ever get that far. He was spent.

"Oh, chicken. Sounds great." Out of habit Rossi grabbed the remote control and put on the news. The local weather person was chirping away. It was a running joke that the easiest job in San Diego County was to be the weather reporter. If there was a gust of wind or a few sprinkles, it would be a heyday for the meteorologists.

"Sure was a nice day, today." Rossi pointed to the television. "She says there is rain tomorrow. Seriously? "He then hit the mute button.

"You know how they get so excited when they think even a drop of rain may be coming. I'll believe it when I see a cloud in the sky, but you better take an umbrella tomorrow. When do you have to be there?" Deborah considered what topics they would cover at dinner. One was unavoidable, the other she'd rather keep to herself.

"Nine o'clock just like today." His eyes were heavy, and sometime between the sports segment and the beginning of the national news, he drifted away, only to shake off the drowsiness when his wife announced that dinner was on the table.

It was habitual to watch the national evening news unless there was a Padres baseball game on tv. With the baseball season for the local team over, the local news was on but muted. So their dinner's soundtrack consisted of some 'smooth' jazz. Deborah smiled as Grover Washington's song "Just the Two of Us" blew into the dining room.

Retirement was a new phenomenon for them. Their two adult children were out and about in the world, with the youngest daughter a year from her college graduation. Both of them were trying to decompress after their last year teaching and all the hoopla that went with retirement parties.

Teaching was a marathon in many ways. Each year brought new challenges, new technologies, new bureaucracy, and more and more students packed into their classrooms. Deborah contended that it was in the last five years that it had gotten to the point where it became difficult to keep up her standards. Tony felt the same. So neither wanted to jump into volunteering until they had time to rest and reevaluate the road they were to travel. But then the jury summons arrived and a path was chosen for one of them. Deborah decided she needed to at least immerse herself, however grudgingly, into the ugly world Tony faced in the courtroom.

From the kitchen she reminded him, "Tomorrow, we are going to your sister's for dinner, remember?" Deborah placed the salad on the table. "I got this chicken today at Seaside Market—it's always so much fresher. "She looked up to see her husband staring at a local reporter outside the Federal Courthouse. The volume muted. The pictures told the story.

Rossi was not aware that protesters had to be quelled by the police, with skirmishes and punches thrown between two opposing factions. Signs reading No Justice No Peace were scuffling with Take America Back banners. Rossi took the remote and pushed the off button.

"Sorry, Tony. I guess we need to pay attention to what's on now—or until you are done." Deborah reached over and touched his other hand. "How did it go today ... in general?"

"Not as bad as that, but close. It is pretty combative and getting more so with each witness." Rossi was not sure if he should say much more. It felt like once he started, how could he stop?

She understood. Better to leave it at that. "Well, tomorrow I will get a break from cooking. Oh, Ann said that she's inviting the Richardsons for dinner, too."

"Good. I can catch up on the latest in the baseball playoffs. Didn't you play tennis with Ann today?"

Rossi and Deborah were also opposites when it came to how a chicken should be enjoyed. Tony used his fingers on the legs and thighs; Deborah's utensils dissected the chicken's breast.

"I did. She was really into it. You know how competitive she can be. God forbid I mess up the score. Anyway, it was good, and I think this is going to be something we can do on Tuesdays when she is off." Ann was a nurse and her husband Ron, a pharmacist. Discussions on Obamacare had to be kept to a minimum. Both couples knew health care was a topic that often raised everyone's blood pressure.

"That's great. Once I am done with jury duty, I'm calling the guys so I can embarrass myself on the golf course like I did last summer."

Silence took hold as the music turned to a guitar solo from Jessie Cook. The quiet could be awkward, strange. Summers always meant visits from their children and family gatherings. They both missed the sounds of their children's voices, chattering away about high school teachers, sports, and eventually college professors, roommates, and when they would be returning for the holidays. Then it became new jobs, new loves, new cities.

Perhaps that was one reason for the news at dinner. They never were at a loss to share the trials and tribulations of the day. However, not having teaching and students and administrative blunders to bat around resulted in either silence, repeating what they said earlier, or mundane topics like how much gas prices had risen. And now an avoidance of the news cycle.

Deborah finished dinner first, as usual. She hesitated to turn back to the topic she knew she had to face. "Tony, I have to tell you something. I hope I didn't make a poor choice."

"I'm sure you didn't."

"Well. Um. Ann asked about you and I just said you had jury duty. And she groaned and I groaned, and then she said something like how she always gets out of it by saying she's a nurse and she can't take time off or something ..."

"And so?"

"Anyway, all of a sudden she looked at me and asked if you were actually on a jury. And I thought about lying, but I am so bad at making something up ... and when I was stammering to figure out what to say, she blurted out, 'Don't tell me he is on that case that is all over the news!'"

Rossi hummed. "Aaannd ..."

Deborah winced. "I told her you ... were. I'm sorry. I should have thought about what I would say if she asked, but she caught me off guard. I'm so ... I should have said you were on something else—a murder, robbery, I don't know. Anything but ... but whatever it is you are on."

She was so flustered that Rossi couldn't help but laugh. "Honey, it's no big deal. Really."

"God, I hope she doesn't bring it up at dinner. You know your sister. She'll just ask about the trial right in the middle of Ron's barbeque ribs!"

Rossi dropped his knife in faux surprise. "We're having barbeque ribs! I love Ron's ribs! It's why I still talk to him after the Obama argument." Rossi smiled.

Deborah knew her husband would not miss an opportunity for a wise crack. "Oh, great. If the trial comes up, we'll change the topic to Trump!" Deborah's eyebrows were triangles peaking up to her bangs.

"No, we will not! That would spoil everything."

"Right. I want to digest my food. Speaking of Trump, did you hear what he said about Charlottesville?"

"Honey, maybe we shouldn't talk about that now either, huh? I kinda need to decompress and remember I'm sort of on this subject all day, you know?"

"Right. What was I thinking?" Deborah finished her chicken and Rossi scooped up her plate.

"Aren't the baseball playoffs on TV at seven o'clock?" Rossi said as he began his nightly battle with the dishes. He knew the evening would be best served chilled with a beer, some peanuts, and baseball.

16

EMI NISHIMURA

Anthony Rossi hopped off the morning southbound Coaster's commute refreshed and hopeful that today's segment of the trial would not tax him as much as the previous day. He wondered if one gets more accustomed to the strenuous nature of listening vigilantly and sitting for long spells. He certainly hoped so.

He walked up to the courthouse at 8:15, hoping to avert the crowd he witnessed yesterday. The space they seemed to occupy had expanded further up both streets and police were already keeping an eye on things. The CNN van now had company with other networks getting into parking stops and a few reporters scouting out places to anchor down their early updates. The protesters themselves were fairly subdued, as signs were being unrolled, flags actually being sold, and only dirty looks being passed from one camp to the other. *Let's hope it stays that way*, Rossi thought.

Rossi quickly passed through the metal detectors with just a quick wand wave of his knees and no line at the coffee and snack cart. He had saved the sports section to read while waiting. On the train ride, he dispensed with the national and local news sections and avoided the story about the Ellis trial located below the fold on page one. He wasn't the only juror with the idea of beating the throng that would likely be appearing soon.

Two of the women on the jury who sat in the row behind him were chatting as they came up to the coffee cart. Placing them in his mind's eye, they were Jurors #3 and #6. He only knew that they were younger than he, likely in their late thirties or mid to late thirties and both brunettes. Juror #3 wore comfortable clothes, sensible but still appropriate for the setting. In sharp contrast, Juror #6, who sat directly behind him, was making quite the fashion statement in black pleated slacks, a silk royal blue blouse, and a matching jacket draped over her arm. Jewelry was on display for her; for her companion, not so much. Both had cell phones twice the size of Rossi's.

Rossi smiled and offered to buy their coffee. The ladies agreed to the deal, but Juror #6 remarked that it would be her treat tomorrow, to which Rossi joked, "Same time, same place." And all three burst into shrewd but controlled laughter.

As the coffees were sipped, Rossi introduced himself. "I'm Tony. You probably know me as the last juror." More nods and smiles. "I know you as ..." he acted as if he was counting in his head, "Jurors #3 and #6. I've never been on a jury before so I don't know the protocol about names but ..."

Slightly taller due to her four-inch heels, Juror #6 sliced into an explanation. "No worries, Tony. I'm sure it is fine. After all, we can't keep referring to each other as numbers, unless we wore uniforms." They laughed quietly. "I'm Melanie." She shook Rossi's hand. Quite professional. A firm handshake.

"Hi, Tony. I'm Kim," said Juror #3. "Do you live downtown?" No handshake.

"No, I actually commute by train from Encinitas."

Melanie raised one brown eyebrow. "Smart man, keeping your global footprint and the driving anxiety to a minimum. I came over from Coronado. The bridge traffic isn't too bad coming into downtown, but that's because it is past the height of the early morning rush."

"We had lunch together yesterday," Kim said. "So we know a little about each other. I live not too far from here in Kensington."

"Those are both nice areas. My wife and I used to go to the Ken Cinema back in the day."

"Oh, it's still there. I live pretty close to it. I can walk there ...actually."

"And Coronado, Melanie, that's our local getaway. The Hotel Del is always our first choice to stay ... if it's not already booked," Tony explained to Kim, who nodded in approval.

Melanie seemed somewhat aloof, looking over Rossi's shoulder at the media that seemed to be coming at them in a rush to get closer to Department 2A's door. "Well, here they come. I hope this doesn't turn into a circus." She seemed overly concerned.

Just then Henry, the bailiff, spotted the threesome and corralled them into a small, rectangular room. Inside they saw two other jurors: the older gentleman who was in the navy, and sitting next to him thumbing through his messages on his cell phone was the Asian gentleman. Rossi found himself resorting to numbers again: #7 and #8. Neither looked up when they entered.

Within the next few minutes, all the other jurors, except Juror #1, had entered the room, most making small talk. Rossi noted that the missing juror was often standing apart from the others, preoccupied with whoever was on the phone. Henry, ever alert, was outside their door, which had a three-by-three window framed at eye level. Rossi checked his watch.

Just a minute before nine o'clock, the last juror burst in, apologetic and flustered. "Oh, God. I'm so sorry everyone. I hope I didn't cause the trial to be delayed. I could not find a parking spot to save my life. I guess I need to leave sooner, but you know how it is with kids." She then tried to put herself together and catch her breath.

Jane, the librarian who sat to the left of Regina, put her hand on the forearm of the young mother. "Relax, dear. You haven't missed anything. It's my experience that the morning session sometimes is delayed a bit. The lawyers are often talking with the judge. You're fine."

Rossi thought, *At least one of them has jury experience.*

As she put her cell phone in her purse, she again apologized. "Well, sorry everyone. And thanks ..."

"I'm Jane. I know how it can be with children."

Rossi overheard the tardy juror tell Jane that her name was Lauren. He noted that the women on this jury generally seemed to warm up to each other quicker than the men.

The door was propped open and Henry told them that the court was ready for them. They marched in through a path made clear by other bailiffs and sat in their seats. Just as it would be for every session, the lawyers stood and smiled. George Ellis appeared to be more buoyant today, wearing a broad, confident smile. *Maybe he was tutored by his lawyer*, Rossi mused. Almost as soon as Rossi sat down, he popped back up when Judge Lewis appeared.

"Welcome back, ladies and gentlemen of the jury. Again, I thank you for your commitment to this trial and your patience. I know you probably have many places to be and business to involve yourselves with, so all of us are grateful for your energy and attention. Counselor Peters, please call your next witness."

———

From the moment FBI agent Emi Nishimura was called to testify, a fracas broke out with multiple objections from Devlin and rebuttals from Peters. Then the judge called both lawyers over for a side bar. That went on for several minutes with their hushed voices inaudible to the jury.

This must have had something to do with the morning's delay, Rossi thought to himself. He surmised the crux of the argument must be centered on how relevant Ellis's past membership in the Ku Klux Klan was, and to what degree the actions of that organization could be included in this trial.

Finally, Judge Lewis sent the attorneys back to their respective corners as if it was a boxing match, and he nodded to Devlin. Whatever had been agreed upon in the side bar discussion seemed to be ignored once Devlin got back to his table because he objected again.

Devlin pointed to his client. "Your honor, as I argued in my earlier motion this is a blatant attempt at guilt by association. My client is not responsible for the actions of a lawless organization despite the fact that this organization still has the right to its ill-informed ideas on race; ideas that drove my client away from the organization."

Peters protested, "Your Honor, that organization, as his counsel so often avoids naming, is the Ku Klux Klan—and the reason they avoid that identification is because of its inherent evil and, as Mr. Devlin admits, lawlessness. Duke Ellis was a member of the Klan and only recently renounced his membership. He refuses to admit how long he remained a member. He has advocated the principles that are at the heart of this incitement charge for years, publicly and privately. The only way to understand his motives is to be informed of his background."

"None of this has anything to do with the actions of September 13th, Your Honor."

"Your Honor, this trial centers on whether or not Duke Ellis should be protected under the First Amendment. Therefore, it is best that the court discovers exactly what he and organizations like his stand for.

"Why? They have a right to free speech." Both lawyers were now yelling at each other, ignoring the judge and jury.

"No. That is what we are trying to establish. Let's find out what we are dealing with here. We are not talking about some innocuous group—we are talking about an organization that will stop at nothing to aid their cause—including murder."

At the word murder, Devlin's voice reached its maximum volume. "This is not a murder trial! This is outrageous and ..."

Judge Lewis decided he had heard enough and slammed his gavel, which froze Devlin in mid-sentence. "Both of you, please stop shouting in my courtroom. Volume does not equate to reason, Counselors."

Devlin was first to apologize with his voice overshadowed by Peters', "Sorry, Your Honor, but ..."

"Counselors, I have heard enough. I thought we had settled this in side bar. I have given you both more latitude than I would normally allow in my courtroom, but I am not going to allow another word out of either of you on this matter. Do not try my patience again." He waited and let the moment settle. The Judge gathered himself, "I assume the defense wants to put this objection on the record. It is so recorded, and I have over-ruled it. I made that clear in chambers and just now. Please, both of you, sit down."

Rossi found himself weighing the choice even though he had no say in the matter. This was the moment that Robert Frost considered so important, for the path of the trial would be altered. Once Judge Lewis made his choice, there was no going back. Which path to take? That would make all the difference.

The judge took off his glasses and turned directly to the jury. "I have overruled the objection of the defense counsel. I feel that in this particular case, it is important for the jury to understand some of the background of the organizations that have been associated with hate crimes and, let me stress to the prosecution, that I want this to be concise and related to the activity of the defendant George Ellis. Jurors, you must limit your use of this information to understanding the organization, and you may not use it as evidence to conclude that he is guilty of incitement on September 13th."

It was with that introduction that FBI agent Ms. Emi Nishimura was sworn in. She was not exactly how Rossi imagined an FBI agent to appear. Again, he chided himself for his stereotyping. Rather than a female crime fighter in a CSI drama prepared to take out any criminal with a single leg whip to the head, Agent Nishimura looked bookish and diminutive as if she had not been in the field in years. Yet it became apparent that she was one of the FBI's top researchers of hate crimes. Once her testimony began, Rossi knew she was a force to be reckoned with.

Peters began, "Agent Nishimura, I have asked you here to testify to the recent history of hate groups in California, and to give us an understanding of their significance across our country, as well as their means of attaining their goals. First, what is their goal?"

Agent Nishimura replied calmly. "The purpose of the Ku Klux Klan is to—and I quote from their literature—'protect the United States from invasion from any source whatsoever.' Therefore, their natural enemies are Catholics, Jews, Muslims, Blacks, and any other 'aliens'—basically anyone non-white. As an Asian myself, I am the enemy. They have splintered off into many other violent groups including Skinheads, Neo-Nazis, and the White Aryan Resistance, to name a few. The KKK has been listed by the Attorney General as a subversive organization because it does resort to violence as a means to their end, as do all the groups I have listed." She cocked her head as if to imply she had much more to say about the subject ... when asked.

"Tell the jury about recent FBI investigations, please, Agent Nishimura."

"Yes, well, I must preface my remarks by explaining that monitoring their activities on social media, in an effort to thwart their violent acts, is problematic since the Justice Department has discouraged collecting information on the internet. This is because the information published on the web can be considered free speech and protected by the First Amendment. For example, we cannot open a terror investigation on that basis. Unfortunately, we have been too late to stop murders that could have been thwarted had we been so empowered. You see, Ms. Peters, as of today hate is not illegal. However, acting on this hate and the tragedies it inspires is both a criminal action and a civil one. In the case of Mr. George Ellis, the speech he gave in the public realm demanded our action. Specifically, he called for his followers at his rally on September 13th to—and I quote—'... kick the niggers out of the state and let's do it now.'"

"And Mr. Ellis's call to action was not a unique one, I take it?" Peters wanted the band to play on.

"Certainly not. I must add that I was not the primary agent following Mr. Ellis's checkered past. Agent Howard Matt is the principal FBI agent assigned to Mr. Ellis. However, let me paint a picture of the racial tension here in California and even in San Diego."

"Do go on, Ms. Nishimura."

"Yes. California eclipses all other states in terms of hate groups and hosts the largest skinhead membership, mostly in Southern California, where Mr. Ellis resides and ran for office." She paused to presumably check her notes.

"This state is the most populist and has the highest population of Jewish and Muslim people, and accordingly it has the highest number of anti-Semitic and anti-Muslim incidents. One of the deadliest attacks was in 2015 when a husband and wife, inspired by foreign extremists' propaganda, murdered fourteen people in a government office in San Bernardino. The

Anti-Defamation League's audit discovered over one hundred incidents in this state that were attributed to a series of robocalls made by one Patrick Little, a white supremacist. This same man, similar to Mr. Ellis, ran an unsuccessful campaign for the US Senate in his attempt to unseat Diane Feinstein, whom he accused of being an Israeli citizen and a traitor to America. His robocalls stated that he intended to—I quote—'rid America of the traitorous Jews.' By the way, he received 89,867 votes."

Peters let that number settle in the air before she prompted Nishimura. "I see. More on the KKK, please."

"Of course. In California, law enforcement keeps tabs on white supremacists, and they have been more active than ever, especially since the 2016 election of the president. At a Ku Klux Klan rally in Anaheim, they fought with anti-Klan protesters. The violence there was replicated in similar brawls in Sacramento at the State Capitol building in 2016, as well as skirmishes in Huntington Beach and Berkeley—frankly, all this has its origins in 1980."

"Explain."

"Back then, Tom Metzger, a resident of San Diego county, was the KKK's Grand Dragon, their term for leader, and he and David Duke ran vigilante groups that 'patrolled the border'—in their words. David Duke created the White Aryan Resistance, and we have been investigating him for decades. In 2012, Wade Michael Page, a member of the United States' largest skinhead group killed six people in a Sikh temple in Wisconsin, but San Diego was the home chapter for his group."

"Thank you for all this valuable information and for all the work you and the FBI do to put an end to this madness and the violence it fosters. Your witness."

James Devlin was deliberate before he asked his first question. Rossi felt he was either unsure how to pursue or playing up the drama.

Remaining seated, he picked up his glasses and for the first time put them on. "Agent Nishimura, let's cover the issue of hatred. You said moments ago that, let me quote your exact words, 'Hate is not illegal.' Hate is an emotion, correct?"

Agent Nishimura couldn't help herself; she rolled her eyes. "Obviously."

"And you went on to say that the FBI is restricted in gathering information in social messaging on the internet because those messages are 'protected speech,' as part of the First Amendment, correct?"

"Yes. We are restricted, unless we are tipped off by a citizen that impending action is forthcoming and that lives are at stake. In many cases, as you know, we have thwarted attacks."

"I see. And the FBI is to be congratulated. However, the First Amendment is a paramount concern to the FBI, I take it?"

"No, sir. Life is a paramount concern." She was determined to set the record straight.

"Of course. Now let's get to the case of Mr. Ellis. You said another agent was the primary officer assigned to my client. Agent Howard Matt, correct?"

"Yes."

"I'll be questioning him later, but in your testimony, you provided no evidence that George Ellis ever murdered anyone. Isn't that so?"

"Not to my knowledge."

"Was he ever arrested by the FBI or the police for anything before these charges were filed?"

"Not by the FBI, sir. Agent Matt can speak to other instances."

"Did my client, to your knowledge, ever physically harm anyone?"

"Again, the word physically is the key, sir. By that I assume you mean did he personally do bodily harm to anyone causing him to have an arrest record. The answer is no."

"So he was arrested on September 13th because of what he said?"

"No. He was arrested for inciting a riot."

Devlin now rose. "Yes, based on what he said—an abstract concept. The state believes his words caused others to resort to violence. That is a value judgment on the state's part."

"Is that a question?" She smirked.

"The arrest on incitement is a value judgment—isn't that so?"

"No. When the defendant demanded at his rally that he wanted—his words, not mine—'niggers kicked out of the state,' that, sir, is not a value judgment. That is a threat and isn't abstract, it is concrete."

"Did George Ellis 'kick' anyone on the night of September 13, 2016?"

"No. Others did his dirty work for him."

"Do you have any idea, Agent Nishimura, why George Ellis left the Klan?"

Peters quickly objected, "It's speculation, Your Honor."

Agent Nishimura replied anyway. "He is your defendant, sir. You'll have to ask him," she shot back.

"He was disgusted with the methods used by that organization. So he left." Devlin paused.

"Sustained. Judge Lewis looked as if he had eaten a slice of lemon as he turned to the jury. "Disregard Mr. Devlin's statement, jurors. Court reporter, strike it from the record. I caution you, Mr. Devlin, you have no authority to speak for your defendant. You know better," he spat.

Devlin apologized. He took a minute to regroup. Rossi wondered if this was how the game was played. The lawyers say things that they wish to plant into the juror's minds, and if their efforts are censored by the judge, they hope a seed of doubt grows fruit. He reminded himself to ignore Devlin's comment, as if that could be easily erased like chalk on a chalkboard.

Devlin picked up some materials from his desk and studied them momentarily. "Have you ever felt like your organization—the FBI—has used methods that you felt sickened you so much that you would consider leaving?"

"What are you asking?" For the first time, she seemed confused.

"It's a simple question, Agent. Do you wish for me to repeat it?"

Peters was on her feet. "I object, Your Honor. What is the relevance? What does Agent Nishimura's opinion of the FBI have to do with this case?"

"Judge Lewis, I asked that same question when we allowed this witness to testify. If we are going down this road, then let's follow it to its conclusion, please."

The judge pursed his lips. "I see your point, Mr. Devlin. Overruled. The witness may request the question to be repeated or reworded if needed."

"Thank you, Judge. Again, Agent Nishimura, have you ever considered the FBI's actions or methods so deplorable to you such that you would consider leaving the FBI?"

"You, sir, are using false equivalents. Comparing the FBI to the KKK is ridiculous. And no, sir, I would not leave the FBI." She raised her voice for the first time since she had taken the stand. She simply could not hide her anger.

"Two things, Agent Nishimura. First, I suggest you recall how your former director Mr. Hoover had FBI agents spread the word that Dr. King had mistresses and that this falsehood was communicated to his wife, Coretta Scott King. Second, that your angry words just now could incite me to react …"

"Objection. He is badgering the witness and lecturing the court …"

Devlin spoke over Peters, "… I know they are only words, emotions. Fortunately, I am a peaceful man, but you could not know that when you spoke, could you?"

Peters tried to get a word in edgewise, "Your Honor ..." But before the judge could rule, the witness rebutted Devlin's harangue.

Agent Nishimura gathered herself. "There is a world of difference between my defense of the department and Duke Ellis's attack on an innocent man and his family, sir."

"Really? I suppose that is yet another value judgment." Devlin bristled and tossed his legal pad on his table.

Judge Lewis again brought his gavel down. "Mr. Devlin, you are badgering this witness. Sustained."

"No further questions, Your Honor." He sat down and readjusted his tie.

"Your Honor, allow me to redirect." Peters was asking, not demanding.

Judge Lewis, perhaps because of Devlin's antics, merely nodded.

"Agent Nishimura, I have read your file and I am quite impressed with your long, dedicated service to our nation; however, when I heard the defense attorney question you about 'hate not being illegal,' I wondered how you have managed to not carry animosity toward the United States government?"

"You must be referring to the fact that my family was put in a Japanese internment camp during the war." Emi Nishimura sat upright and responded to her own rhetorical question. "My parents were instrumental in teaching me and my siblings that hate is a pointless, dark place, and that if you dwell there, you'll never be able to see the light. People make mistakes, as do governments. My parents emphasized that to be wise, one must learn from those errors in judgment. And that is a value I hold dear."

"Thank you ... very much, Agent—Ms. Nishimura. No further questions."

As he did the first day of the trial, Judge Lewis thanked the jury for their attention and cautioned that they should not discuss the trial with each other or anyone including family during the lunch break. He ended by explaining that at least one other witness would be testifying in the afternoon. With that, he adjourned the court.

In the time he took to explain these points, Anthony Rossi used every second to scribble down points he did not want to forget. Anything particularly important would be underlined ... sometimes twice. In this case his emphasis: <u>false equivalents</u>.

17

RONALD PAUL ROBERTS

The bailiff took roll, as he did each day before letting the jury into the courtroom, but this time Anthony Rossi paid close attention to putting a name to a face. Then when he entered the courtroom, he made a chart in his notebook so that when the time came, he knew who was who. Better, he thought, to call someone by their name. At that point, he realized he was creating a seating chart. Old habits never die. He charted the jurors as they were seated:

#1- Lauren- the woman who was late; has children; always on the phone.

#2- Jim- worked as a manager at Sears, maybe? Wears a tie ... a wide one.

#3- Kim- lunched with Melanie; friendly, down-to-earth.

#4- Russell- goes by Russ; wears athletic clothing; a coach, perhaps?

#5- Adam- youngest; local college student?

#6- Melanie- had lunch with Kim; well off? Definitely over-dressed.

#7- Heroyuki Sato- Henry called him Mr. Sato; sports coat and tie.

#8- George- oldest member probably; retired Navy. Very quiet.

#9- Joe Garcia- owns a landscaping company; self-made man.

#10- Jane- been on juries before; retired librarian ... for county or school?

#11- Regina- real estate agent. Intense. Professional.

Rossi finished writing just as Judge Lewis was entering the courtroom. He apologized for the slight delay, thanked everyone, and asked the prosecution if they were prepared to call their next witness.

"Yes. We call Ronald Paul Roberts to the stand."

Roberts was by far the tallest person in the room. Rossi concluded that with Roberts' frame and size, he had to be an athlete or at least a former one. He looked to be in his mid-thirties. Roberts wore a tie, but Rossi couldn't help feeling that this was not his uniform of choice. No sooner had he taken a seat, he loosened his tie and unbuttoned his clearly too-tight collar. He winced at the effort. Rossi glanced behind him to the juror in the fourth seat, Russell, who seemed to be taking in the measure of Roberts' demeanor.

Roberts brushed back his hair the way Robert Redford did in the movies. He had what some might describe as rugged, movie star looks. Then he gave a broad pearly white smile to no one in particular, but Rossi spotted an indication of nervousness, which he made more obvious as he rubbed his palms against his slacks. *Sweating already?*

"Mr. Roberts, you were present at George Ellis's rally on the night of September 13th, 2016, were you not?"

"Y-yes, I was there."

"What was the reason you were in attendance?" Peters was glancing at her yellow legal pad.

"Um. Well, it was my assignment."

"Please, sir, explain for the jury."

"Right. Well, for the last five years I've worked for the FBI as a sort of ... a consultant."

"No. No. No. Mr. Roberts, before the defense even objects, allow me. You are an informant for the FBI, isn't that so?" Peters dropped the legal pad and also nodded to Devlin. *Professional courtesy*, Rossi figured.

"Uh, yeah."

"And your file shows that you were a drug dealer selling first to sports teams and eventually to the ... Aryan Resistance, did I get that right?" Peters was being coy.

"Yes. That's true, but can I say something? I wasn't one of those skinheads and I don't believe in that ... s-stuff. It was just business. Bad business, I admit. And I got caught and ... well, because of my connections, the FBI offered to drop the charges if I cooperated with them on a few cases ... for a while, anyway."

"Right. I'm glad that you have seen the error of your ways, Mr. Roberts. And one of those cases involves the defendant, Duke Ellis, correct?"

"Yes." He took a deep breath. "I've been 'acting' like I'm a Klan member and going to all the rallies ... even helping Ellis's campaign. This was what I was told to do by my agent, Howard Matt, who was my contact person."

"Your boss. All right, please tell the jury about what they are about to see on the television screen, Mr. Roberts."

Up until now, Rossi hadn't noticed the large television screen. It was set back by a partition. As Peters spoke, two bailiffs were moving it into place and making sure all the jurors had a clear vantage point.

"Okay. Well, I had made some voice tapes of Ellis when I talked to him. I wore a wire so that the FBI could hear. Anyway, Ellis was never saying anything that was too bad ... racist stuff but not physically threatening, I guess. At least Agent Matt didn't think so. But on this night—the 13th of September—I had a cell phone ... a better one than I usually carry ... that was given to me by Agent Matt, who wanted me to record what happened. Get a video recording, I mean. That's what they're gonna see ... on the night when Duke Ellis spoke to the guys, mostly guys, at his rally."

"Before we show the jury, explain the Ellis campaign's techniques for gathering votes."

"Oh. Okay. Well, most of the time I was given orders by Bud Temple—he was kinda second in command. People called him the campaign manager. I don't really know if that's what he did. He was more like security, in my opinion. There were times when he and the guys, me included, would cause trouble for some of the Curtis people, mostly the blacks. Bud said that Duke figured if less blacks vote, then he would win. Duke told Bud that whatever they do—he would say be nice—but I know what Duke really meant. Duke was smooth like that. Smart. He didn't want his hands dirty."

"Objection. Judge, this witness is speculating. He has no direct evidence my client actually said that he wanted to 'keep his hands clean' or suppress the vote." Devlin acted nonchalantly.

"Sustained. Stick to what you know factually, Mr. Roberts." Judge Lewis looked directly at him.

"Sorry, Judge. Well, so I went along with stuff like putting posters on cars saying things like 'Black lives don't matter' or 'White Power.' Sometimes we wrote on signs, 'Niggers belong in Africa.' There was even one about Obama that said, 'A village idiot's gone missing in Kenya'—stuff that I knew was bad, but I had to do it because, like Agent Matt said, I had to get their trust. The whole thing makes me sick, now. But shoot ... I didn't want to go to prison, you know?"

"You had direct conversations with Duke Ellis, correct? Some that were on voice recordings?" Peters prompted her witness.

"Yeah. Duke was always the fightin' sort, if you know what I mean. He talked tough. Bragged is a better word. He told me that Christians need to stick up for our rights even if it means with our fists. 'Kick some ass,' was what he said. He told me one time that we'd been pushed around by the government too long and that laws were written by Jews for blacks and that just meant that white people always got screwed."

Peters asked this question of the witness, but her eyes were on the jury the entire time. "What did Duke Ellis say about Dr. Martin Luther King, Jr., Mr. Roberts?"

"Duke said that King wasn't a hero. That he was just someone who made white people feel ashamed 'cause they're white.' He said King was a communist agitator."

"I see. Judge Lewis, may I ask the bailiff to play the tape of the rally that Mr. Roberts recorded, please."

———

At first, the screen shook and was out of focus. It appeared Roberts held his phone near his hip due to the angle of the images. Roberts was off to Ellis's side so only half of Ellis's face could be seen when the video began. Ellis wore black pants and a white long-sleeved shirt. He had on a fire engine-red hat. As he pivoted, it was clear it was a "Make America Great" Trump cap. Other men were talking briefly, but then a voice, not captured in the video, boomed out: DUKE ELLIS. Ellis's voice dominated the scene.

"Tonight, I want to talk about your duties as Americans. Loyal, true Americans. Born here and raised here. Patriots. We know who used to be the enemy—the communists. And we thought they were defeated a long time ago. But that is far from the truth. They have been planning their comeback. They have slowly taken over our government. Obama has seen to that. He is a socialist and his Obamacare is just one of the things that his liberal Kenyan brothers have plotted. They are in control of most everything in government. They want abortions legal, but they outlaw our prayers in schools. They want to take away your guns so that you cannot defend yourselves. And most dangerous of all is that they have complete control, almost complete control of the media—the newspapers are all fake news. Liberal bullshit."

Rossi could tell from the video that Ellis had his audience mesmerized. Their off-camera vocal exhorting of Ellis, often repeating what he was saying or shouting obscenities at those he was vilifying, was chilling. To call their outcries vulgar would be an understatement.

"Liberals want to tax you and then give your money to the lazy niggers and other wetbacks who cross our boarder and want to get everything for free. Your taxes pay for their babies, their kids go to your schools, but do they pay any taxes? NO. They just take and take. The Mexicans are drug dealers and rapists like the President said. You know he's right. The niggers get away with all sorts of crap in the once great cities selling the drugs. You can't put enough of them in prisons—which your taxes pay for, too. The Jews launder all the money and control the banks and the courts. Almost every lawyer is a Jew, and let me tell you, they watch out for their own. The Chinese take our jobs and we let them. They make cheap junk, and we can't keep our jobs because of them."

There is a pause as the crowd grew raucous with each new riff that Ellis delivered. His voice grew louder. He rose to his tiptoes, and as he pointed to the sky, his face turned crimson.

"Well, it's time we take back our country. We gotta shut down the 'deep state.' We gotta stop listening to the fake news —shut it all down. We gotta clean out the swamp. We gotta fight for our rights—our white rights. It's gotta happen with this election. Trump is right. Hilary Clinton is the devil and we need to lock her up. LOCK HER UP! We gotta make sure that

Curtis does not step foot in our Congress. We gotta kick the niggers out of this county, this state. It's them or us. And LET'S DO IT NOW!"

The picture jostled and then abruptly ended. The courtroom was dark. Rossi was stunned.

18

REBUTTAL

The lights blinked on and while the bailiffs were removing the television screen, Rossi peered to his left and took a quick inventory of his fellow jurors sitting in the first row. In the furthest chair, Mr. Heroyuki Sato was pokerfaced. George had his hands on his thighs, unblinking and pensive. Joe Garcia was trying to hide his anger but wasn't succeeding. Jane had her hand over her mouth and was clearly shocked. Regina was the easiest to read. Her arms were crossed; her attitude screamed, *well, we finally caught them in the act.*

Rossi tried to remember that closing one's mind off to all the information was never the right way to make any decision.

Peters looked at Judge Lewis, "No further questions for this witness."

Devlin approached the lectern and faced Ron Roberts with the charm of a cobra rattling its tail, ready to strike. "Let's get a few things straight, Mr. Roberts. You are an FBI informant, correct?"

"Yes, sir." Roberts was wary. *As he should be*, thought Rossi.

"That's because you were a drug dealer, an intermediary to the Mexican cartels, correct?"

"Well, I got my drugs from lots of sources ..."

Devlin had a file tucked under his arm, which he withdrew and then placed his glasses back on. "Says right here, 'Mexican drug cartels' as part of your file that the FBI provided to the defense after we requested it. You were a user, too—which is typical of dealers. Isn't that correct?"

"Um. Yeah. But I've been clean since I started work ..."

"Since you were caught, arrested, and worked out a deal with the FBI to catch bigger fish. Mr. Roberts, I know just how the game is played." Devlin placed the folder on his table, returned to the lectern and turned toward the jury to frame the next question. "It was in your interest to give the FBI the best evidence, correct?"

"Um. I don't understand."

"Sure you do. You just said that you wore a wire, right?"

"Yeah."

"But you didn't record the audio of any of the alleged conversations you testified to before the videotape was made, correct?"

"Well, no. But they happened."

"Really? I guess we will just have to take your word on that —the word of a motivated informant." Devlin paused.

Rossi half expected an objection from Peters, but none was forthcoming.

"Let's get to the night in question that you filmed on your phone. Did Mr. Ellis's speech convince you to go to the Curtis home?"

"Well, I-I didn't go."

"Why not? Wouldn't that have been in your job description to get the dirt on Mr. Ellis?"

"Well, I was supposed to follow Duke Ellis around. Ellis didn't go."

Devlin pounced. "How do you know that?"

"Um. Well. He didn't. I mean, I kinda lost him in the crowd."

"Oh. I see. Still, why didn't you go to film the event? Seems like you should."

Roberts swallowed, and despite his efforts to remain poised, he acted as though any minute his chair would fall right through the thin ice forming below.

"I don't know. I mean ... I just didn't. I mean, I-I'm not like them. Besides, I didn't stick my nose in to find out if there was gonna be some riot. I just did what I was told to do. Stick with Ellis ... until I lost him in the crowd like I just said."

"You seem to be contradicting yourself. It was your job to act like them and you did participate in some of the actions that you found to be wrong, correct?"

"Well, then I hadda do that, like I said to get their trust ..."

Devlin leaned over the lectern and directed fire at Roberts. "How many people were at Mr. Ellis's speech? Was it a public event?"

"Yeah. It was public because Ellis posted it to his social media, and, you know, racist websites from out of state, too. So anyone could come, but mostly his people locally came. His campaign staffers were there."

"And how many was that?"

"I dunno. I didn't count."

"Really? Take an educated guess, Mr. Roberts. More than ten, twenty, thirty ... fifty?"

"I guess ... about forty, maybe." He glanced at Peters and Rosen. They were impassive.

"Well, the police arrested two people at the Curtis home, and they questioned witnesses and the men that they captured. At most we are talking about ten to fifteen showed up at the Curtis home on the 13th of September. Seems like Ellis didn't incite a high percentage of his 'people'—and not even you, sir."

A beat.

"Last question. Did Mr. George Ellis ever tell you directly to injure, kick, hit, or physically attack anyone, Mr. Roberts?"

"Well, Bud Temple, he told us that Duke said ..."

Devlin pointed at Roberts. "Oh, sir, you did not hear what I asked you. I'm not asking about Bud Temple, we will deal with him later. Did Mr. George Ellis ever directly tell you to physically attack anyone?"

"No, sir."

Devlin removed his glasses and looked at Judge Lewis. "No further questions."

Peters was shaking her head and rising simultaneously as Devlin removed his glasses. "Your Honor, redirect, please."

"Granted."

"Mr. Roberts, you videotaped Ellis's speech and within the hour people were amassing at the Curtis home, isn't that a fact?"

"Yes, that's my understanding."

"Thank you, sir. No further need for questions, Your Honor."

"Mr. Roberts, you are excused. Counselor, do you have any other witnesses to call?"

"No, Your Honor. We have made our case clear. The prosecution rests."

Judge Lewis took a moment to whisper instructions to the bailiff, then turned to the jury. "Members of the jury, I want to thank you for all your attention ..."

Anthony Rossi was not listening to the genial appreciation of the judge. Instead, his eyes were glued to the defendant, Duke Ellis. Ellis had leaned back in his chair and was smiling as he flattened his tie against his protruding belly before buttoning his coat. He seemed aloof to the sober atmosphere in the courtroom. Ellis looked back to a woman, presumably his wife, and gave her a wink. She did not react at all. Devlin glanced over at him and then quickly placed his hand on Ellis's forearm.

Rossi turned his attention to the judge, then quickly

glanced to his left at his fellow jurors on his row. None seemed to have noticed Ellis's behavior, he thought, until Jane, two seats over, shot a quick look at Duke Ellis. She saw.

"... and so, court is adjourned until nine o'clock tomorrow when the defense will present its case."

Henry's voice resounded: "All rise."

19
_____

DEBORAH'S CLASSROOM

Deborah Rossi knew her husband better than he knew himself, so he wasn't surprised when she put her wine glass down and touched his forearm.

"You seem miles away, Tony."

He sighed. "I'm sorry."

"You have nothing to be sorry about. I think I have a pretty good idea where your mind is. After all these years, I spot the signs. You're playing with your food. Your eyes are unfocused. I know you, Tony. The gears are turning." She pointed to his head. "And I know you're not supposed to talk about the trial, but I want you to know that I have been watching the news, and I have some idea what's going on in there." She released his forearm. "It must be upsetting."

He let out a sigh and picked up his white wine. "Yes, it is. It was an ugly day. I wonder where this country's"—he drifted for a moment—"moral center has gone, you know? We live here in California and we think, well, this is 2017. This isn't the Deep South. But then a day like today comes, and it reminds me of how far this nation still has to go.'

"I know."

Deborah did not want to let on to what she was learning as she read various articles off the internet. The President's words had encouraged and emboldened white nationalists. The furor rose from anger about the removal of Confederate statues, but it had been fanned by the administration's remarks about globalism and 'America First'. All this, Deborah came to conclude, was being twisted into the idea that America is a 'white' nation and that ordinary 'white' people were getting ignored or even discriminated against. How ironic!

Deborah's reading indicated that white nationalists groups were coming out of the woodwork. The Southern Poverty Law Center's website claimed 155 such groups existed in most states. They were not including the obvious suspects like the Ku Klux Klan, racist skinheads, and neo-Confederate groups, all of which also express some version of white supremacist beliefs. Each organization had a deep seeded fear of demographic change. Pluralism was the common enemy. Even evangelical Christians had extremist views, many intolerant of other religions.

She had to force herself to detach from the screen. It made her sick—physically. She could not shake it off like it was some version of a horror film that was all pretend blood and screams. Is Anthony seeing some version of this macabre world?

It was so overwhelming. So disheartening. So contrary to what she valued as an American and as a teacher. Deborah began to wonder if she had been living in a bubble. She taught innocent ten year olds. Her curriculum introduced them to the American Revolution. To colonists' courage as they rebelled against the British. She did not dodge the fact that America's founding fathers had a blind eye to the profits reaped from slavery—it was, she explained to her fifth graders, "America's original sin."

What she taught was secondary to how she taught the children and what she expected of them as they interfaced with each other in her classroom. She encouraged each student to treat others with kindness and to support each other, especially those who struggled. She expected them to root for the under-dog. They were a team, and she wanted them to pull together like one.

She hoped they would be more prepared to enter a world in which working together and with mutual respect for others are the attributes that are valued, rewarded. Tolerance was part of the curriculum. Compassion and unity were embedded into her lesson plans, not just during Black History Month, but in every month.

Deborah Rossi's students put push-pins in her world map where their families may have immigrated from. She told her students, "Other than the American Indians and the Mexican people who lived in the Southwest, we are a nation of immigrants."

Had I been naïve? Which America was real to my students when they walked home from school? What would happen when my students grew up?

A beat.

Deborah repeated, "I know, Tony. I really do."

Tony looked up at her. "I know you do. And then I think about how I need to just be there to listen and not jump to conclusions. And I am trying. I am." Tony speared his grilled shrimp.

"Of course you are, Tony. It's not easy. I see what they are showing on TV and I worry about all of this ... and you." Deborah looked away. The catch in her voice could not be disguised.

"Don't worry about me, Hon." Tony seemed at a loss to form a cogent sentence that could quell the anxiety of the moment. So he opted for quiet.

James Taylor's soft voice seemed to be calling their names. "I love this album."

"I know you do, Tony. Why do you think I put it on?"

"Remember when we saw him in concert last summer?"

"Yes, I do." Deborah leaned toward him, and with powers only she possessed, she drew her husband's eyes up from his wine glass, or wherever his mind had wondered, to her own brown eyes. Then she whispered, "My favorite song of his is 'Whenever I see your smiling face' ..."

And she finally got Anthony Rossi to smile.

20

THE DEFENSE

Juror #1—Lauren —sat away from everyone in the hallway. She had taken her phone out, put it back in her purse, and a minute later grabbed it again. After checking the screen, she let out an almost silent *damn* that Rossi could hear as he wandered near her. It was in his nature, a teacher habit, to watch how people reacted, and he had a feeling that Lauren could use a little encouragement.

"Morning, Lauren. I'm Tony. Mind if I share the bench?"

"Oh, sure. Of course. Here let me move my bag." She slid down a few inches.

Rossi sipped his coffee. "We sure do a bit of waiting, especially in the morning."

"Yes. At least this time I'm here and not running late." She smiled. Then she started to say something but stopped abruptly.

"What were you going to say?" Rossi asked this innocuously so as not to pry.

"Oh. It's nothing, really. Tony, aren't you the high school teacher?"

"Ah, present tense, Miss Lauren. I am retired—so I was the high school teacher." Rossi grinned.

"Probably English, huh? That was my worst subject."

"Mine, too." They both chuckled.

"Oh, you're just being nice. I bet you're really smart. I watch you taking notes. I started to because of you," Lauren admitted.

Rossi rolled his eyes. "God, I hope people don't think I am trying to teach people how to be a juror. I've never been on a jury, and this case is ... well, let's just say my gray hair may tell you something about my memory. At least that's what my wife says."

"I bet you were a great teacher. No really, I can tell. You know, what I was going to say a minute ago was that my old band teacher used to have a name for me. Remember the movie *Dances with Wolves*?"

Rossi twisted himself slightly so they were looking at each other and not the dull, beige paint on the corridor wall. He nodded. "Sure."

"Well, Mr. Stephenson, the band teacher, used to kid around with us. He was really a good conductor. Well, anyway, he used to call me Running Late because I was always ..."

"... running late." They both had a quiet laugh. Rossi allowed this light moment to linger before he remarked, "I overheard you tell Jane, the woman that is two seats from me, that you have teenagers."

"Yes. I do. Two girls. A junior and a freshman in high school. It's a crazy time. Driving, college, grades, their friends—the hormones ... I am sure you know exactly what I mean."

"Yep. My wife and I have three adult 'kids,' recently out of college and employed thankfully. But it wasn't easy. High school itself isn't, and I taught juniors for twenty years. It's a particularly challenging time for them, and for their parents." Rossi finished the last sip of his lukewarm coffee.

"I mean they're great kids, really, but there are times when my husband and I are just so frustrated." She looked at Rossi. "But you and your wife got through it. So we just take it day to day, you know?"

"That's my advice. Just be there for them." Rossi noticed the doors open and Henry was about to call the jury in.

"Tony, it was so nice talking to you."

"Same, Lauren."

"Okay, well, here we go. I'll remember to take notes." She grinned as she grabbed her purse.

————

That was his wife. Rossi recognized the woman whom Duke Ellis had made eye contact with at the conclusion of yesterday's trial. She was being introduced as Mrs. Maureen Ellis, the wife of the accused. She was dressed conservatively in a dark blue dress that dipped just below her knees with a red shawl wrapped around her shoulders. No flashy jewelry. A patriotic color scheme. Her hair was so blond it appeared nearly white. Rossi surmised a shoddy bleach job, perhaps. She was quite attractive but her make-up was overdone. It took away from her natural beauty, but it may have been her attempt to make herself look younger than her mid-fifties.

James Devlin stood from his table and got right to the point. "On the 13th of September, last year, your husband was with you in the evening, correct, Mrs. Ellis?"

"Yes. Of course. He was always home in the evenings as long as he did not have campaign meetings."

Devlin moved swiftly to clean up her answer. "Yes, but on the night in question, when was he home?"

"Oh. Right. Yes. He was home for a late dinner that I warmed up for him because he missed dinner with me and the girls."

"Right. But when exactly?"

"Oh. Okay. That was eight o'clock, around." Rossi got the feeling they had practiced this question and answer, but Mrs. Ellis was struggling to remember exactly what her answer was supposed to be.

"And he never left the house for any reason, correct?"

She acted as if she remembered a point she had been coached to do because she made it so obvious to Rossi. Up until that time she looked directly at Devlin. But for this question, she paused just long enough to shift her body so she could face the jury and emphatically announced. "Absolutely not!"

"Thank you, Mrs. Ellis. I have just a couple of other questions." Devlin was being deliberate, giving her time to think. "You and your husband have been married for over twenty years, and in all that time has he been, let's say, violent or involved in any scuffles or even any verbal attacks with people of which you are aware?"

"Mr. Devlin, we have been married for twenty-four wonderful years. He has been a perfect husband and father for our children. He has never been in any fights or done any of the things that those men who attacked the Curtis home did. Not that I know much about that, just what I heard in court. And we never have had any fights or that sort of thing. It is ridiculous to accuse him of these things."

She was on her high horse Rossi thought.

Devlin's body language gave Rossi the impression that Mrs. Ellis was elaborating far too much, but he could not stop her once she got on a roll—doing so would have been rude.

"And no one is accusing him of any sort of violence." Devlin looked toward the jury. "So he was not at this incident. Had he mentioned to you that he had any suspicion that a protest would develop after his rally?"

She jumped to the answer before he could get the question out. "No. That's because he never did."

"I'm sorry, never did what?" Devlin stopped and wanted to clarify her remark.

"Never did ... what you said he did." Mrs. Ellis confused herself. Her nerves were exposed and her high horse suddenly bucked.

Devlin rebounded. "So he never spoke to you about inciting his men to be involved in a disturbance ... that what I was asking, Mrs. Ellis."

"That's what I said ... isn't it?" She glanced up at Judge Lewis who was impassive.

"Well, yes. I think I confused you. I apologize." Devlin was trying to get his witness back on track.

It was at that moment that Rossi understood Devlin must have been considering his strategy: the less said the better. After all, she had given the alibi he wanted the jury to hear. Ellis was not there. He did not say anything about his speech or any of the violence at the Curtis home. Maybe that was all he really needed her to say. Any more could muddle things.

"No further questions, thank you, Mrs. Ellis." Devlin sat down and looked at his client in a manner that communicated *your wife is doing fine. Don't worry ... and keep a straight face.*

Patrick Rosen handled the questions for the prosecution. *Interesting change.*

Rosen went to the lectern. "Mrs. Ellis, we have had a few conversations as well, and we appreciate your willingness to speak to the issues." He was playing the good cop. "Would you say that your husband is easy going?"

"Um. Pretty much. Yes."

"Not much of a temper?" Rosen was picking up the pace of questions.

"Not really."

"No arguments with neighbors?"

"I don't ... think so. No."

"And you and he see eye to eye on things, I take it."

"Mostly."

"Have you been to his rallies?"

"You mean when he is speaking to people in the campaign?"

"Exactly." Rosen kept the pace up.

"Most of the time. I think. I mean there were so many times he was out there."

"Of course. And someone had to be home with your children, obviously."

"Naturally, yes, of course."

"Would you say you were there maybe half the time?"

"Maybe."

"Sounds like you're not sure. Maybe less than half?"

"I don't really know. I didn't keep track." She glanced at her husband for the first time. Rossi thought, *maybe she was told to not look to him*—it would mean she did not know her own mind.

"Did Mr. Ellis discuss with you his platform?"

"His what?" Her eyes shot back at her husband.

"Platform. What issues he was campaigning on, emphasizing?" Rosen did not want the pace to let up.

"Oh, um, not really. I mean, Duke ... my husband and I are very conservative. We support the President." The answer was the only thing she knew to say, it appeared to Rossi.

"Conservative about what?"

Devlin was on his feet. "Objection. Mrs. Ellis is not on trial and neither are her political beliefs, Your Honor. This is way out of line."

Rosen rebutted Devlin. "Judge, we are merely trying to understand what this witness actually knew about her husband's actions and his intentions. We are not contending that she is mistaken regarding her testimony about Duke Ellis being home."

Judge Lewis pointed at Rosen. "I am aware of what you are doing. I do not want this witness badgered or made to look ...

uninformed. So I will overrule the objection, but advise you, Counselor Rosen, to get to the point very quickly. If you don't, I will excuse the witness. Understand?"

Devlin rolled his eyes, but Rosen apologized for ruffling feathers.

"Mrs. Ellis, is it fair to say that your husband, wisely, kept politics and his personal life at home with you and your children separate?"

"Well. I'm not stupid, Mr. Rosen. I know why my husband thinks he should be elected. I don't pay attention to all the fake news and mean things people in the press say, but I know right from wrong and my husband is right."

Rossi wondered: was she aware that Rosen was making her out to be left in the dark regarding Duke Ellis's real political views?

"Right about what, Mrs. Ellis?"

The next few minutes were a flurry of objections and rebuttals with each ensuing remark growing in volume. Rossi glanced at Jane, who raised her eyebrows and widened her eyes. Rossi thought, *Jane knows this is turning into a dog fight.*

Judge Lewis gaveled the commotion to an end and his instructions were blunt. "I think Mrs. Ellis has told this court and this jury all that is needed with respect to the charge of incitement. The objection is sustained. Mr. Rosen, you don't have any further questions unless you are moving to another lane, do you?"

"No, Judge. You have been very understanding. I think the witness has testified to all she knows."

Indeed, thought Rossi.

———

It was inevitable. Deborah had her cell phone in one hand and the remote control in the other as she switched from channel to channel. Her son was calling from New York City. Her two daughters had already called.

"Yes. I am watching it now. I know. The police have already arrested people. No, I don't know if anyone is hurt ... well, yes ... that's true. The local reporter said two protesters had been hit and then people were throwing things ... bottles or whatever."

Deborah kept creeping closer and closer to her television. The local news anchor cut to a young female reporter wearing a TV8 baseball hat and yellow jacket. Her head was on a swivel, as she looked back at the camera and returned quickly to the skirmish some thirty yards down the street. "... and so as of now several people have been taken to get medical attention. The police have apparently made arrests of at least seven protesters. I believe some of them were part of the Black Lives Matter group over there across Union Street ... but from what I am hearing it was in retaliation for objects being thrown from the group who are closer to the courthouse entrance ... you can see the Tea Party flags along with MAGA signs. Several of those people I saw handcuffed. One woman who was walking past me about ten minutes ago was bleeding from the head and people were trying to attend to her ..."

The news anchor in studio took stock of the situation and looked to her partner in the studio and reported the obvious: "Tempers are short and the police are doing their best to keep both groups as far away as possible. Let's hope they can keep things under control."

Deborah muted the television so she could respond to her son. "Your father is in the courthouse, and I am sure they have no idea what's going on outside. So don't worry. I'll call as soon as I hear from him. If your sisters call, just tell them to sit tight and I will let you know as soon as I know something. I don't want to be on my cell when Dad calls."

21

JUDGE LEWIS

Bailiff Henry Lamont was moving quickly up to the judge's bench. Judge Lewis was understandably taken aback. He pushed his microphone, which he hardly used, off to the side and covered it with his palm while his senior most bailiff leaned toward him. The judge's face slowly transformed from slight annoyance to consternation. Henry finished his message, stepped back, arms behind his back at attention, and awaited the judge's instructions.

"Counselors, would you please approach the bench for a sidebar?" he requested.

Both attorneys glanced at each other, clearly in the dark regarding the news the bailiff had delivered to the judge. For a full five minutes, the four of them huddled with the judge, who was making it clear that he was calling the play. The others involved nodded. Rossi looked at some of the other jurors, who seemed anxious to know what this was all about.

Once the lawyers left the bench, Judge Lewis made the announcement. "I am asking the bailiffs to escort all visitors out of the court using the main entryway. Thank you for your cooperation. The court reporter will note that I will be giving instructions to the jury and the alternates momentarily, with only both counsels in the courtroom. Thank you for your cooperation." Then, in his effort to assuage the jury's apprehension, he waited patiently while throwing a taut smile toward them, assuring that he still had everything under control.

Once the room was occupied by only those the judge allowed, he began again. "Members of the jury, I am sure you are not oblivious to the publicity that this case has garnered from the media. That was a concern of mine as the bailiffs have guided each of you around various public demonstrations that have ensued from all the reports generated in the media." He cleared his throat. "However, events today have taken a turn that I had hoped would not become a reality. Comments made by some public officials about the nature and existence of this trial have caused a serious disturbance outside of this courtroom, and I fear those protests have grown even more ... volatile in the last hour as word has spread of some comments made on social networks."

He quickly took a sip of water. "I am forced into a position I feel is necessary to preserve the safety of the jury and the neutrality of this trial. Thus, I am excusing the jury and the alternates at this time and delaying this trial until Monday morning at ten o'clock. This court will remain dark on Friday so that other matters can be attended to. This will give you time to prepare next week for the likely conclusion of the trial and deliberations. During this time, I have several requests I must make of each of you fourteen jurors, and I must emphasize that in the event one or two of you cannot meet my request, for reasons I will understand completely, our two alternates, who have been so kind as to stay with us during these first days, will be asked to step forward."

It was clear to Rossi that what Judge Lewis was about to say was disdainful to him. "I am going to sequester this jury starting Monday evening and through the conclusion of the trial. What that means is I am asking each of you to make a commitment to not return home after Monday; instead, the court will provide transportation, meals, and accommodations for you for the duration of the trial. Furthermore, I am asking each of you to not discuss this trial with others and to refrain from watching the news or exposing yourselves to articles on social media that pertain to this trial. I realize that may be difficult for you, but I am confident that your vigilance in this matter will allow this trial to remain focused only on what has appeared before you here in the courtroom. If you feel you cannot meet this requirement, I will ask you say so and it will not be a reflection on your integrity but rather on the realities of your own circumstances. I know this is asking a great deal of each of you."

The seriousness of the judge's tone and his implications were not lost on Rossi. The sacrifices he was calling for were no small matter for many of the jurors. On the other hand, Judge Lewis could not have been more considerate Rossi thought. *We all have an out.* Rossi realized that with the media so ubiquitous, it would be nearly impossible to ignore whatever the disturbance was outside the walls of the Federal Courthouse.

Judge Lewis then explained the situation further. "I am not inclined to order this action unless provoked, as I am. I am doing so for the safety of the jury and the impartiality of this trial. I have conferred with counsel, and I've been given assurances that this trial, barring a uniquely long deliberation, should take no longer than five additional days. So I will ask each of you if you can make that commitment—understanding its daunting nature. Let me emphasize that there will be no cost to you. My bailiffs will make sure that all luggage is taken care of once you have checked in Monday morning here at the courthouse."

The jurors looked around at each other in what seemed to Rossi to be a way to get their bearings.

Judge Lewis then looked at the jury and the two alternates and asked, "First, do any of you have any questions?"

Juror #5—Adam, the youngest juror—raised his hand. "So, we tell our family that we are not going to be back home for what ... five days starting next week, Judge?"

"Yes. It may be less time, perhaps. But as I have cautioned, none of you should discuss the events of this trial, nor should you discuss the issues in this trial with each other until you go into deliberations. At that point, our alternates will be excused from service. Does that answer your question, sir? It was a very good thing to get clarified." Judge Lewis was conciliatory. "Any other questions before I ask you all if you wish to continue serving?"

Lauren raised her hand. "Judge ... Your Honor. Um. I have to check with my husband about my children. But ... I really want to see this through. What can I do?"

Judge Lewis looked at Henry. Their non-verbal message was clear. The judge explained to Lauren, "I understand. Please take your time and consult with your husband, Madame. My bailiff, Henry, will take your information and you and he will be in communication. Will that be satisfactory?"

Lauren seemed relieved and smiled at Henry. Henry grudgingly nodded back. The judge took a scan of the rest of the jury.

Silence. Finally, Juror #2—Jim —asked, "Judge Lewis, I take it something bad happened today. Is it something I ... we should know about? I mean, I have been here all these days, and I want to see this case through. My employer—Sears—is very supportive of jury duty. So, I guess, I'm asking what happened that made all this ... have to happen?"

Without giving anything away, the judge replied, "That is a fair question and I cannot say precisely what occurred, but events outside this courthouse have become far more contentious ... if you get what I mean." He measured his words with a degree of caution. "Let me say that I do not want any of you to feel pressured or intimidated by the actions of people outside of this courtroom, and I want to assure you that your anonymity will be protected. Does that help you to see the situation, sir?"

Jim nodded. "Thanks, Judge. I get your drift." Then he made a valiant attempt at humor. "I guess the folks outside are getting noses bent outta shape." Several jurors suppressed laughter that would have grown into a fuller voice had the tension not been so palpable.

Judge Lewis merely nodded. "I believe you've hit the nail on the head." He leaned back. "Please, do not feel you must commit to these restrictions. If this is not something acceptable, please let me know. Any of you?"

No one moved a muscle until Mr. Heroyuki Sato raised his hand. Until this point in the trial, Rossi had only heard him utter a word or two when roll was taken. Once acknowledged, he announced, "Your Honor, it is my duty to serve. Thank you for your offer of this court's protection and hospitality."

On that note, eleven jurors and both alternates nodded while Lauren and Henry whispered.

———

"Hello, Deborah."

"Anthony?"

"Yes, it's me. I just wanted to call you ..."

Rossi didn't have a chance to finish his sentence. "Anthony, what is going on there? I'm watching the news now and they are showing this ... I don't know what to call it ... a protest outside the court. It's nuts down there. Are you all right?" Deborah's words came out in a rush. It was in her nature to keep a cool head, but she also knew that her husband would easily try to downplay when things were dicey. And things had leaped past dicey to dangerous in the last two hours.

"Hold on. Hold on. Here is the situation. I don't really know what is going on outside the courthouse, but I can assume it is pretty crazy. That's why I am calling you."

"But ..."

"Wait, Deborah. I'm trying to explain. The judge told us to go home now and that he is sequestering us for the remainder of the trial ..."

"Wait. What? What are you saying, Anthony?"

"He is not allowing us to go home after the weekend. So starting Monday they are putting us up in a hotel for the next five days until the trial is over," Rossi explained.

"Can the judge do that? I mean, isn't that really extreme?"

"You tell me. You're the one watching the news. He seems to think it is necessary. Look, here's an idea I have. My train doesn't leave for two hours so I am stuck. Why don't you hop in the car and head down, okay? We can have lunch downtown and then we can figure things out."

"Anthony, considering what is going on down there a lunch date doesn't seem too bright. You aren't seeing what I'm ..."

Rossi cut her off. "I have a pretty good idea what you are seeing. Henry has warned us, but the thing is I have to get home and the train that stops in Encinitas won't leave for hours. I can walk far away from whatever is going on. Trust me. Okay. Can you get down here?"

Deborah had already bounded off the dining room chair, and with phone in hand, she turned off the TV and searched about for her jacket, purse, and car keys. "Of course. Of course. I can leave right now ... wait. Where are you?"

"I am at the courthouse. Henry is directing us out from a side exit like he did yesterday. We aren't going to be anywhere near where all the protesters are. Look, I'll meet you at Buon Appetito on India Street. Don't rush. It will take me at least a half-hour to get there, so no need to get a speeding ticket." He tried to make light of the situation.

"All right. I'll meet you there. But be careful, Tony. I'm serious. Okay? Whoever gets to the restaurant first, grab a table and I think a drink will be in order ... Wait. Who the heck is Henry?"

"Oh, Deborah, I've made all sorts of new friends here."

22

THE PRESIDENT'S TWEETS

While they sipped their chardonnay and nibbled on their appetizer, lightly battered fried calamari sprinkled with sea salt, Deborah discussed with her husband what Twitter revealed earlier that afternoon. Twitter zeroed in on the reason for the mayhem that had caused the trial to go off the rails earlier.

"Anthony, I know we can't talk about the trial, but you can at least know what happened this morning, don't you think? There were several tweets sent by the President, and it blew up along with a video that was leaked to the media."

"Wait, what video are you talking about?" Rossi took a bite of one of the calamari Deborah didn't care for because it looked like a miniature octopus. It always grossed her out.

"The video that you saw—I presume—in court—of Duke Ellis's rally. CNN is reporting that it got leaked to them during the night and by morning it was all over the news, just like the video of the Charlottesville protests with all the torches and the Nazi and KKK marchers in Virginia last month."

"How in the world could that happen? I mean, I don't get it. We just saw it, and now it's on the news? Impossible." Rossi shook his head. "Well, I know you want me to be aware of what's going on, but I really should not know what the President said. I'm not saying you shouldn't see the news and Twitter, but the judge told us not to discuss this case or read about it. I know you know that."

"Of course I do. Tony, I am just trying to get you to understand that this is getting out of control, and you have to be very careful. What if you got involved with the protesters? I know you, Anthony. You think that nothing bad can happen to you, but unless you understand how dangerous this is becoming ... my point is that you can't be too careful. In any case," she hoped she had said enough, "I'm sure it will be all over the news—which we are not watching. But the President has already tweeted and that's what made this all go viral." She slipped her phone over to him as if she was implying read it yourself.

Rossi picked up the cell phone and put on his glasses to read the small text.

What's going on in California! These poople are crazy. They lock up a Republican politician because they don't like what he said. I hear video is a fake. This is why you cannot trust DEEP STATE!

"He spelled people wrong."

"Yeah, I know. Is that all you're going to say, Anthony?" She was beside herself.

Rossi sighed. "I probably shouldn't read that stuff at all. I know you want me to know what happened, and I am glad you do, but it is about the trial. Anyway, now I know why so many people showed up at the courthouse."

Deborah thought twice before adding, "And now you know why the judge ordered you guys to be sequestered. I mean, look what just happened in Charlottesville last month. That nutcase rammed his car into the crowd and killed a woman and a dozen others were injured." She wanted him to fully grasp the danger, but she also knew that she had to not discuss issues that could pertain to the trial. "Anthony, this morning ten people were arrested and two had to be taken to the hospital. You just need to be very careful … that's all I am saying, okay?"

"Okay."

"Okay."

A beat.

They both made an effort to talk about anything other than the events preceding lunch.

It was a gorgeous day downtown. Tourists were milling about in the Gaslamp District, which had been restored from a blighted area two decades before with the construction of Horton Plaza and then Petco Park, where the Padres played. It made the area a destination for tourists who could easily ferry over to Coronado Island as well. Little Italy, where they were dining, had grown from a block on India Street to several square miles of cafes, restaurants, and boutique shops, not to mention fashionable bed and breakfasts. It was the closest thing to a European ambiance this one time navy town could muster.

The waiter arrived. He had split the lasagna as they asked, and it smelled delicious. The bolognese sauce cascaded over the noodles, and the parmesan cheese made for a cream-colored summit. Deborah knew it was Rossi's favorite, but it was far too filling for one person. They silently enjoyed the aroma. The truce regarding how much information could/would/should be shared about the events of the day was broken by Deborah.

"Five days, huh?"

"Yes. Maybe fewer, I hope." The lasagna was piping hot. Rossi ate around the edges.

"And none of the other jurors took the out?"

"Not so far. I think they all want to see it through. I know I do."

"Well, no matter what, I think that you are just the person

who should be on that jury. And I won't bring up anything else about it." The lasagna had cooled enough to begin cutting through the layers.

"Deb, I think that ..." He stopped himself. "I think the judge is right. It's best for me to just hear the facts and decide what the law dictates should happen. I know that this is not going to be easy." He chewed slowly and his eyes were not focused.

Deborah knew the signs. He was in his head. At least he was getting a good meal.

———

Rossi carried his suitcase up to the second level of the Coaster. Fewer people today. He placed his suitcase next to him, skipped over the front page of the *San Diego Union-Tribune* newspaper and the local news section, and opened up the sports. The Padres had imploded, again. Wait till next year ... or the year after that. He loved baseball and now that the playoffs had begun, at least he would have something to watch in the evening since the news was out of bounds.

The weekend was strange. He knew that his sister-in-law Ann and her husband, not to mention the other couple, knew about the trial. Deborah had delivered the message loud and clear—DO NOT BRING UP THE TRIAL. He also knew that the ladies had to be chatting about it in the kitchen while he nursed his beer at the grill. Ron's barbeque ribs did not disappoint.

Maybe it was his imagination, but he could not help but get the feeling that the guys were giving him a look that implied *Sorry, Buddy, but I'm glad it's you and not me.* Knowing the politics of both men, Rossi had to concur.

———

Deborah drove him to the train station Monday. Neither said much on the way. What more could they say? She decided she would wait for the southbound train. He said it was not necessary. She said it was. They sat on the cement bench. The wind had kicked up from the ocean. Winter weather along the San Diego coastline. They sat closer and both sipped coffee from his thermos. Rossi actually saw his breath. As the train's brakes screeched and the Surfliner paused in Encinitas, they stood and they embraced. Her last words to him were, "Do your duty, Tony. You'll know what is right." Then she kissed him and turned away before he saw the tears forming. She walked to their car. She did not pull away until the train left the station and her tears dried.

Rossi knew exactly why Deborah's words were terse and her exit quick. Poignant moments materialized as goose bumps that percolated on his arms. Goodbyes turned to tears. As he looked for a seat, the lump in his throat reminded him of how rare it was that he would be away from her, how strange it was to not have her seated next to him. How lonely it would be without her nestled in bed next to him. More than three decades of marriage and selfless devotion could not be taken too lightly. He reached in his back pocket for his handkerchief.

Rossi watched the beaches of Del Mar disappear and the green valley that separated the north coast from downtown materialized. He opened the sports section, but watching him closely, one would notice he never turned the page. His eyes were focused out the window just as buildings began to blur past.

23

DESIREE OWENS

The next witness for the defense did not need an introduction for Anthony Rossi. Desiree Owens was a most recognizable face to a San Diego jury, as for many years she was the anchor for the local news, as well as a graduate from the local university and high school. Her homegrown status only lasted a short time. It did not take long for the national networks to recruit her, first with CNN and then MSNBC. Ms. Owens had been on the election beat for the western states in 2016 and, because of the notoriety of the Curtis/Ellis Congressional election in a swing district, she spent time following both candidates, as the jurors were soon to discover.

Devlin traced her background and then quickly got to the crux of why she was subpoenaed to testify as a hostile witness. "Ms. Owens, please inform the court how many months and how often you reported on George Ellis's campaign."

Owens was a striking woman; her long blonde hair and green eyes may have gotten her noticed, but as she spoke, it was clear she was nobody's fool. And although she was testifying for the defense, technically, she had no intention of painting

Ellis with even a single stroke of sympathy as she explained the internal workings of the Ellis campaign machine.

"Once it became clear," she began, "that Ellis's district was going to be a tight race, our network was alerted. Remember that the House majority was still up for grabs. With Hilary Clinton on the top of the ticket, the Democrats were fully convinced that a landslide would sweep the nation and at least carry the House of Representatives for them. So this race, so close to Orange County, which is traditionally conservative, was on everyone's radar."

Owens paused momentarily and sat back in her chair. The anxiety of being on a witness stand had subsided. "Once the media reported on Mr. Ellis's background, being a former member of the Ku Klux Klan, and Mr. Curtis being black, there was a flurry of reporters on this beat. I was involved more so as we got into the fall months, from mid-August through the November election. I observed six rallies that Mr. Ellis was a part of—never as a single candidate—but part of a slate of Republican candidates."

Rossi took note of the fact that Devlin never left his seat at the defense table. He appeared to make every effort to be pleasant to her. "And what was Mr. Ellis's message to his audience when you observed him?"

"Well, as I just said, I saw him with other candidates so he mostly delivered boilerplate messages consistent with the conservative Republican audience's preconceived attitudes."

Owens was experienced with lawyers like Devlin, Rossi noted.

"So you never heard him curse, use bad language, or make racial slurs?" Devlin's question aimed at the jury, rather than the witness.

"Not that I observed. But he behaved differently from the other candidates." Now Owens also pivoted her answer to the jury. "He acted like he was quite macho. A tough guy. His body language was interesting, jacket off and sleeves rolled up. He talked tough and he got angry ..."

Devlin countered before she could elaborate. "Tough talk is the bread and butter of every candidate, wouldn't you say, Ms. Owens?"

Owens shook her head. "No. I wouldn't agree with that. Some politicians have 'an edge' and your candidate—client now—wanted to make sure voters knew he meant business."

"I believe all politicians mean business."

"Ah, but Mr. Ellis's appeal, as I witnessed, was distinctly anti-immigrant, much like the current administration's position. And mind you, he decried Affirmative Action, and I personally interviewed him on the subject of racial discrimination. He claimed that racism was 'a thing' of the past and that blacks and other minorities had it pretty good for the last few decades. He told me it was the white people who were suffering. That's what I mean by 'different', sir." Owens was calm but direct.

Devlin ignored that remark and instead rose from his seat. "I believe there are a majority of Supreme Court judges who agree that we are in a post-racial America now, isn't that so, Ms. Owens?"

"I'm sorry. The Supreme Court's views are not my beat, nor am I privy to their views."

"Ms. Owens, you know quite well where the Supreme Court stands. The *Shelby v. Holder* decision in 2013, authored by Chief Justice John Roberts, explained that the times have changed and that this nation is 'colorblind.' So was it out of line for Mr. Ellis to claim that racism was antiquated and that policies that gave preference to people of color are unnecessary?"

Peters' voice reached maximum volume. "I object, Your Honor! This line of questioning has strayed from the point of this trial. The defense counsel is questioning Ms. Owens, their

own witness, on subjects on which she has already said she is
not well versed."

Devlin's facial expressions conveyed the pain of one innocent of all charges. "Judge Lewis, my client is being painted as a
racist and an instigator of behavior outside of the norm of political rhetoric. I wish to find out how that could be so."

Rossi couldn't help but wonder, Is this part of courtroom
theatrics, or does Devlin believe that discrimination disappeared with a wave of the Supreme Court's gavel?

"Objection sustained. Mr. Devlin, this isn't a law school
review session, and Ms. Owens is not a lawyer. Just get to your
point, please." Judge Lewis was not at all happy with having to
scold Devlin.

"Fine. I'm sorry, Judge. So let's cut to the chase. First, you
were not there when George Ellis delivered a speech on
September 13th of 2016 that allegedly incited a riot, correct?"

"Correct. The mainstream media was not there because the
Ellis campaign did not inform or invite us. So, therefore, I was
not there." Owens' answer was frosty.

"And when you were present at his rallies, you didn't hear
any of the alleged remarks that Mr. Ellis has been accused of,
correct?"

"If you mean calling black people the N word and remarks
about 'kicking them out' of roles in government, no, your client
is far too smooth for that. He picked his time and place, didn't
he?" The frost turned to razor-sharp ice.

"And never once at any of the speeches he made was there
ever a"—Devlin used air quotes to sarcastically indicate his
next word—"riot, correct?"

"No. But I will add that ..." She was cut off as Devlin's voice
trumped Owens' when he announced that he had no further
questions.

Peters' shrewd follow-up did not miss a beat. "Please finish what you were about to say, Ms. Owens. I have a feeling the court would like you to finish your answer."

Owens nodded. "Thank you. As I was about to say, I was in the crowd of his avid, or I should say, rabid supporters. It opened my eyes to their anger, compared to many political speeches in which the supporters were enthusiastic. In my opinion, these people were a powder keg ready to explode."

Now Devlin's voice rose an octave. "Objection! Mere speculation on this witness's part, Your Honor."

"Sustained. The jury will disregard Ms. Owens' description of the Ellis supporters."

Peters asked. "I'm curious, Ms. Owens. Did they chant 'Lock her up!'?"

"Of course."

"What about posters? Any 'White Power' posters?"

"Honestly, very few. When I saw one or two, they were quickly taken away and rebuffed by party officials. That was something I specifically reported on in my segment for the news."

"Yes. I know. I watched it, Ms. Owens."

24

BUD TEMPLE

There was a brief thirty-minute recess. In the interim, the jury had a chance to stretch and was provided with beverages and snacks. Henry insisted that they take every chance to "refresh" themselves, implying that the morning session may last longer than usual. Rossi took the hint. The bailiff also told them that lunch would be made available in one of the rooms used for deliberations. At that time, they would be informed which hotel they would be sent to once the afternoon session had concluded.

The jury had been warned numerous times by Judge Lewis to not discuss the trial until deliberations began, which wasn't the easiest thing to do since they were standing around munching on granola bars or sipping coffee or juice. So the small talk condensed even further. Rossi took the opportunity to thank Mr. Sato for speaking up yesterday and echoing his feelings about the duty of citizens to serve the justice system.

Mr. Heroyuki Sato slightly bowed and told Rossi he appreciated his words. "I learned long ago that citizenship is too often taken for granted."

Heroyuki Sato was a man of few words, but his wisdom needed little explanation.

———

After the recess, the defense called its next witness.

James Devlin had the look of a man who was about to take a bite out of something he found disgusting—but it had to be done. "The defense calls Mr. William "Bud" Temple to the stand, Your Honor."

Rossi tried to not judge a book by its cover; however, this witness made that very difficult indeed. He walked up to the witness stand as if he had just dismounted from a long day's ride out on the range, and his body language was like a cowboy strutting into a saloon to order a whiskey. His too-tight blue jeans forced his bulging gut to protrude over his knuckle-sized silver belt buckle.

Rossi realized this couldn't be Temple's first courtroom appearance because an ankle bracelet, indicating he was under house arrest, was hovering over his right cowboy boot. His body type, certainly imposing enough to make those Curtis campaign workers rattled, would be an understatement.

Devlin tried to not make eye contact with Temple until he finished his opening question. "Mr. Temple, you have been mentioned numerous times already in this trial, so I want to clarify one thing: you are known as Bud Temple, correct?"

An enthusiastic reply, "Yes, sir. I was named after my daddy's favorite beer—an American beer." Temple smirked.

"All right. So that's clear. Now, Mr. Temple, I want to ask you to tell the court why you are wearing an ankle bracelet, if you please." Again Devlin wasn't looking at him. Instead, he flipped through what appeared to be his notes at the defense table.

"Sure. I got arrested the night at the Curtis home. The cops charged me with 'disorderly conduct' and 'disturbing the

peace'—which I don't really think was fair—or true. But whatever. My lawyer told me to just to take a plea and, since I hadn't
done nothing really wrong that night, the judge just sentenced
me to six months with this damn doohickey on my leg."

Now Devlin looked at him. "Let's not discuss that any
further since it has no bearing on this case. Instead, here is why
I have called you to testify. Did George Ellis, your boss and the
candidate for Congressional office, order you to go to the Curtis
house on the night of September 13th, 2016?"

Temple replied with an indignant "No!"

"Did he ask you to lead the men to the Curtis house that
same night?"

"Of course not." Equally indignant.

"Did he incite you to become angry and therefore take that
anger out on the Curtis family?" *Devlin was not fooling around,*
Rossi surmised. *Just get the facts out with short answers.*

"Duke, er ... George, he never told me nothing of the sort,
sir. He just gave a speech is all."

Bud Temple followed orders. He had been coached. Say less
and get off the stand.

Devlin had only one last question. "So you and some of the
others just went to the Curtis home ... why, Mr. Temple?" This
was the question Devlin must have thought would be better
coming from him first, rather than from the prosecution.

"Look. It's a free country. We just wanted to let people
know what we stood for. I didn't have nothing to do with
those stupid Nazi clowns and a few skinheads ... who, you
know, did stuff that was ... um, bad. They were the ones who
got busted. We was just exercising our right to free speech.
I'm sorry it got outta hand." Temple tried his best to look
sincere.

Devlin quickly sat down. "No further questions."

Peters and Rosen conferred and after a minute, Peters rose
to cross-examine Temple. "We've got a lot to cover, Mr. Temple.

Were you dishonorably discharged from the United States Army for continued fighting and assaulting an officer ...?"

Before she could finish, Devlin popped up with what would be a series of objections. This one centered on the irrelevance of Temple's previous military service. After quarreling with Peters, Judge Lewis called both lawyers to the bench for a sidebar. Rossi understood what she was after. Temple was a hothead, ready to use his fists and could be easily provoked.

After a brisk and animated whisper session, Judge Lewis sent both lawyers back to their prospective respective tables and turned to the jury. "The objection is sustained. Members of the jury, ignore the comments of Attorney Peters regarding Mr. Temple's previous military service. It has no bearing on this trial of Mr. George Ellis's actions. I hope each of you understands my instructions. Ms. Peters, please continue your cross-examination."

"Thank you, Your Honor. Mr. Temple, you were arrested and charged with 'disorderly conduct' and 'disturbing the peace.' But you seem to think you didn't do anything—your exact words here in court to describe what occurred at the home of the Curtis family are limited to one word—bad. However, the police report indicated a more sinister picture. For instance, explain why the police found a cross in your back seat—two of them to be exact, both the same size and shape as the cross that Frank Templeton pounded into the Curtis's front lawn." Peters stood next to her table with her index finger pointing to documents lying open on the table.

"Well, those were for campaign posters." Again Temple smirked.

"Really? In the shape of a cross?" She tilted her head in disbelief. "But there were no posters attached to these 'crosses,' were there?"

"Not yet."

"And the lighter fluid also found in the trunk of your car—

were you and the boys planning a barbeque?" The overt sarcasm was a first for Peters.

"No. We had one before and I ... always come prepared." Temple made it obvious that he thought he had outsmarted the lawyer.

"Ah, the question is for what? But let's talk about your behavior. The police reported you were obstinate, vulgar, hostile, and physically aggressive with them. Now, how do you account for your behavior since you seem to be claiming to be an innocent bystander?"

Again, objections and explanations were slashed back and forth between the lawyers. Rossi had trouble separating the sparring attacks. Devlin kept repeating that Bud Temple wasn't on trial, and Peters insisted that she was establishing an out-of-control angry mob had a leader in Bud Temple. Judge Lewis gaveled them to order. This time he overruled the objection, thus deciding in Peters' favor but cautioned the prosecution to stick to the affairs of September 13th.

"You were George Ellis's so-called 'campaign manager.' How many people reported to you, sir?" Peters began a new line of questions.

"I don't know exactly. We had names in our computer, but Duke's staff was about twenty of us guys, I guess." Temple showed his first signs of concern.

"The police report matched the names of the men at the riot with your staff and, more or less, it's a match—even Frank Stapleton who has already testified to this court and is in jail as we speak. Now, you are telling this court that even though you are the campaign manager and Mr. Ellis's top assistant, that you never organized this trip to the Curtis home? You expect this jury to believe that?"

"What is there to believe? I told you I didn't tell anyone to do anything. The boys just showed up, is all. Just like me." His voice rose and his neck reddened.

"Sure. Just a coincidence. Did Duke Ellis tell you ..." Peters closed a report, presumably the police report to which she was referring, and she now strode toward the lectern which closed the distance between her and her witness. It appeared she was going to try a different approach, Rossi deduced.

Peters began slowly, but as each question volleyed back to the witness, her pace and intensity increased. She started factually. "Mr. Temple, do you agree with what Duke Ellis said about blacks: that 'they should be kicked out of the state?'"

"Yeah."

Curiously: "Aren't the Latinos and the Jews also a problem?"

"Yeah. They should go back where they belong." He arched his back and shook his head back.

Brusquely: "Like send the blacks back to Africa and the Mexicans back over the border, right?"

"Damn right. They're just a bunch of rapists and drug dealers."

Suggestively: "And where do we send the Jews? To Israel?"

Temple inched to the edge of his chair, his finger pointing at Peters. "That's where they say they belong, so get out of MY COUNTRY!"

Egging the witness on: "Are these minorities just trash, pulling America down, living off of your taxes, and getting everything handed to them?"

"You got that right. Give 'em an inch and they take a mile, I say. They steal and kill and spray their graffiti all over our cities 'cause they are in a gang! Look what they do to their women!"

As if unaware: "What is that?"

"They get 'em pregnant and then take off. Or they turn 'em into prostitutes and make 'em get abortions."

Knowingly: "That's why the prisons are packed with them, right?"

Bud Temple reached his epiphany. He was seething. "See,

they can't control themselves. They're like the President says, 'An infestation!'"

Peters makes her final push, ignoring Devlin's objections. "Kick them out, right?"

"Yeah, all of 'em. They never did a damn thing for this country—get rid of the Chinese, too. They just take all our jobs and make a bunch of crap. But the nig ..." He catches himself, if only for a moment. "... the blacks are the worst. I HATE ALL OF 'EM!" His face is contorted and he slams his hand on the wooden banister caging him in.

With satisfaction: "I bet you do."

Devlin protested, "This is outrageous, Your Honor." But his words were white noise. Even Judge Lewis was focused on Peters, unwilling to intervene until the time was right.

Peters turned to face the jury. "Ladies and gentlemen, I submit that it takes very little to incite these men to anger and rage that makes violence inevitable."

Devlin objected again, claiming it was argumentative. Judge Lewis sustained the objection and instructed the last statement to be struck from the record and ignored by the jury.

If only it was that simple.

25

SEQUESTERED

Judge Lewis made it clear that he did not wish to hear any more speeches from Attorney Peters; instead, he looked to Devlin and said, "Do you wish to redirect?"

Rossi figured after the skirmish between both lawyers, the judge was giving Devlin a chance to do damage control.

Devlin took the opportunity. "Mr. Temple, at the risk of having you repeat yourself, let me again put this to you: did Mr. George 'Duke' Ellis order you to round up people to go to the Curtis home and involve his campaign workers to commit any acts of violence?"

"No, sir. He did not." Temple shook his head in the most bovine manner.

"Did the defendant imply you should act in the manner I just described?"

"No, sir. We did what we did because we wanted to do it. It had nothin' to do with Duke."

Devlin didn't like part of that answer, it appeared. He followed up: "I did not ask you why you went to the Curtis home. I asked if you were encouraged to go by the defendant."

"No. Sorry."

"Thank you ..." Before Devlin could dismiss the witness, Bud Temple put his hand up.

"Sir, can I say one thing?"

Devlin turned back and for a split second, he seemed unsure of how he should respond. "No, thank you, Mr. Temple."

Peters jumped in at redirect. "I would like to hear what he has to say."

Judge Lewis in a tired baritone allowed it. "Go ahead, Mr. Temple."

Temple seemed confused but decided his proclamation was too important. "I just wanna say that I'm not a racist. What I am is a proud American." Temple puffed out his chest and nodded at Duke Ellis.

Devlin merely turned away and headed to the defense table.

Duke Ellis stared at Temple and kept his face as impassive as possible.

Even he knew not to react to this bravado. Rossi heard Regina beside him clear her throat. He would not glance at her. He didn't have to. There was something akin to heat rising to his left.

———

Judge Lewis asked for the bailiff to clear the courtroom of all observers. He also explained to both legal teams that he was going to explain the procedures under which the jury would be sequestered. He made a point of thanking Lauren, Juror #1, for agreeing to commit to the trial after conferring with her family. It was the only smile he revealed all day.

Once the courtroom was empty, Judge Lewis pivoted to the

jury and the two alternates and explained that Henry, his senior bailiff, would be with them throughout the evening as well as the morning. Henry would be explaining all the specifics regarding accommodations, meals, and the allowable communications that each of the fourteen representatives would need to know.

"I must require each of you to refrain from discussing this trial with each other and with any family members that you may communicate with this evening." On this point, the judge's sternness was most acute. "Also, you must refrain from watching the news or viewing the news reports on social media via the internet. Newspapers are also to be avoided. I know these restrictions may seem both inconvenient and extreme. Only during deliberations, will this case be discussed. Is that clear?"

All jurors affirmed his wishes.

Then Judge Lewis made one last point. "I know what an inconvenience this is for all of you. I do not issue an order for sequestration without knowing I am asking a lot of you. You are each to be commended for your willingness to go the extra mile to preserve a fair and untainted process. It is rare for a judge to do what I have done, but this case has drawn so much media and public attention that I want to keep you away from all the difficulties that this attention can bring."

The judge took a moment to ponder whether he had forgotten something. Then there was a flicker of a grin. "I leave you in the very capable hands of my head bailiff. Please stay seated—no need to rise on my behalf. Good evening." With that, Judge Lewis quickly scampered off the bench and exited to his chambers, as did the attorneys and Duke Ellis.

Henry and another female bailiff, whom he introduced as Rose, stepped before the jury. "Folks, I can only imagine how much you want to get up and stretch. Been a long day for you.

I'll keep this brief. Rose and I will be with you 24-7 and your security and wellbeing are our first concern. We will be traveling together in one vehicle to the hotel. Your luggage is there, and I will let you know your room numbers when we arrive. I will give you two vouchers for dinner and breakfast. You may choose to dine at the restaurants listed on the vouchers or head out on your own, but that will be on your tab. I strongly advise whatever you do, please stay clear of this courthouse."

Henry thought for a moment before making his final comment, "Oh, and I want you to know drinks are on you, but I suggest you not indulge too much." He grinned. With that, the tension released like a deflated balloon and a few jurors muttered that they sure could use a drink.

Anthony Rossi was one of them.

———

"Deborah, yes, I'm walking." Rossi's huffing and puffing was a sure giveaway. "I just had to get out and get some fresh air, and I just can't sit anymore." The evening rush hour was just beginning and Rossi decided to head south toward the Padres Petco Park instead of west to Little Italy. It was all downhill from the Holiday Inn on Sixth Street. He was approaching the House of Blues with the U.S. Grant Hotel one block west.

"So you are at a swanky place, huh?" Deborah was relieved to hear from him since they had only had a brief chat at 11:30. "Did you eat yet?"

"Well, the hotel is fine. I guess that the taxpayers don't expect us to be in the lap of luxury. We piled into a van and our bailiffs were very helpful getting us all set up with rooms and such. We are all on the same first floor so we don't see too many folks."

Deborah decided to ask if he had seen the protesters when they left the building.

"Well, not really," Rossi lied. "We took the long way around to the hotel. So I didn't see much." He had seen the crowd as the van crossed Broadway. Each of the jurors craned their necks out the windows to see what was happening. The van was at least two city blocks away. Rossi thought that the size of the protest was at least two, maybe three times what it was in the morning. He glimpsed at the banners and television news vans, but their view was fleeting and the next intersection north had nothing of note.

Rossi waited for the light to change as he stepped onto the crosswalk. "As for dinner, well, I just wasn't hungry then. I just got into the room, unpacked, and flew out of there. The others were discussing getting dinner, but I'd just as well be on my own."

"Oh, sure. Well, I assume they provide dinner, right?" Deborah was playing with her chicken soup and watching developments on the news that she wasn't planning on sharing with her husband. Naturally, the trial was the first story covered in the local news.

"Yep. I have a voucher for a couple of places. I'll just mosey down to the ballpark and see what I feel like. If I don't see anything, I'll head back and go to one of the places on the voucher. By then, the others will probably be done with dinner. I tell you what. I'll call you when I stop for a bite and then it'll be a lot quieter, okay?"

"Tony, that's fine. Or just call when you get back to the hotel and I'll catch you up on things ... that I can catch you up on."

"You know, that is a better idea. I married a smart gal, didn't I?"

"Yes, you did, Mister Rossi. Someone has to be the brains behind this operation." Deborah laughed. Rossi loved when she chided him. She was the practical one. He was the dreamer.

Rossi headed down to First Street where he knew that the Sofia Hotel was adjacent to a Tender Greens Restaurant. He just didn't want to eat anything heavy, and the voucher options seemed limited.

On the way down, he passed the various government buildings and could not help but notice lawyers conversing on their cell phones, carrying thick briefcases and looking haggard. It was interesting for him to compare their sober trudge to whatever obligation was next in their queue. This contrasted with the exit he made from his high school classroom.

His school's campus had changed drastically with remodeling and such, but one thing remained constant—the parking lot. There he would often catch up with colleagues, discussing the highs and lows of their day. Usually, laughter emanated from the conversations, but occasionally tears surfaced as the pressures of teaching became overwhelming.

Then there were the students parading between the cars, milling about, often flirting, or exhausted but also pumped up from the day's sports practice. Sometimes during the September months, he would stride over to the tennis courts to watch the kids play. He and Deborah loved playing doubles in those heady days when they could move effortlessly on the courts; those days were fading quickly as their knees and shoulders groaned. At the tennis courts now, he would cheer on his students and chat with the coaches.

In the winter afternoons, he would wander over to the gym when a basketball or volleyball match was underway. Oftentimes, he had promised his students he would be there, even if he just made an appearance, which was what he would tell Deborah when he was home later than usual. She was often marking fifth-grade math homework, and he would massage her shoulders, knowing that her tension was spreading along her neck to the base of her skull.

As the seasons passed, and with it the years, the football, lacrosse, baseball, softball, and soccer players would smile, wave, or hoot and holler when Mr. Rossi came into view. That was what he remembered when walking away from school each day.

It was a far cry from the image of the attorney, dutifully meeting obligations that the justice system demanded. He was reminded of his decision, back when he was in college, regarding a career in law or teaching. When asked why he wasn't a lawyer, he told his fiancée Deborah, "I guess that I want to defend the innocent. And the classroom is my court-room." The American saga, with characters, heroic and vile, became his witnesses. Rossi aimed to win his students over to the idea that, although far from perfect, the American experiment of self rule as a republic was the beacon of hope to so many people around the world who thirst for freedom.

His teaching centered around one principle: Teach to kids, not at them. He focused on reaching his students where they sat—in their ever-shifting world. They needed to know that what he was teaching them mattered, but more importantly, they needed to understand that he personally was invested in them. Each year success was measured by his students' faith that they could think for themselves and answer life's most abstract and illusive question: What do I believe and why?

———

As he paid the check and exited the restaurant, he knew that for once he was in the students' seats, listening to those polished lawyers making their case. This time a man's fate was on the line. Perhaps society's values were being put to a test. *What will I believe and why?*

When he sat on his bed in his hotel room, he called Deborah and she told him that their adult children knew he was serving on a jury—this particular jury. She wanted to encourage him since he sounded weary, "They are so proud of you, and they said—Who could do a better job than Dad?"

He smiled. They wished each other a good night's sleep, and Rossi promised to call in the morning. He fell asleep watching a baseball game. He didn't sleep all that well in hotels.

Who does?

26

DOC

Cafe 222 was Rossi's favorite breakfast treat when he was downtown. The trek to Second Street was just what he needed, some fresh air after a night of stale air conditioning. Downtown was just starting to shake itself awake as he sauntered past hotels and shops. As usual, Café 222, a pillar of local lore, was already crowded. The waitress showed him to a counter that had a few openings, and at one stool there appeared a familiar face.

Juror #8 was holding the rather extensive menu. He peered at the cornucopia of waffle selections with his reading glasses perched on his nose.

"Good morning, George." Rossi's warm greeting couldn't have been less threatening. "I hope you don't mind if I take this stool ... but if it's a problem ..." Rossi was quickly cut off.

"No. Of course not. Please grab a seat. Maybe you can help me decipher this confounding menu. I've heard from my buddies down here about this joint." He threw a nod to the kitchen. "Figured I'd wander down. I'm George, by the way." Rossi let him believe that his name was new information.

"Tony." They shook hands. "I've been here a couple of times with my wife, and we love the place, but the menu is kinda overwhelming."

"Well, for an old guy who is a ham and egg man, this certainly is different. What do you recommend?"

Rossi took a quick inventory of the menu and reported back. "George, as a ham and egg guy, the All American breakfast is the safe bet. Waffles are what they are famous for. I am partial to the pecan waffle, myself. Not too sweet or filling."

"You know, I am always getting the same darn thing—my wife always chides me for that. So I'm gonna give the pecan waffle a try. Thanks. By the way, most folks who know me call me Doc."

"All right, Doc. I remember you are retired Navy, right?"

"Yes, sir. And if memory serves, you're a school teacher."

"Right. And because the government knows we are retired, here we are on jury duty."

Both men chuckled. The waitress filled up Rossi's coffee mug and orders were given in duplicate.

"You seem on the young side of retirement," Doc ventured.

"As a matter of fact, I retired this year. Didn't take them long to snatch me up." Rossi assumed ten years separated the two. "Did you work out of Balboa Naval Hospital, Doc?"

Doc took his time before answering. He sipped his coffee and rearranged his silverware. Rossi guessed that since he seemed fairly reserved during the trial, perhaps he was someone who calculated just how much of himself he would offer to the world.

"Balboa was my final stop after many others. It's a great facility. My wife really wanted us to stay here after traipsing all over with different assignments. Managed to keep her here for a good fifteen years." He stared up at the kitchen where the cooks and waitresses were like buzzing bees.

"I see. Well, San Diego has always been a Navy town."

They both fixated on the hustle and bustle on the other side of the counter. There was so much to watch. Everything sizzling. Grills being scraped. Orders being shouted out. There were five huge waffle makers in constant use with batter splattering over the sides. And when a waffle popped out, then the toppings had to be layered just right. Strawberry. Peanut butter. Bacon. Bananas. It was all part of the formula.

"They sure do pile it on, huh?" Doc noted.

"Sure do. The batter is made of pumpkin or blueberry mix ... whatever the chef wants to whip up." Rossi let the action speak for itself.

"Coffee's good."

A beat.

"Doc, you sleep well?"

"Nah. You?"

"Never really do at hotels," Rossi answered.

"Cars, sirens, and people walking on the floor above with the TV blaring. Besides, I never sleep more than five hours most nights nowadays." The Doctor realigned his silverware.

"I know what you mean. I'm not used to having the whole bed to myself," Rossi admitted.

"Took me a long time to get used to that."

Rossi let the sadness of the moment settle. "I'm sorry for your loss."

Doc took another long sip of coffee and placed the mug down gently. "She was a terrific woman." He placed his glasses in his front pocket. "Forty-seven years. She spoiled me rotten." He finally turned to face Rossi. "But that's life, Tony. She made me promise to not stop living. I told her I wouldn't. I still pop over to the hospital every so often ... Oh, and she was a teacher, like you, except kindergarten. God, she loved those little rascals." A smile.

Rossi allowed enough sand to run through the hourglass as a sign of respect.

Then the waitress presented the plates with one thick slice of warm buttermilk in the blueprint of a waffle. The pecans drizzled over the top. Vermont maple syrup was provided in two miniature bottles.

"Holy cow, Tony, this is something."

"Eat up, Doc. This has got to hold us over. I think it may be a long day."

"Oh, my. This is delicious. Thanks for the heads-up. Never had anything quite like this in the naval hospital." Doc attacked the waffle with abandon.

"I know what you mean. Hospital food leaves much to be desired." Rossi was relieved his partner was gleefully enjoying this breakfast treat.

Out of the blue, Doc said, "I was a radiologist. And then in my later years, I was teaching the newer doctors how to prepare for their oral exams to be certified. That's part of why I have so much respect for teachers. Some of my doctors were so darn stubborn that you couldn't tell them a thing. Then if they failed, well, all of a sudden they were finally listening."

"I see. Sounds pretty familiar, Doc. Guess we each had a few knuckleheads. But I will say that the kids I taught made my day. They kept me young ... at heart anyway."

Doc chewed and rummaged around, considering something before speaking. "I can tell when a person has a sense for people. How they listen. What details they notice. I have a pretty good idea you were a heck of a teacher, Tony. For example, I noticed you taking notes and I also realized that you knew my name ... before I even told you. My wife Margaret was like that."

"Thanks, Doc. I appreciate it. I imagine you two were quite a ..." Rossi stopped. He didn't want to stir up memories. "Anyway, I just bet your Margaret had kids who loved her. I know my wife's students do. It's a passion. That's for sure."

They chewed quietly. The waitress asked if everything was all right and Doc winked at her. "Couldn't be better, miss."

And with that, the two men headed off to the hotel before embarking on the next act of the drama that played at the Federal Courthouse.

27

SOPHIE AND GINA

As Anthony Rossi walked with Doc back to the hotel, Deborah Rossi was picking up her phone. Her two daughters, Sophie and Gina, were on a joint call.

"Mom," implored Gina, "Pete told us this morning that Dad's jury was being sequestered. Really?"

"Yes. I talked to him an hour ago, but when your brother and I talked yesterday, I didn't get into that with him because we were just talking about how Dad was doing and why the protests had grown because of the President's tweets. He was busy then and I just didn't want to go there ... yet." Deborah muted CNN, which had covered the morning developments in San Diego. "So, yes. Your father is on a sequestered jury."

Sophie lived in Denver and Gina was in her final year at Berkeley. "Wait. Mom, how long will the jury be sequestered. I mean a few days or what?"

"Wait, wait, wait. Mom, when did this start?" Gina, the youngest daughter, had insisted that Rossi use Goggle maps to walk to the courthouse. She had no idea he was on a jury. She also was miffed that her older siblings had discussed this, and she was just now getting into the loop.

"Hold on, Gina." Deborah drifted to the couch and knew she had to calm Gina down. "So you know that last week Dad went to jury duty. Right? So, that day he was named to the jury. Then there was a day of the trial ... I think, Yes. So the next day is when the media got wind of it and it blew up to a national story. You know what I mean ..."

"Because of the President's tweets?"

"Well, right and because it's a civil rights story ... it's politics and racism and ..." Deborah was cut off.

"Hate crimes, Mom." Sophie did not mince words. "The Ellis trial is all about a racist jerk who incited a riot and lost an election to a black man. It's a hate crime, period. Let's call it what it is."

"That's probably so. I agree. But, girls, we can't talk to your father about it and he can't be exposed to the news or read about the protests. The fact is that I haven't talked about all this with him either. What I knew was that it was the Duke Ellis trial and he did tell me that it might get pretty ugly. You know Dad, he downplayed it."

Sophie again, "Ugly. Do you mean outside the courtroom or what ... inside? Because the news said there were arrests and what I saw looked like the violence could get way worse."

"Sophie, when your father went to the courthouse on the first day, it wasn't anything to worry about he said. He told me the morning looked pretty tame with both sides just setting up their banners."

Gina was still puzzled. "Do they know he's on the jury? Because if they do ..."

"No. Of course not. Let me finish. Once the court officers realized what might happen and they saw that the news media became alerted, that's when the judge told the jury they were to be sequestered. That was last Thursday. We had Friday to get organized because the judge thought they needed the weekend to get organized. So he packed for a week."

"So Monday he left and then that night, last night, we talked. This morning he called me and said he was getting breakfast. The officers are taking them to the courthouse and then back to the hotel. He says they feel perfectly safe, but you know your father. A bomb could go off and he wouldn't tell us because he would be afraid we would worry. I know he knows that things are bad enough to be careful or else they wouldn't be in this situation."

"He better be careful because those right wing loons are crazy. You saw what happened in Virginia. One of them drove their freaking car and ran over people and killed a woman," Sophie warned.

Deborah sighed, "Sophie, I know. He knows. But I want to tell you both that we don't know what the facts are about this trial. Right? Just because people are protesting or that some extremists are out there ... that doesn't mean that this Ellis character is guilty of a crime. He's presumed innocent and that is what your Dad has to remember ... and we need to keep that in mind, too. So ..."

"Mom, come on."

Gina's sarcasm pushed Deborah's button. "Gina, you and your sister need to not get involved in this."

"But we are involved."

"Gina, we are not. You father is. And the other jurors. Look, what I am saying is this is not something we discuss in public or with friends. You know how social media is. If you write or speak about this in any way, it will only make things worse for your father and our family. We will know what we need to know when your father can speak of it—if he wants to."

A beat.

"Of course, we aren't going to say anything, Mom. I mean we are not that naïve."

Sophie's awareness settled Deborah's nerves. "I know you know. Look, I will let you know the moment I can share what your father tells me. Do yourselves a favor and don't obsess about this whole thing. The news media is going to make things look worse than it is."

"That's easier said than done, Mom. But you should do the same, right?" Sophie countered. "I mean, you sound awfully upset yourself." She paused to consider if she should pursue this further and decided it was necessary. "Did you sleep okay? Cause you sound tired."

Deborah knew she was rattled by the week's events. Sophie usually tapped into her emotions better than her other two children. "I'm just flustered a bit, but seriously, I am trying to keep this in perspective. Your dad's doing what he needs to do and I—we—need to just trust he is being careful and, you know, listening to both sides ... which I know he is."

"Mom, he is the best person to serve on a jury, "Gina blurted out, "if anyone can be on that jury and do the right thing, it's Dad ... and you, too."

For the first time their mother laughed. "Oh, you couldn't get me on that jury if you paid me a million dollars. Forget it. I am having enough of a time just watching and reading about all this in the newspapers."

"Make sure you tell Dad that we are all really proud of him ... both of you, Mom."

"I already have, Sophie. Do either of you need anything ..." And the conversation drifted to the usual topics: relationships, work, and school.

When she finally put her cell phone down, Deborah felt spent. She flipped off the television and made another cup of coffee. She wondered why she felt she needed to defend Duke Ellis to her children. Perhaps she wasn't actually defending Duke Ellis but reminding herself that in this country people have the right to speak freely. But if those words encourage hate or violence, then what? She noticed that her hand holding the coffee mug began to shake. She quickly put the mug down on the counter.

And perhaps more perplexing for Deborah Rossi was the anxiety she felt when she and her husband had to confront anger and hatred, knowing that whichever side wins there will most likely be a price to pay.

28

HOWARD MATT

I f there was to be any sense of decorum in the courtroom, Judge Lewis had to come down firmly and decisively with one swift ruling.

"I will overrule the prosecution's objections regarding the testimony of the next witness. While I agree that the actions of organizations like the Ku Klux Klan are not the primary focus of this trial, I allowed witnesses to already testify about the FBI's involvement in curbing activities that are deemed to be criminal in nature. Besides, this witness has already been referred to in previous testimony."

"But, Your Honor," Patrick Rosen complained, "the witness has been forced to …"

"Mr. Rosen, sit down and do not interrupt me again. I am well aware that this witness has been subpoenaed by the defense. He is a hostile witness. If the defense wishes to question him, that is their prerogative." Then the judge turned to the jury. "Members of the jury, please ignore these objections. I have overruled them. Give your attention, instead, to the examination of the witness."

Rossi concluded, *And that was that.*

He sensed that the prosecution had fair warning that something FBI Agent Howard Matt may be compelled to testify about wasn't in the government's best interest. If not, why make such a fuss over the agent who had overseen the actions of their informant, Ronald Roberts?

Devlin began, "Thank you, Your Honor. Agent Matt, we have established that you recruited Ronald Roberts to be a mole in the Ellis campaign, and, in fact, Roberts went so far as to claim to be a Klansman. Did you know if George Ellis was aware that Roberts was an informant for the FBI?"

Howard Matt appeared right out of central casting. Tall and lean. Horn-rimmed glasses. Dark suit. Thin-striped tie. Grim-faced. A full head of salt-and-pepper hair. Clean-shaven. He answered questions in a terse, clipped manner. In a sense, there was no fat, no-frills, and no fooling around when it came to Agent Howard Matt.

"Certainly not, Mr. Devlin. Duke Ellis, to the best of our knowledge, did not know Mr. Roberts was working for the FBI." His intense stare remained focused on Devlin. It quickly became a brusque battle of wits between lawyer and detective.

"Did Roberts tell Mr. Ellis he belonged to the KKK?"

"Yes."

"And Mr. Ellis never asked him to leave the campaign, is that correct?"

"No. The matter was never discussed again, to my knowledge." Matt was unaffected.

Rossi felt that Devlin had scored his first point.

"Did the FBI have any surveillance of Mr. Ellis other than what was supplied by informant Roberts?"

"Yes."

"Can you explain what and why?"

"No and no."

Devlin was coy. "I'm sorry, why not?"

The agent responded in the matter-of-fact manner his

training demanded. "It is a policy of the FBI to not reveal its methods."

"Oh really. Why is that?"

"Because it can be a matter of national security." Howard Matt's stone face could be carved into Mt. Rushmore.

"National security? This is a Congressional race for the House of Representatives. Surely, the FBI did not think it was dealing with a Russian spy ring."

Silence. Rossi counted to ten.

Then, dry as a recitation of the dictionary, Agent Matt parried. "Your question is ... what, sir?"

"Why is this super top-secret investigation into my client, George Ellis, occurring? That, Agent Matt, is my question." Devlin had thrown up his arms in exasperation.

"Mr. Ellis was deemed by my superiors to be dangerous. He had been fermenting anger and violence. His opinions being voiced publicly and privately were becoming dangerously close to incitement—until he actually achieved his goal. Thus, the government has charged him ... and I am here to testify to this incitement charge."

Devlin looked at the jury. "Agent Matt, explain to this jury the definition of presumption of innocence."

"I believe that is your responsibility, counselor." The duel was far from its apex.

"You say your superiors deemed Mr. Ellis to be dangerous. What evidence did they have to drive this opinion and therefore begin an investigation?"

"I believe you have already seen the videotape, sir."

"Ah, but before that date, Agent Matt, before the videotape, you had him under surveillance. You were already tapping his phone, isn't that correct?"

"I cannot say. That is classified information."

Rossi deemed it a draw.

Devlin turned back to the witness. "I see we will not get past the secure borders of your superiors. So let me ask you about BAMN—the investigation's acronym for By Any Means Necessary. You have worked in California for how long, Agent?"

"Twelve years."

"What can you tell us about BAMN?"

If he was surprised that the line of questioning had veered into uncharted waters, Howard Matt showed little concern. "Not much, sir. Most of it is classified."

"Please, Agent, at least explain why the FBI would have an organization named after one of the most famous, or dare I say infamous, statements made by Malcolm X, whom I believe the FBI investigated and harassed." Devlin was back on the offensive.

The FBI agent decided a strong volley was called for. "All I can tell you is that when right-wing organizations like the Aryan Resistance, the so-called American Nazis, and the Klan, as three examples, are protesting, there are counter-demonstrations often by left wing organizations that oppose these racist groups. Unfortunately, violence can become the inevitable result, as has occurred in Charlottesville in which a deranged man drove his car into the crowd of protesters, killing one woman ... as you know."

"Isn't it true that the FBI has been more vigilant about infiltrating these, as you call them, left-wing organizations?"

"I cannot speak to that. The FBI is vigilant about any and all groups that are not peaceful."

Rossi was starting to see Devlin's strategy. First, discredit the FBI. Second, make the point that protesters of any political persuasion could be potentially dangerous if given enough provocation.

Devlin made his strongest attack. "Perhaps your tight-lipped testimony is not all that this jury will hear. The FBI researched the BAMN website. The FBI knew that BAMN's message encouraged their supporters to protest against the

Klan and other white supremacists. For example, it featured slogans like 'No Free Speech for Fascists!'"

Devlin was reading from his notes, "The website went on to celebrate 'the mass, militant demonstration that shut down the neo-Nazi rally at the California State Capitol Building days before. The FBI reported that 'it was possible the actions of certain BAMN members may exceed the boundaries of protected activity and could constitute a violation of federal law.'"

Agent Matt remained stoic. His only response: "What is the question, sir?"

Incredulous, Devlin spat out, "Are you aware of the FBI's decision to label counter-protesters as dangerous?"

"I am not privy to the information you are addressing. And if I were, I could not comment because it is ..."

Devlin beat him to the punchline. "Classified. I know, Agent. I know. So it seems it is open season for the FBI to investigate all organizations who want to voice their displeasure with the government, is that correct?"

"No, sir. We investigate when there is cause. I will remind the counselor that the Klan has been responsible for literally thousands of murders."

"Strange, Agent Matt, that other than this videotape, the FBI has not presented any other concrete evidence of Mr. Ellis's so-called racism or hatred."

"I do not believe it is at all out of the ordinary for certain individuals to keep their real intentions, shall I say, under wraps." Howard Matt delivered the final words toward the jury, whereas all his previous responses had been laser-focused on Devlin.

"One last thing, Agent. Your informant, Ronald Roberts, was recruited by the FBI because he was arrested on numerous counts for dealing large quantities of drugs over a two-year span, isn't that correct?" Devlin was heading back to his table, preparing to sit next to the defendant, Duke Ellis.

"Yes."

"Took you two years. Why so long?"

"Some fish take a while to catch and reel in."

"So you had a lot on him? He must have faced a long time in prison."

"I was not in that courtroom, sir."

"He sure was motivated to be a very resourceful snitch."

Agent Matt, for the first time, leaned forward, cleared his throat, and declared that he was about to draw the line with Devlin and the defense. "The video Ron Roberts provided speaks volumes. That is all I will say."

"No further questions, Your Honor." Devlin had extracted what he planned and seemed satisfied.

Rising from his seat, but remaining behind the table, Mr. Rosen was quick to his mark. "I'd say the videotape certainly makes Duke Ellis's intentions crystal clear. I sense that the defense has some issue with the videotape. Let's set the record straight. Was it doctored in any way?"

"Of course not." Agent Matt was pleased to be playing with the home team.

"That is the work of Ron Roberts, and there have been no alterations then?"

"Mr. Roberts made the recording. No alterations at all."

"And the FBI investigates organizations that either promote violence or plan an event that is likely to provoke a violent response?" Rosen was cementing his rebuttal.

"Absolutely. That is often the true motivation of a so-called protest. These groups will use social media to inflame the situation. We have discovered that the activity on social media is not always homegrown."

"Meaning?"

"The websites and internet chatter can be sponsored by

nations that are at odds with the United States' interest. Many players are trying to stir discord here. The Klan is just one of the players—albeit, it is one of the oldest and most vicious."

"Vicious." Rosen made sure that the jury allowed Matt's final word to saturate the proceedings. "Thank you. No further questions."

Judge Lewis looked to Devlin. "Redirect?"

"Yes, Your Honor. Agent, George Duke Ellis was not a member of the Ku Klux Klan when this incident occurred; furthermore, he had renounced his views of the Klan publicly, correct?"

"That is what he claims. It is not what the FBI believes to be true." Agent Howard Matt had a smug look on his face.

"Fortunately, the defendant will not be judged by the FBI, but rather by a jury of his peers. No further questions." Devlin glanced toward the jury.

29

MURRAY STEINMAN

J udge Lewis ordered a recess. Henry offered the jurors snacks and beverages in one of the rooms where they would likely deliberate. The other bailiff, Rose, explained that lunch would be provided and she passed around a menu of sandwich choices. Each of them filled out their preferences.

Time seemed to stand still. Rossi looked at the clock, which reminded him of the one in his classroom. It was government-issued, and the minute hand jumped from one small black minute dash to the next with no second hand as guidance. During his days teaching, time just flashed past. One of his students described it one day: "Mr. Rossi, I come into class. Sit down. Take off my backpack. You start teaching, and bang, the bell rings. It's like I just blinked my eyes." Her name was Solmaz. Mr. Rossi remembered the freshman well. He also told her at the time what a nice compliment she gave him.

If only time could move at that speed now. Instead, he heard the ticking of the clock, the salty chips and crackers crunching around him, and the sterile metal chairs squeaking as the others moved about, trying to keep their legs from tightening up from the constant sitting. Rossi decided to inquire with Henry about the delay.

"Well, Tony. This is life here in court. As they say, 'The wheels of justice grind slowly.'" Henry was placid.

Rossi bobbed his head in acquiescence. "Not like my old job. My day used to have so much going on that I'd barely finished lunch and next thing I knew the last bell would ring."

Henry looked left and right, as if their conversation could be viewed with suspicion. Then he smiled and said, "You were a teacher, right?" His question was rhetorical. "I can see how that would be a lot of fun, if you could have the energy for all those kids, I mean, students. Many years ago, I thought about teaching when I got out of the service. The army would have paid for my schooling. I went into law enforcement instead. No regrets though. It's been a long ride."

"How long have you been a bailiff ... if you don't mind me asking?"

"Okay, as long as you don't go blabbing to the others." That joyful grin reappeared. "I'm just joshing with you, Professor."

"Oh, I'm a professor now, huh?" Rossi jabbed back.

"Hey, I see you taking notes there in the box. Smart. Lots of folks don't and then either they can't remember important events or mix everything up. Anyway, when I retired from the police force, I thought this here would be a good opportunity for me. I'm coming up to seven years." Then he whispered, "My wife told me if I didn't get off the street beat and retire, she'd stop cooking me dinner." He patted his stomach, which showed evidence of her culinary skills. "You know what they say, 'Happy wife, happy life.'"

"You got that right, Henry." Rossi glanced back at the clock and wondered if maybe the power had failed. It just seemed frozen. Henry noticed and took the hint.

"I'm going to pop in and check with the judge. See if things are on the move soon." Then he made a similar announcement to the jury. Rose would hold down the fort. Heads nodded, and Jane, who had been watching them, gave Rossi a look that indicated good move.

————

Twenty minutes later, the court was back in session, and it did not take a detective to surmise what had forced the trial to skid to a halt. Judge Lewis apologized for the delay and, as usual, gave sincere thanks for the jury's patience, even if they had little choice. He then explained the delay.

"In criminal trials," he began, "both counsels are required to provide a list of witnesses before the court embarks on the proceedings. However, on occasion, a witness is called who has not been listed. This is for a variety of reasons. In this case, the defense needed more time to locate the witness you are about to hear from, and I have allowed this and explained my rationale to the prosecution."

It was at this point that Rossi noticed, for the first time since the trial began, that Devlin was joined by the man who had sat next to Duke Ellis on the first day of the trial: the man who didn't quite fit the description of a lawyer. A bodybuilder was a more apt depiction of the burly character, who consumed the entire space toward the end of the defense table.

And that was the prologue to the appearance of Murray Steinman. Mr. Steinman's body was the personification of an antique resurrected from the bowels of a downtown alley. He wore an obvious shiny, silver toupee that did not match his dull gray hair residing around the bowl of his head. His glasses were black-rimmed and thick, making his eyeballs appear as large brown bubbles. His cheeks sagged and became a matched pair with his rubbery jowls.

However, his physical appearance belied his vigor and showmanship at suddenly becoming the star witness—at least as he perceived the situation. He used a cane to take the exceedingly measured shuffle to the witness stand, whereupon he placed his hand on the Bible and pronounced in a loud and unmistakable Bronx inflection, "I do!"

Devlin began. "Mr. Steinman, thank you for making the journey here and taking the time to testify before the court. I am sure everyone here appreciates your commitment to these proceedings."

Steinman shrugged. "No problem. You paid for it."

The gallery and a few jurors chuckled, Rossi included. Rossi knew right then and there that this octogenarian would be what Hollywood would call a *character*.

"Yes, that's right. It was our pleasure. Now, sir, this trial deals in many ways with language, specifically words. In this case, the words of my client George Ellis. I've called you here because of your, shall we say, background when it comes to language and its impact on one particular person you have represented. You are being called as both an expert witness and a person who has dealt with this issue of censorship in the past." Devlin was taking an argument and folding it into a question to spring on the court. "So please, tell us your background and how you became involved in the issue of language and censorship."

As if a spotlight honed in and the cameras rolled and the director called out action, Murray Steinman took the stage. "Well, okay. So I gotta go back many, many years to when I was breaking into comedy, back in the Fifties. I never made it big on the stage, and I quickly figured I'd be better dealing with the talent, as an agent—if you know what I mean. So, this kid—he was pretty young when I first met him—this kid went by the name of Lenny Bruce ..."

Rossi almost rose from his chair. Lenny Bruce! Not only had Rossi read about him, but he was a fan. He had seen a documentary about the controversial comedian as well as the film that starred Dustin Hoffman. *What in the world is Devlin up to?*

"... now Lenny was one of my first clients, and I loved the kid. But he was raw. Let's say coarse ... vulgar, some thought. But he was funny as hell, I tell ya. And stubborn as a mule, too. Anyway, the bigger he got, comedy-wise, the more controversial he became because in his act he cursed a lot." Steinman was rolling, but Devlin wanted him to stay on course.

"Yes. What kind of language did Lenny Bruce use, Mr. Steinman, and what was the result?"

"Oh, well, okay. Besides cursing—and I am sure you know what that got him, usually busted by the cops for obscenity, of which I had to bail him out—his act often was political or racial. For example, he had this bit about President Kennedy. It killed me. He said something like: suppose Mr. Kennedy got on television and brought out some fellas who were workin' in his cabinet. And then the President introduced them sayin' 'here's a kike, a wop, a greaser, and a nigger.' And Kennedy kept going on saying 'nigger, nigger' so often that it don't mean nothing anymore. Then Lenny would say, real serious like, 'Then, you see, the little black boy don't go home cryin' cause somebody called him a nigger at school."

Devlin interjected, "And his point was ..."

"Lenny Bruce believed, as I do as well, that when you suppress a word that is what gives a word its power. See what I mean?" Steinman rearranged himself on his chair, almost like he was milking his lines and didn't want his scene to end so fast. "So, naturally, people didn't like what he was saying and," Steinman slapped his hands together, "bang, he was back in the slammer. And then I hadta bail him out ... again." Mock exasperation followed.

"I see. Was Lenny Bruce a racist?" Devlin feigned ignorance.

"Lenny? Are you kiddin' me? Lenny was the most open-minded guy you would ever meet. He had this funny bit about Kate Smith, you know, the gal who belted out 'God Bless America.' She was a fat, um ... okay, let's say hefty woman. I'm not sayin' she wasn't talented—amazing! She was amazing. But there was a lot of her, if ya know my meaning. So anyway, Lenny, he says, to the audience real sneaky like: 'If you really believe in segregation, and you'd fight to the death for it, here's your choice. You can marry a white, white woman or a black, black woman, only the white woman is Kate Smith ... and the black one was Lena Horne! Lenny'd look at the men in the crowd and say, 'Okay, boys, make your choice.' Remember, back then Lena Horne was a black woman and drop dead gorgeous. So the place went nuts. That is what Lenny Bruce thought of racist bigots."

"So Mr. Stienman, is it your opinion that words should not be censored because that just makes them more powerful, and if we had not censored Lenny Bruce's words, then a word like nigger would not have the impact it has today? Am I correct?"

"Well, yeah. And Lenny wouldn't have died at forty because he wouldn't have been treated like a criminal, for God's sake." Murray Steinman was trying his best to defend the honor of his client, several decades removed.

Devlin was tying the two together as best he could. "My client used the word nigger, as you know. What is your opinion of that?"

"Well, look. I don't know your guy. But I will say that if someone called me a name because I'm a Jew, I wouldn't make a federal case outta it. I mean, it's just a word. Whoever called me a kike—I'd figure he's a shmuck. A jerk, if you don't know Yiddish. I don't mean to offend. But instead, you got this trial and look at all the publicity he gets. Publicity. You'd kill for it in my line of work."

"Thank you, sir. Your witness." Devlin sat and seemed quite pleased with his surprise witness's performance.

Just as he was finishing, Patrick Rosen, who was absent from the prosecution's table, had slipped in relatively unnoticed. Before Peters proceeded, she looked at a memo he slid over to her. Peters absorbed it quickly and greeted Murray Steinman warmly.

"Thank you, sir, for coming all the way to San Diego. I want you to know that I also was a fan of your client, Lenny Bruce. Of course, as you point out, his words were not intended to be racist, just the opposite. Now, Mr. Steinman, as an agent to many stars, you must have worked with a great many controversial people over the years. Were any of them members of the Ku Klux Klan?"

"Are you kidding me? I worked with a lot of people who weren't always the brightest candle in the candelabra, if you know what I mean, but the Klan, no way. Those guys didn't go in for comedy." The audience tittered.

Peters knew what she was doing. "Tragedy, more likely."

"Yeah. Exactly. Politics more their style." Even more chuckling. Judge Lewis was vigilant. He peered out to make sure his courtroom did not turn into the Murray Steinman Theater.

"Are you aware that Duke Ellis claims to have rescinded his membership in the Klan?"

"Good for him, Counselor. Everybody can be a horse's ass once in their life." The audience was doing their best, as well as some on the jury, to contain themselves.

"Speaking of making a fool of oneself, I assume you know that Duke Ellis is charged with inciting a riot at the home of his opponent in a Congressional race?"

The bait was on the hook, Rossi surmised.

"Well, I heard something about that. But I spoke with Mr. Devlin there, and he says that his client didn't mean that to happen. I mean, that's what he told me."

Murray Steinman could not be more transparent.

"I see. And you believed Mr. Devlin? Hmm. If someone called you a name, I believe you used the word kike, and started to encourage others to do the same, how would you feel?"

"I don't know. When I was younger I'd pop him one." He made a fist and pointed it at what he would likely call his kisser.

"And if that wasn't possible, if these people then soon began threatening your family, that would not be acceptable, would it?"

The fish was on the hook.

Rossi leaned in and looked at Devlin. Rossi surmised that Devlin knew where this was going. It was a calculation. Devlin hoped he could either nip in the bud, or else hope that the element of surprise would never allow it to come to fruition.

"Objection, Your Honor. Speculation and relevance ..."

Judge Lewis stopped him quickly. "I allowed you to take this court down a road that I had cautioned you about, Counselor. I'm afraid you have to ride it to its conclusion. Overruled. Continue, Ms. Peters."

"Thank you, Your Honor. Let me repeat the question, Mr. Steinman. If fighting off the offender wasn't possible, and these people, who were egged on by that person, then began threatening your family, that would not be acceptable, would it?"

"It definitely would not," Steinman responded brusquely. He seemed unaware of the destination.

"And I object again, Your Honor. A lay witness cannot answer hypothetical judgments."

"Overruled ... again." Judge Lewis's irritation was obvious.

"If they did damage to your home or your loved ones, you would take them to court, I suppose?"

"You're damn right I would. I'd sue ..." He paused. "In a New York minute," he reconsidered. "Of course, this is all ..." Steinman smirked, "hypothetical."

"Oh, I am afraid not, Mr. Steinman. There was a man who managed to do just that in 1933. And you are right, he was a politician. No further questions."

30

JOE GARCIA

Rossi needed a break, as did the other jurors. Apparently, Judge Lewis was of the same mind. He excused them and called for a recess. Henry quickly herded the fourteen into a different room, where Rose already had their lunches ready for them, along with an assortment of beverages.

As sandwiches were distributed, Rossi took inventory of who was sitting with whom. He waited for everyone else to get settled, needing to stretch his legs anyway. He made a calculated decision to sit between Jim, who managed a department at Sears, and Mr. Garcia, the owner of a landscaping company. The two men had been chatting at various times and seemed to see the world in the same manner: work hard, reap the benefits, and expect that of others. *Honorable, for sure.*

"Mind if I squeeze in, guys?" Rossi was already maneuvering the chair, the question being a mere formality. Necessary, since he had not really spoken to either of them.

They nodded and accorded him a bit more room. Both men's girth consumed more space than either would probably care to admit. Rossi introduced himself and Garcia shook hands and told him, "I'm Joe."

"Jim." Another hand came over after wiping his fingers on his napkin. "Sorry, too much mustard for my taste."

Joe Garcia chimed in, "But I gotta admit, these are very good. Can't complain about how they're treating us. You sleep okay, Tony?"

"Well as can be expected in hotels. Never been easy for me. How about you guys?" Rossi took his first bite of a BLT.

Again heads nodded. Jim spoke as he reached for a can of Coke. "Yeah. Same here. My wife's happy though. She said this was her vacation from me."

All three chuckled and chewed.

Jim turned to his left and started a conversation with Jane, the librarian, about his wife and how, after this, maybe they should take a much-needed vacation. Jane gave a series of affirming nods and remarks. It was apparent that Jim's decades of sales experience allowed him the gift of gab.

Rossi remarked to Joe, "I heard when we first got on the jury that your son is overseeing your business. That has to be very gratifying, having him keep the business on solid footing?"

"Oh, yeah. Joey ... I shouldn't call him that. He gets ticked off. He says, 'Dad, I'm almost thirty, man.'" Joe paused. "It's a habit. Anyway, to tell you the truth, he really is terrific at the business. He's good with people. Me, I'm old school. I stick to my lane. My son, he is great with customers, and he gets all the computer stuff that I hate. Billing, you know. You have kids, Tony?"

"Yep. Two are out of college, have jobs, and are independent, too. My youngest daughter is a senior in college. So it is just my wife and me. Empty nesters."

"Grandkids? I have four. Love 'em to death."

"One, so far. My daughter has a two-year-old girl. She's adorable. I just retired, so when this is over, my wife and I will be heading out to Denver to see them."

"Nice. Grandkids are the best. I always feel like I need to

appreciate my time with them because when my three kids were little all I did was work, work, work. You know what I mean, right?" He had finished his sandwich in one large gulp.

"Oh, I get that. I was lucky in a way because for a while my wife took time off; she was a teacher, too. And I tried to get home from school to relieve her in the early days." Rossi reached for a bag of chips.

"What did you teach?"

"High school. My wife taught fifth grade, mostly."

"Oh, man. Those high school kids must have been a challenge. I know I wouldn't have the patience. I know I could be too tough. My sister says I was a disciplinarian. But I had to be. You know, respect. They gotta respect their parents. In my case, mostly me."

A brief hesitation from Rossi. Joe's last comment was just hanging there. *Should I ask?* His question was moot.

"Jeez listen to me talking. Sorry. I guess I should explain that my wife died when the kids were young. Cancer." Joe paused in thought. Rossi let the moment settle. "Anyway, my sister and brother-in-law, they really helped. I don't know what I would've done. You know?"

Rossi was reminded of his time back in his classroom after school speaking with the numerous single parents who, for various reasons, had the burden of being alone, trying their best to make everything right for their son or daughter.

"Joe, I'm sorry. I have spoken to so many parents who were in a position where they needed help. Divorces usually." Then Rossi let a moment pass before he said in earnest, "Sounds to me like your wife would be so proud of you and your sister ... and, of course, your kids. How old are they?"

"Thanks, Tony. That's nice of you to say." Again he took time before responding to Rossi's query. "Geeze, the older I get, the harder it is to remember. Joe is twenty-nine; Nina is a year younger. She has two kids. Leticia is ... hmm, twenty-five, I think. And Ronnie ... he's twenty-three, no twenty-four. Yeah, that's right. He's married to a great gal. They have the other two kids."

Just then Henry entered the room. "Everyone, I hope lunch was to your liking. The judge says in about thirty minutes he is going to get started. So I guess this is a good time to, as they say, 'empty your tanks' and stretch your legs. I have the feeling that because you are being sequestered the judge wants to move things along. I'm sure you all appreciate that."

Lots of heads nod. And then each started to head for the restroom.

"Nice talking to you, Joe."

"Same, Tony."

Rossi finished his lunch and then sat back to consider his conversation with Joe. *Joe Garcia contradicted every stereotype that too many Americans had of Mexicans, especially lately.* Just having one meal with this self-made man, whose shoulders were strong enough to endure unimaginable loss, told Rossi all he needed to know about Joe Garcia, juror #9.

31

GEORGE 'DUKE' ELLIS

R ossi watched George Ellis take the witness stand, which surprised him. *In the movies and television shows, the defendant usually doesn't testify ... unless they need to.* Rossi closely observed his body language. He did not have the strut of Bud Temple, nor was he as nervous as Ronald Roberts. He presented himself to the court with a slight smile but composed and not overconfident. He nodded politely to the judge. His uniform *de jour* consisted of a dark blue suit, white shirt, and wide red tie, which completed his patriotic theme along with a sizable America flag pin on his lapel.

Rossi thought that Duke Ellis's persona sharply contrasted with Ellis's campaign rally persona: the raging maniac on videotape, a man crimson-faced and screaming at the top of his lungs. That night Ellis was fire and fury. Today he presented himself as placid and pleasant. *Was he coached to act in such a manner?*

Devlin began with the question that Rossi first considered. "Mr. Ellis, you did not have to testify, since it is the burden of the prosecution to prove you incited a riot—something they clearly have not done ..."

"Objection."

"Sustained."

"Fine. So why did you agree to take the stand, sir?"

"Thank you for allowing me to explain, Mr. Devlin," Ellis began. His voice was smooth and measured. "I am aware that I don't need to testify. However, I feel it is very important for me to speak directly to the court ... to the jury, and to my supporters to tell them that in no way whatsoever did I intend to begin a ... let's just call it a protest or a disturbance, at the Curtis home. I am deeply sorry anything like that occurred. I apologize to the Curtis family—specifically to Mrs. Curtis, whom I am sure is a fine lady."

Somehow the word *fine* didn't sit well with Rossi. He could not put his finger on why.

"Well, I am sure that the Curtis family and this jury appreciates your statement, Mr. Ellis." Devlin moved forward. "Just for the record, can you tell me why, since the prosecution seems to think this is incriminating, you joined and then subsequently left the organization known as the Ku Klux Klan?"

"Certainly. I was only a member for a very short time. Actually, *member* is really a vague term. I went to several meetings and such. I was curious about what they stood for and how they tried to accomplish their goals. Once it became obvious to me that there was a history of violence, well, I just felt that these people, this organization basically, was too extreme. I have not had anything to do with them for several years."

"What about other white separatist organizations like the Aryan Nation or the American Nazi groups?" Devlin wanted to cover all the bases.

"No. I definitely had nothing to do with this crazy Nazi movement, nor would I be associated with a foreign nation's influence. I consider myself an American—through and through."

Again Rossi wondered about Ellis's version of *an American*.

"What do you make of the media's coverage of the protests that have occurred recently—for example, in Charlottesville?"

Rossi felt that Devlin believed it may be better for him to wade into dangerous waters before the prosecution inevitably covered this subject.

"Sensationalism. How can the news sell if it doesn't have something sensational in it? Had the media not made this protest a 'breaking news event,' perhaps some of the tragic actions would not have been taken." For the first time, Ellis's smugness rose.

"How did you see your candidacy? What did you attempt to achieve?"

"Political influence for the white man. As I just said, I admonish violence. I believe political strength is the best road for progress to be made for the white man." Ellis said this in the same manner one would order a ham sandwich. *"I'll have mine with mayo and hold the mustard."*

Rossi threw a glance to his immediate left. Regina had stiffened.

"I see. Did you ever encourage your staff to do any physical harm to anyone?" Devlin needed to make this clear.

"Of course not."

"Did you ever threaten anyone?"

"No."

"Thank you, Mr. Ellis, for your frankness. No further questions at this time." Devlin took a seat and immediately jotted something down.

Attorney Peters began, "Let's begin with your last point about the *white race*, shall we? Do you feel persecuted by other races, especially the black race?"

Ellis cocked his head as if assessing the direction her question was taking. "Persecuted. No. I just feel that our laws should be fair and balanced." A slender smile.

"Now where have I heard that before ...? That's not a question." Peters quickly reloaded. "Then if that is so, why did you scream out 'kick the niggers out of the county, out of the state'?"

"Well, it was just a figure of speech."

"Pretty ugly figure, wouldn't you say?"

"That depends on one's point of view, madam."

"Let's go there. What is your *point of view* regarding separation of the races? There have been quite a few times when you have made provocative statements about the subject."

"First of all, I have the right to say it ..."

"That is part of what this trial will decide."

"... and I have the right to my beliefs. I believe that the black man and the white man will never live in peace. There will always be confrontation and, although I disdain it, violence. It has been going on since the nation was formed. Secondly, the laws of the nation have been unbalanced. Affirmative Action is one example. Obamacare. Welfare, in general. These programs are created for black people who are simply not up to the task in our country. If they can't pull their weight, well, then they should go back to where they came from. Simple as that."

Again, he was not angry, just polished. *This was part of his stump speech*, Rossi concluded.

"Would that be Africa, I assume?"

"Yes. That is where they came from."

"Well, that tells us quite a bit about you, doesn't it?"

"You really don't know me at all, Miss Peters." A flash of anger.

"Let's learn more then. Your military record indicates that you were given a 'General Discharge,' which, as I read the military code, means it is, and I quote, 'given to service members whose performance is satisfactory but is marked by a considerable departure in duty performance and conduct expected of military members.'" She looked up at Ellis. "Would you like to explain why you are part of the roughly nine percent of service personnel given this discharge, rather than an 'Honorable Discharge'?"

Ellis was unfazed. "That was decades ago. As I recall, my commanding officer and I had several disagreements and, frankly, I felt I was treated unfairly."

"Actually, you have left out two important details. First, your CO was black. Second, you fought with other black people in your unit, and you showed, according to the letter written by your CO, Sergeant Michael Strom, that you called him and others '*niggers and jungle monkeys.*' Did I get that right, Mr. Ellis? By the way, I'm introducing this letter as Exhibit B."

Devlin pleaded. "Your Honor, I object. This has nothing to do with the charge of incitement to riot. Judge, this was, presumably, when my client was twenty years old."

"Overruled. It speaks to impeachment. It directly challenges his testimony on the point. You will respond to the question, Mr. Ellis." Judge Lewis made it clear that he wanted to hear Ellis's explanation.

Ellis grudgingly began, "Like Mr. Devlin said, I was a young man with a lot to learn. I was sometimes brash, but I had my reasons. Some of the blacks in my company were not exactly taking too kindly to me, a white man. They called me a *cracker, whitey,* and other obscene words that I will not repeat here in court. I talked back and then it got a little heated. That's all there was." Ellis downplayed it.

Peters followed up. "Sergeant Strom's letter indicates several fights occurred, and that you called him a *nigger.* That's not just a little misunderstanding, is it?"

"Like I said, they called me names and I just gave it back to them. That's just the Army."

"Obviously your *general discharge* indicates that the Army didn't agree. Let's move to another confrontation. Wayne Sims testified here that you were involved in an incident years later in which you were an instigator in vandalizing a Chinese man's business with spray paint while you *were* a member of the Klan in 2013. Care to explain those actions?"

Ellis could not remain calm. His anger materialized in both pitch and volume. "First, Wayne Sims is a joke. He is just trying to make up for what he did back then. When he found Jesus, his wife made him 'repent' because the truth is that *he was the real racist.* He was caught up in the whole thing. I was not, and the police report shows that I did not do anything. I was just there. That's when I realized the Klan was trouble. He makes it out that he was the hero or something. Check the police report, Counselor. I did not do anything." Ellis was adamant.

Peters would not let him off the hook. "You were there and the police reported that you *were involved*; that's why you are identified in the police report, sir. You were not charged with any damage to property, but you were part of the group that went there. Sims said you brought the paint cans."

More anger. "No, I didn't. He is a liar and he can't prove a thing."

"More recently, Susan Hall testified about your implication that Jews were not welcome in *your neighborhood* while she and Jacob Rosen were working for Congressman Curtis. I quote, 'We don't want any trouble *with their kind.*'Why did you say that and what did you mean?" Peters kept pressing.

"I don't know what you are talking about. I have no memory of her or her friend or that incident."

"Well, they sure did. But let's move on to the night in question. During your *private meeting* with your campaign supporters, why did you use the word *nigger*?" she stabbed.

Regaining composure. "I could have said *blacks*. These are just words. When I speak to different groups I use different words. Words are not harmful. After all, blacks themselves call each other *nigger*, don't they?" A smirk.

"And you don't consider it offensive, then?"

"Why should I?"

"That's right," Peters mocked. "You are not a black man being called that by a white man." She fired another shot. "Why did you use the word *kick*? Isn't that an action? A rather violent verb. 'Kick the niggers,' those are your *words*. What were you trying to accomplish with that expression?"

Straight faced. "Enthusiasm. Enthusiasm for the campaign."

Peters turned to the jury in disbelief. Her eyes delivered a clear message: *did you hear what he just said?* Peters was incredulous. "Are you serious? You want this jury to believe this was a chant at a pep rally?"

Ellis stiffened as he perceived an insult. "Running for the United States Congress is serious business. I am attempting to regain political influence for the white man. Political strength is the road I travel, one without violence. Besides, no one says anything when someone shouts 'Kick Obama out of office.'"

"Oh, I wouldn't be so sure, Mr. Ellis. Death threats against President Obama were a common occurrence. But let's stay on point. You say you wanted to use *political strength*. How do you accomplish that?

"By winning the election and convincing like-minded patriotic colleagues to feel the same." He had finally managed to neutralize his voice. Smoother.

"I'm not so sure that is what you mean by *strength*. You were very straightforward on Twitter recently. Isn't it true that you retweeted a message to your followers about Tom Metzger's views about what a racist truly is?"

"I have no recollection about that."

"Let me refresh your memory. You posted this Tweet. Quote: 'Tolerance toward an invader or enemy ... is suicide. An invader of the gene pool cannot be tolerated in any way.' For the benefit of the jury, Metzger was the head of the Klan in California many years ago. Is this part of your *political pressure*? To not tolerate others who don't belong to your *gene pool*?"

"Those are not my words. I do not remember any such ... tweet." Ellis was hesitant.

"Wouldn't that make you a racist?"

"Well, first off, that is not a crime."

"You didn't answer my question."

Ellis reacted quickly. "Maybe I am. That is my ... prerogative."

"Do you want people of color to *fear* you then? Isn't that what you mean when you say *pressure*?"

"Fear? Did I say fear? I want *power*, Counselor. And if I get it, then I want to create a nation I am proud of."

Peters went in for the kill. "Then you must not be proud of our nation as it exists today. That must be why you have to 'kick the niggers out of the county, out of the state.' Isn't that so, Mr. Ellis? Isn't that the *fear* those men were trying to ignite at the Curtis home when you finished your speech by yelling to them, 'let's do it now!'?"

"No. I do not condone their actions." Anger began to bubble up again.

Peters pushed him further. "FBI informant Ronald Roberts testified that you wanted blacks to fear you."

"Fear me winning the election. That is what I meant."

"Why was your speech that night not an open invitation to mainstream media? Why was it only offered on the internet to right-wing organizations that were hostile to people of color?"

"Because ... I ... it was. And I wasn't hostile to anyone. I just wanted to thank my staff and my *loyal* supporters. I needed to rally them for the last push to the election."

"And wasn't it odd that every single one of those men the police rounded up at the Curtis home were at your speech that night?"

Catching himself. "Coincidence. Merely a coincidence."

"And your campaign manager, Bud Temple, leading the

charge was just a *coincidence*—you expect this jury to believe that?"

"I am going to repeat, I did not direct those men to do ... those things they did." He regrouped. "To go to the Curtis home ... look, I was *not* there. I was home. I had nothing to do with it. What more can I say?"

She looked directly at Rossi. "Oh, I think you have said plenty, Mr. Ellis. One last question: were you inciting them to vote or to harass?"

"To vote. I was inciting them to ..."

As Ellis finished his sentence with the word *vote,* Peters cut in, "So you admit your purpose was to *incite*. Did you have any doubt that they were not *already* going to vote for you?"

"Don't put words into my mouth." His temper flared again. He appeared to be of two minds; practiced poise was being choked by a burning, pent-up rage.

"I don't need to, sir. Your mouth has uttered enough *words.* No further questions." Peters' disgust was evident.

Judge Lewis was momentarily frozen, as if he had to pull himself away from the theater on display before him. He looked at Devlin. "Redirect, Mr. Devlin?"

Devlin rose only to say, "None needed, Your Honor. The defense rests."

"Fine. Fine, then. The witness is excused and this court will reconvene at nine o'clock tomorrow." He then gave the same instructions to the jury as he had the day before. He also waved the bailiffs, Henry and Rose, toward the front and told the jury to follow their instructions.

While all this transpired, Anthony Rossi was writing furiously in his notebook. One word was underlined. *Intent.*

32

CALLING HOME

A s the jurors filed into the mini-bus that would take them to their hotel, Anthony Rossi realized something that had not occurred to him in thirty-seven years of marriage. It came to him as he sat next to Melanie, Juror #6, whose bulging diamond ring was prominently affixed to her ring finger.

Rossi turned to her. "Well, calling my wife will be very ... strange."

Melanie looked from her ring to Rossi's. "Why is that?"

"Because of this trial, for the first time I can't tell her much about what happened to me. Weird, huh?" Rossi glanced out the window and then back at her.

"Oh, well. That's par for the course for me," Melanie replied. "My husband travels all the time ... lately. Ever since he sold his business and has been consulting at seminars, there are weeks when he is out of town, and we just catch up when it is over." She sighed.

"Oh." Rossi was not sure how to respond or if he even should. *Does she realize what she just revealed to a relative stranger about the state of her marriage?*

Finally, Rossi said the polite thing. "What business was he in, if you don't mind me asking?"

"Oh, not at all. He was a plastic surgeon."

The last of the jurors squeezed into the mini-bus. Everyone was settling in.

Melanie continued, "So now my husband attends conferences and lectures to doctors, mostly on how to run a successful business ... and then he plays golf with them." The last remark was delivered with a snarky tone.

Melanie looked down at her ring. Her nails were perfectly manicured and painted mauve. To Rossi, her wardrobe gave the impression she was someone with expensive taste. She had worn knee-length dresses with boots each day, always with a matching jacket and scarf to complete the ensemble. She was the only juror giving off this well-heeled vibe. Even Regina, the realtor who sat next to Rossi in the jury box, had toned down her look, from a business suit on the first day to fashionably comfortable clothing.

Rossi ventured forth one obvious point to Melanie. "Well, right now, talking to my wife about the trial, politics, and the news is out of bounds, I guess. But our jobs made it habitual for us to catch up on the day since we were both teachers."

"Oh, that's right. Kim told me she thought you taught at the high school. That must have been challenging, I suppose."

Challenging. Code for "I pity teachers who have to deal with those unruly kids."

Rossi also recognized the disingenuousness that sometimes accompanies statements similar to Melanie's. Some people cloaked their reaction to teachers in buttery polite words and forced condescending smiles. And no matter how it was disguised, after decades of experience, it was easy to tell the difference between appreciation and insincerity. Rossi decided to give Melanie the benefit of the doubt.

Next to Melanie, near the window, was Kim. Melanie

looked at her as she made one last proclamation about the teaching profession. "We must value teachers, of course. They sacrifice so much." Her last remark was directed toward Kim. "I could never have been a teacher. It must be rewarding ... but teenagers can be a handful with all their problems. And the parents! I don't envy you. How did you ever do it?"

Rossi understood her question was more rhetorical than interrogative. He decided a cliché was called for. "It's not for everyone."

A beat.

Kim decided to break the silence. "My kids love their teachers. This year the teachers seem to be more understanding of the homework load. For me, being by myself, it was overwhelming ... last year, especially."

Rossi did not want to say too much about Kim's situation, so he circled back to what started the conversation. "I understand. Anyway, it will be good to find out what's been happening on the home front. And, I must say, we've been sitting, it seems, all day. I need to move around."

Both women nodded. Fourteen strangers on a bus can make for awkward conversation when they have spent days watching something they must avoid talking about.

It's just human nature.

———

"So, I take it you've had quite a day."

Rossi leaned his head back and rotated his neck, trying to loosen the tightness. "That would be an understatement, Deborah." He placed his feet, sockless, on the bed while he kicked back and tilted the swivel chair. "And I'm tired of sitting. That's for sure."

Deborah had the news on softly, keeping a lookout for

stories on the Ellis trial. "Well, it was pretty boring here without you to pick on, dear."

"I'm sure. Since we can't talk about the trial, tell me what you did today. Oh, and anything new with the kids?" Rossi still referred to his threesome as *kids*. Hard to break the habit.

"Nothing to report with them, really. No news is good news, I guess. I'll remember to text all three tonight and update you tomorrow. By the way, when do you think you might be home? I mean, if this keeps going, would they keep you there over the weekend?" Deborah cringed, anticipating the response.

"That's a really good question. Our bailiff, Henry, is here at the hotel. If I can catch him, I'll ask. What I think will happen tomorrow is closing statements will be made. At least that's how it works on *Law and Order*." Rossi's habit of turning on the television and channel surfing to the news took over, and just as quickly he pushed *off* on the remote.

"Hmm. If that's true, is it possible that you might deliberate on a Saturday?"

"I can't imagine so."

A beat.

"Let's talk about your day. What did you do?" Rossi could already guess her answer as they both were transitioning to retirement and trying out new routines.

"Yoga this morning, and after that three of us headed to the French Pastry Shoppe. One of the ladies has taken up paddle boarding, you know what I am talking about?"

Deborah realized that the local news switched to national news and the anchor opened with: "*Breaking news from San Diego's courtroom where the trial of George 'Duke' Ellis is wrapping up ...*"

"Yeah. You've been talking about paddle boarding. I hear it is harder than it looks. You should go for it. Just make sure you fall into the water, not on to the board. Remember, that's how your sister hurt her back." Meanwhile, Rossi absent-mindedly flipped through the hotel's channel guide.

Silence. More silence.

"Deb, are you there? Deb?" Rossi looked at his phone. She was still connected. "Deborah ...?"

"Oh, yeah ... um, sorry, Tony. I thought I heard the doorbell. It must have been the neighbors."

Rossi was not the slightest bit fooled. He knew his wife was a terrible liar. It was exactly six o'clock. "You're watching the news, right?"

"Anthony! No, I'm not."

"I take it our trial is on the evening news, right?"

"Um." She gave up. "Yes. It's the lead story. But that's it. I won't say another word."

Rossi considered his options. He knew that the route taken to get to the hotel was even more circuitous than the day before. He knew why. He heard murmurs about crowd size from Henry to the van's driver and when he glanced down Broadway it was evident that the commotion had grown much larger. The blue flashing lights of patrol cars were ubiquitous. He could faintly hear bullhorns blaring out angry messages to the crowd. But again, once they had crossed Broadway and moved north to C Street, there was only a scattering of people.

Instead, Rossi took a detour from the trial. At the same time, Deborah resisted asking him about his experience. Then Rossi offered, "Okay. Honey, let's talk about what we are going to do when this is all over. Okay? Like what we are going to do to celebrate." The pages of *San Diego Magazine* lying on the desk featured plenty of tourist hot spots.

Silence again.

He knew she was still listening to whatever the news was reporting. He couldn't blame her.

"Tony, sorry. I am pausing this. No. I am turning it off.

There. Ah, look, if you turn to channel 4 you can watch *Jeopardy*."

"Deborah, I don't want to watch anything that requires me to test my brain. I have a thought that would be fun to do when this trial ends. We can go down to Coronado Island and treat ourselves to a night at the Hotel Del. Then we can stroll the beach. How's that sound?"

Deborah was coquettish, her voice dropping an octave. "It sounds absolutely ... dreamy."

"Definitely." Rossi wished he was holding her instead of his cell phone. "I miss you."

"Of course you do. That's why I love you so."

"I'm gonna grab a bite to eat. I'll call you to say *goodnight*, okay?"

"You better, Juror #12."

They laughed. Loneliness can be crazy.

33

JEAN PETERS

Henry called roll in the adjacent waiting room. All fourteen were present, albeit a bit tired from four days of intense proceedings. Nevertheless, they were eager to get underway.

Rossi asked the question most were whispering to each other. "Henry, since today is Wednesday, do we serve on Saturday if this trial goes that far? I mean, you had us check out of the hotel and ..."

Henry knifed into his query. "You beat me to the punch. The judge will be asking you what you all would prefer to do today. He instructed me to tell you that the trial will finish in the morning session, most likely, with the closing statements. Then deliberations will begin. Judge Lewis will explain the choices that this jury will have to consider. I hope that satisfies everyone ... for now." He saw heads nod, but their faces seemed somewhat perturbed.

Jane spoke up. "Just one thing, sir. Will there be a chance to go home over the weekend?" She paused. "I'm asking for a friend." She smiled, injecting a bit of levity.

For once everyone, including Henry and Rose, smiled and

laughter fluttered around the packed room. Henry looked to Rose and then summed up the situation: "The answer is way above our pay grade. It's my experience that the judge wants you all to be in the best frame of mind possible. That's as much as I can say."

Diplomatic, Rossi concluded.

————

Judge Lewis began the day with jury instructions. Rossi listened carefully because now he and the other eleven jurors were going to have to decide Duke Ellis's fate.

The judge began, "Members of the jury, you must decide on the one criminal charge that George Ellis is faced with: incitement to riot. It is imperative that you understand what the law says regarding the charge before the prosecution argues it has proven its case beyond a reasonable doubt and the defense argues otherwise."

Then Judge Lewis got very specific. "Allow me to define this term so you understand what it means. Inciting a riot is generally defined as *the negligent irresponsible action of one person which, done purposefully, causes physical harm.*

"The defendant is charged with one count of inciting a riot under *Title 18, United States Code, Section 2101,* which makes it a crime to incite a riot. For you to find the defendant guilty, the government must prove each of the following beyond a reasonable doubt: first, that the defendant traveled in interstate or foreign commerce, or used the mail or any facility in interstate or foreign commerce; second, that the defendant did so with intent to: 1. incite a riot, or 2. organize, promote, encourage, participate in, or carry on a riot, or 3. commit any act of violence in furtherance of a riot, or 4. aid or abet any person in inciting or participating in or carrying on a riot or committing any act of violence in furtherance of a riot."

After putting some notes aside, Judge Lewis returned his gaze to the jury. "I know that was a lot to grasp. You will have time to consider the entire definition of incitement and if you have any questions or need of clarification, of course, I will provide that to you.

"So the first order of business is for you to decide on a foreperson. My bailiffs, Henry and Rose, will be available to you at any time. You may direct questions you have to them and they will consult with me. You may ask for the transcripts of the trial to be read to you by my court reporter. These transcripts can also be provided to you in writing. You may ask for the videotape to be re-shown as well." Then he got the attention of Henry and they quickly whispered to each other. "If you cannot reach a unanimous verdict today, you will be returned to the hotel and deliberations will continue tomorrow, and so on until a verdict has been reached. Needless to say, you are to not discuss this trial with anyone other than your fellow jurors and you must refrain from news and social media until you have completed your service. I am aware at this time that this limitation is difficult to follow, but follow it you must. Now you will hear the closing statements of the prosecution and then the defense. Again, thank you for your attention."

Judge Lewis told District Attorney Jean Peters she had the floor.

Peters did not use notes. She stood at the lectern. She wore an elegant black suit with a white blouse. Rossi wondered if the colors were symbolic. Her eyes scanned back and forth. She didn't look at their faces; she focused on their eyes. The eyes of a juror can tell so much. Do they stay focused on her, or drift away? Do they look down, as if they are pondering something? Do the eyes pull their head up and down, unwittingly affirming what she is saying? Or is there a roll of the eyes or an unfocused, bored look that is worrisome? Can she spot the leader's eyes, the one who will dictate the deliberations directions? Is there some set of eyes so hardened that the mind is closed? If that person is working against her, can she direct her attention to that juror and make every effort to convince? She knows she has no room for error. It's not a civil case. It's criminal and it must be unanimous to convict.

"Members of the jury. There is the rule of law and the spirit of the law and both are required to prevent lawlessness. Lawlessness is what occurred on the night of September 13, 2016. The physical damage is repairable, but the psychological pain inflicted leaves a scar that cuts deeply, not just with one family, but in the hearts and minds of all people of color. Some of those rioters have been punished. More will be. But what you must decide is whether the ringleader should be held responsible for this despicable assault on the home of Congressman James Curtis, one that his wife Roberta Curtis and their children will not easily forget.

"So let's begin with the rule of law. Did George 'Duke' Ellis, in fact, *incite a riot*? When this trial began, Judge Lewis explained that incitement to riot is defined as 'the negligent irresponsible action of one person which, done purposefully, causes physical harm.' Remember those words when you go back to deliberate because those words will seal Duke Ellis's fate. Ellis said, and I quote, 'We gotta kick the niggers out of the county, out of the state and let's do it now.' Now, does this sound physical? Does it sound violent? Does it sound irresponsible? Does it sound negligent? You bet it does! Why? Because Duke Ellis fully intended that riot to happen while he sat at home thinking he had an alibi."

She let a moment pass for the jury to absorb her opening attack. "Why deliver his speech in a semi-private setting? Why not at a fully public event that the mainstream media could attend? Because if he had, he would most assuredly be on trial as he is today. He tried to be secretive and never considered that the media would find out because he never thought that someone from the FBI would be videotaping his virulent, hate-filled message. Ask yourself, did Ellis commit any act of violence in *furtherance* of a riot from his pulpit? When he yelled out, 'Let's do it now!' what do you think he was demanding of the men who then did their best to instill fear into the hearts of his black opponent, Congressman James Curtis, as well as his family? Oh, he most certainly knew exactly what he was doing.

"What if he had done so in a transparent, public manner? Well, then all of America would see him for what he is: a racist of the first order. Duke Ellis never counted on the FBI producing *evidence of his crime.* That is why he sits at that table knowing that his former KKK involvement and his continued race-baiting have finally caught up to him.

"What was his intent? To incite fear. Simple fear. Ronald Roberts testified that was Ellis's objective." Peters pointed to the witness stand. "'Fear,' he said, 'is the weapon of the Klan, and words are the tools they use.' And use them he did. They have their own twisted, sick version of what a *true American* is, and they surely do not want people they view as inferior to ever vote, let alone hold a position in government. Ellis hopes that *the fear* will make them just leave—the county, the state, the nation. That's what Duke Ellis is all about.

"You see, the spirit of the law is also on trial. The inspiration to create 'a more perfect union' is the heart and soul of our Constitution. The spirit of our laws dictates 'all men are created equal,' and through Constitutional amendments that right was extended to race and sex, as well. But Duke Ellis does not *accept* that idea. No. He believes in white supremacy: one race of people, superior to others. Ladies and gentlemen, where does that lead? Just look to the Civil War and World War II. Americans have fought and died to defeat leaders who incite that insidious propaganda."

She leaned over the lectern and pointed back to the defense table.

"If you decide that Duke Ellis is innocent, he will be viewed as a hero. That must be going through his twisted mind. And now the defense wants to *whitewash* his crimes, to make this riot about 'free speech' instead of violence. They want to white-wash the legacy of racism in our nation. To pretend that, what Ellis said that night—'we gotta kick the niggers out of the county, out of the state'—was just a 'figure of speech.' No, it is not. You know that in your soul. If you allow justice to be white-washed again, you will be disgusted with yourself at what you have done. You will have set a precedent that others like him will follow."

Peters took two steps back and reached for a legal pad on the table. It was obvious to Rossi that she was transitioning from an emotional appeal to a historical perspective, in that she became the storyteller rather than the sermonizer.

"You will not be acting alone in your verdict of guilty. The United States Supreme Court stands with you. In 1969, the Court held in *Brandenburg v. Ohio* that inflammatory speech is protected under the First Amendment *unless* the speech 'is directed to inciting or producing imminent lawless action and is likely to produce such action.' Supreme Court Justice William O. Douglas explained that the First Amendment is not absolute when he wrote for the Court: 'The question in every case is whether the words used are used in such circumstances and are of such a nature as to create *a clear and present danger ...*' I believe that the words of Duke Ellis represent a clear and present danger. I think you already know that."

Peters was coming to the climax.

"Members of the jury, stand together against hate. Be unanimous as one voice that will not tolerate this evil. You know exactly what Duke Ellis was calling for people to do. When you go to deliberate, imagine *you* are the person that Ellis wants to scare. Duke Ellis is pointing at *you*. It is you who cannot live in *his country*. It is your house, your children that he threatens.

It is you who must explain to the generations that follow why you allowed justice to be denied, again. Think about the burning crosses, the bombed-out churches, the Aryan arrogance, and deliver a guilty verdict."

Peters scanned the jury one last time. Then she returned to her seat.

34

JAMES DEVLIN

J udge Lewis was deliberate. He surveyed his courtroom, signaled to the bailiff to approach the bench, and whispered instructions to him. Rossi figured Judge Lewis was allowing time for the jury to absorb the prosecution's argument and giving James Devlin a moment to gather his thoughts. The judge cleared his throat and then asked for the defense's closing statement.

Anthony Rossi leaned forward. His notebook was opened just as it was during Jean Peters' closing. His pen poised.

Devlin wore a gray pinstriped suit. He did not use his glasses as a prop. The contrast in presentation was noticeable to Rossi, as was his tone. Softer, less theatrical. He was a mixture of polite but confident. Everything about his manner and tone was calculated to convince his jury of one simple fact: the law states that you cannot incite a riot if you are not there and never directly instructed anyone to take a riotous action. He made every effort to keep the facts clear and irrefutable.

He began speaking at the defense table. It would take the full length of his oration to land at the lectern where Peters had spoken.

"Members of the jury, I thank you for your unfailing attention. Let me be brief. George Ellis did not incite a riot. There are three questions in my mind right now, and these will be the three questions you will be considering shortly. To each question I answer a firm *no.* Let me tell you why. Question number one: Has the prosecution justified censorship of my client? I say *no.* You may not agree with Mr. Ellis, you may hate him or love him, but that is what this nation's Constitution guarantees —the freedom to think and to speak one's mind.

"Question number two: Do you have any reason that compels you to gag my client? No! If you silence him, you would have to round up every militant, dissenter, protester, or revolutionary—you would have to lock them all up for life because they will try and try and try to exercise their Constitutional right to free speech. The protesters who chant 'Black Lives Matter' or the people at political rallies who repeat 'Lock Her Up'—and every cause you can think of in between—those two political polar opposites will be frightened to speak out. Why? Because they will be frightened of what could happen. Someone might throw a punch. A brick may be thrown. A fire could start. There could be looting. The police may be hurt. And none of this was the *intent* of the speaker's words, but of someone's irresponsible, possibly criminal actions. We've already arrested those people—Frank Stapleton and Bud Temple. However, you will be the ones to decide *what can and cannot be said.* I don't think any of you are ready to accept that responsibility.

"My final question is this: Did my client incite a riot? In order for you to believe he did, the burden of proof has to be met. And that burden is a high bar, and one that the prosecution has not come close to meeting. Let me explain. George Ellis's speech is, by law, labeled 'political speech.' It is the most protected type of speech—constitutionally. In order for my client to be guilty of inciting a riot, he would have to have *the knowledge that his followers would act.* In simple terms, his followers would have had to come up to him and say, 'Tell us what to do and we will do it.' It did not happen. Not one of the witnesses can testify to that. Why? Because George Ellis did not say those words. That is the test the *Brandenburg v. Ohio* case established. It is how the law defines *incitement to riot.*

"Let me also state, emphatically, the Supreme Court case Ms. Peters referred to decided that Mr. Brandenburg, a member of the KKK, gave a *constitutionally protected* speech and the Supreme Court overruled any of the Lower Court's incitement charges. That's right. *Overruled.* Brandenburg's radio speech, just like Mr. Ellis's rally speech, did not explicitly tell people to violate the law. Mr. Ellis had no knowledge of the actions of the rioters. He was not even there. Think of the witnesses you heard from. Reporter Desiree Owens denies that he incited the riot. Bud Temple, his campaign organizer, told you that my client did not tell him to act as he and others did. If the prosecution's only proof is that, well, 'George Ellis was a Klansman,' as I said at the very beginning of this trial, his right to free speech cannot be quashed because of his membership in any organization, even the KKK.

"George Ellis gave a *thought*-provoking speech. His *speech* did not explicitly provoke violence. And there is a world of difference. That is why my client is innocent of the charge."

With this last understated sentence, Devlin spun and returned to his seat next to George "Duke" Ellis.

35

ROSEN'S REBUTTAL

Judge Lewis took a look at his notes. He was being very deliberate. Then he explained, "Members of the jury, the prosecution in a federal criminal case has the burden of proof but it also is allowed the final word ... or rebuttal. In this case Attorney Peters has asked Attorney Rosen to speak to the defense's claim just now. So, Mr. Rosen, you may proceed."

Rossi took measure of the Riverside United States Attorney. Rosen was more bookish and rumpled—less the leading actor, but clearly an important player in the drama. He stepped to the lectern with a large book and legal pad in hand. He cleared his throat. "Thank you, Your Honor. Members of the jury, I will be brief and to the point. The defense is misleading you and misrepresenting the opinion of the United State's Supreme Court. They posed three questions. The first: did we justify censorship? That is not the principle this trial seeks to answer. Duke Ellis has a right to say what he pleases. He also bears the responsibility for those words. In this case the responsibility is that his free speech incited a riot. Period. Full stop. Second, do you have a reason to 'gag' Mr. Ellis? Yes, you do. Why? Because his speech's purpose was to incite a violent act. It matters *not* if he was or was not there. The point is that the event would not have happened if he had not advocated these exact words 'kick the niggers out of the state, out of the county. And let's do it now!'"

Rosen assessed the jury's reaction so far. Rosen nodded to them. "I think you know exactly what Duke Ellis wanted them to do." Then he opened the thick book he was carrying against his chest. "I want you to know that the defense has not been forthright in the explanation of *Brandenburg v. Ohio.* The majority opinion which was penned by Justice Douglas concluded, and I quote, 'the First Amendment is not absolute.' Why did they then allow Mr. Brandenburg off the hook, so to speak, for his racist comments? Answer: because he did not cause a riot. It was a radio broadcast and no riot resulted from his radio speech. That is *not* the case here. The Supreme Court took years to reverse the evil that is rooted in racism. I do not need to give this jury a civics lesson to prove that point. We are one nation, 'indivisible, with liberty and justice for *all.*'" Rosen closed the book with purpose. The sound echoed forth throughout the courtroom.

36

THE JUDGE'S INSTRUCTIONS

J udge Lewis straightened up in his chair and rolled his shoulders. Rossi couldn't tell if he was trying to relieve stress or gather his forces for what would be his final instructions to the jury. One thing Rossi knew for sure: the level of tension in the courtroom had reached a zenith. He looked to the packed gallery and all the onlookers were still. One could hear a pin drop. Since there were no cameras allowed in the courtroom, the faint sounds of pencils sketching the scene reminded him of students penning answers to his quizzes. It took several minutes for the judge to gather his notes, survey his courtroom, and then turn to his jury.

Judge Lewis began: "Members of the jury, you must now decide on the one criminal charge that George Ellis is faced with: incitement to riot. Allow me to again define this term so you understand what it means. It is defined as *the negligent irresponsible action of one person which, done purposefully, causes physical harm.*"

Judge Lewis then paused to review his notes before continuing. "I must add that both the prosecution and the defense have brought into the trial the United States

Supreme Court's decision in the case of *Brandenburg v. Ohio*. Since both parties wanted to discuss this, I will add that the Supreme Court gave its definition of *unprotected* speech. The Supreme Court ruled in 1969 that the First Amendment protects speech unless the speech is directed to *inciting or producing imminent lawless action and is likely to incite or produce such action*. This information may help guide you in deliberations. The facts in the *Brandenburg v. Ohio* case were that the defendant, a leader in the KKK, did indeed speak in a radio broadcast. His speech was indisputably racist, however, did not meet the Court's standard for incitement because there was no imminent riot or one planned. Thus, the Supreme Court did not find the defendant, Mr. Brandenburg, guilty of incitement."

Judge Lewis then clearly looked at his own notes as he read, "The US Supreme Court noted that speech could be prohibited if it was directed at inciting or producing lawless actions and it was likely to incite or produce lawless actions." The judge cleared his throat and straightened his shoulders before making one last point. "The opinion of Justice William O. Douglas regarding when incitement *does occur* is relevant today because Douglas argued that the First Amendment is not absolute."

The judge took a deep breath. Rossi reasoned that the pressure of this trial was weighing on him. The judge wanted to make sure there were no mistakes on his part since how he ruled throughout the trial would be examined under a microscope by legal scholars, no doubt.

"Let me remind you that the first order of business is for you to decide on a foreperson. My bailiffs, Henry and Rose, will be available to you at any time. Naturally, you are not to discuss this trial with *anyone* other than your fellow jurors, and you must refrain from news and social media until you have completed your service."

He looked at Henry, who motioned to Rose, and both strode over to the jury box.

"So once again, I entrust you into the hands of my fine bailiffs. I know that lunch is in order. So please take your time before beginning deliberations to refresh yourselves. Thank you very much. This court is in recess." He picked up the gavel and forcefully struck it against its wooden base.

Rossi was the last to rise. He was preoccupied with finishing a final thought he was scribbling in his notebook. He underlined Brandenburg decision.

37

DELIBERATIONS: DAY 1, HOUR 1

Henry took lunch orders and Rossi took in the lay of the land inside the deliberation room. It was as one would expect. Thin, rectangular, with a long generic table for twelve. A restroom toward the back of the room. A long whiteboard on one side. A large television up front in the corner with a DVD system below. The clock near the television mirrored the same state-issued one in the anteroom they had been in earlier. It ticked loudly. No windows. One door. Not a lot of room between the walls and the chairs, such that people needed to scoot around to get past each other. If you had a problem with claustrophobia, you were out of luck.

Rossi recalled that the judge said that they should not start deliberations until after lunch and once everyone had had a chance to stretch their legs and use the restroom, but it was the first unanimous decision reached that afternoon.

He noticed that along one wall was a thin counter with a coffee maker, and coffee was already brewing. *Good,* he thought, *I need to stay awake.* Afternoons were his weakness. He was a morning person who gathered his second wind around four o'clock, so the next hour would be a time when his eyes drooped. Coffee would help. Lunch would also, as long as it wasn't too heavy. A pastrami sandwich worked; he mostly ignored the potato salad.

They dropped their notebooks helter-skelter on the table, but that wasn't to be their final resting place. Once lunch ended, Russell asked everyone if they could get started. Rossi noted he was the most eager as he clapped his hands together.

"Let's kick this thing off." *He had coach written all over him.*

When the question of who would be the foreperson came up, everyone looked around. It appeared there was no one eager to take on the task. Adam, the youngest, asked who had already been on a jury before. Doc, Jane, and Heroyuki all raised their hands, but none immediately volunteered.

Heroyuki demurred.

Doc said he was too "damn old"—everyone chuckled.

Jane, the librarian, finally agreed. "Well, I guess I am elected. I just want to say, if anyone else wants to ..." They cut her off. It was obvious she was their choice.

Henry the bailiff settled the issue, "Okay, Jane, you get the honors. Here is my cell phone number. Call me for anything you need. I'll come to you. Here is a list of the jurors' names. I believe we are all present and accounted for. Coffee and snacks on the counter, folks. The television is set to play the videotape if you wish to see it. If you want to review an exhibit or piece of evidence or have testimony read back to you, send a note to me and I'll relay the message to the judge. I can provide transcripts to you if the judge prefers. Other than that, you are all set." He smiled and exited stage right.

Jane began with an ask. "Everyone, can you indulge me in one favor? The last time I was on a jury, I found it strange that all the women sat together, as did the men. And the frustrating thing is that they often talked among themselves. We were always asking what the other group was saying. And worse than that, we also found that the voting was men one side, women the other. So I was thinking, can we sit just as we sat in the jury box, please?"

People looked around and all acquiesced to her wish.

"So, Lauren, you are here," Jane pointed to the first seat on one side of the table, "since you are juror number one. Then Jim and Kim, next. Russell, you are number four, right?" He nodded taking his seat. "Okay, um, Adam and then Melanie. On the other side, right across from Melanie is Heroyuki ..."

Heroyuki quickly interrupted. "Please, Jane, everyone, just call me *Hero*. Nobody really uses my full name. Thank you." Smiles all around.

"Right," Jane continued the roll, "Doctor ..."

Doc interrupted. "Nobody calls me Doctor, either. Just Doc. Thanks." Again smiles. Nervous laughter.

At that point, Russell piped in. "Just Russ, here ... or Coach. Only kidding about that."

"All right. This group has a sense of humor. I think that will serve us well," Jane chirped. "Joe, you're next to Doc and then me, and Regina and Tony. And that's a wrap."

Everyone sorted themselves out and a few handshakes were exchanged.

"So the next thing to decide is do we discuss the case first or do a preliminary vote? What do you folks think?"

Melanie spoke up. "I think we need to talk a little first. Don't you? I mean, this is pretty complicated. I felt one way for a while, and now, well, I really have no idea what I think." This was followed by rousing agreement.

Doc said, "Maybe we ought to write on the whiteboard the exact charge and what the judge said it meant." More agreement.

Russ shot up. "I'm good at whiteboards—all that coaching. If you don't mind I'll be the scribe."

Jane proceeded to read out the definition the judge had

given them. "*The negligent irresponsible action of one person which, done purposefully, causes physical harm.*"

"Okay, got it. Whew. That's a mouthful." Russ made sure he omitted nothing. And all faces stared at each word. "Mind if I underline a couple of things, folks?" Heads nodded. He underlined the words *negligent, irresponsible,* and *purposefully.* "Okay. There. I think those are pretty important." Russ took his seat.

Joe Garcia: Well, this Ellis guy sure gave a pretty nasty speech. I kinda think he knew what he was doing."

Melanie: "But that's the problem. Was he firing up his troops or inciting them to ... like it says there ... *cause physical harm?* I think that is the question."

Jim: "Agreed. I mean, the whole thing comes down to his intent. How can we know that? I've been in sales all my life, and I can usually read a customer, but it's hard when you're not there. You know what I'm saying?"

A collective *hmm* circled the table.

Rossi: "Maybe we ought to see the videotape again. That is the only direct evidence of what he said that night."

All agreed. Lauren, closest to the television, hit the *play* button and then turned off the lights.

———

All twelve jurors fell silent as the video ended. It was as if that vulgar night flooded the room with its ominous presence. This reminded Anthony Rossi that what he saw wasn't just something one could glance at on the television news and then ignore.

Rossi knew that this trial encompassed far more than the fate of one man—George "Duke" Ellis. This trial's overtones could reverberate well past the anguish felt by one Congressman's family. The twelve jurors were listening to the speech that justified the Civil War, the Jim Crow laws, and the reason

Martin Luther King, Jr. felt the need to tell Washington, D.C. that he had a dream one day that all men, black or white, would be truly equal. The fact that the Civil Rights Movement was cemented in the shadow of Lincoln's Memorial was more than symbolic of one day's march. It was generational. Rossi's calling to become a teacher sprung from the image of Dr. King challenging the culture and conscience of a nation. The blurry black-and-white footage would forever frame the face of a white policeman standing by Dr. King's shoulder. That officer broke into a grin at the climactic moment when Dr. King uttered, "Free at last, free at last, thank God Almighty, we are free at last."

'At last.' Now that was irony.

Rossi scanned the room. The table. The whiteboard with a definition written in black marker. The video frozen on a tubular screen. Eleven pensive faces staring in various directions. Only one thing was certain: they were lost in thought.

Outside, the media waited impatiently for their verdict. All of it drove home the sobering fact that this verdict would speak to far more Americans than he could have imagined. He could not be certain that the others grasped this, but he couldn't avoid the subtext. So it began.

Jane: "Well, observations?"

Kim: "I don't know about you all, but that just gives me chills." She looked at Regina, as though she wanted the only black person in the room to comment. Regina crossed her arms and pursed her lips. *She wasn't ready to speak.*

Lauren: "Yeah. I know what you mean. Um. I couldn't help but look at the other men at the rally, as much as the camera allowed, seeing how they reacted. It seems to me that they were, um, really, like, getting riled up. Do you guys agree?"

Adam: "Yeah. But to be the devil's advocate, no pun intended, that's the point of all these political rallies. I mean, look at Trump. He is ... maybe this is off-topic, but he is all over the place saying crazy stuff and the crowd eats it up."

Jim: "I'm not sure we should get into politics here. Trump is Trump. And I think we shouldn't go there."

Some nodding.

Rossi spoke. "I agree we should not be debating the merits of President Trump. However, the defense attorney raised the question of 'political speech' versus a speech that is 'actionable speech,' and that is something we do need to deal with. Did Duke Ellis call for action and what kind of action did he intend?"

Jim: "Right. And that's the problem. How do we *know* what he intended?"

Doc: "I guess that is why we are here, isn't it? This whole trial has every network staked out in front of this building to find out what we all think about free speech."

The room settled into a quiet pause with the only sound emanating from the unstoppable ticking of the clock.

Jane looked around the room. All seemed to be contemplating what to do next. "I'd like to encourage others to share their thoughts. We need to know what everyone's reaction is ... so far."

Joe Garcia broke the ice. "Look. I know racism when I see it. And I hear it loud and clear every day, okay. I work landscape and my company employs many guys from Mexico. I think you all know that. All of them have visas or are US citizens. And I'll be straight with you. I don't know for sure if the documents they have are legit, but I do know they work their butts off. And I also know that they, like me, are insulted by a lot of racist people. It's frustrating because we are hired because we can charge a little less than some companies, big ones, with—I don't mean to offend—with mostly white workers, or at least white front men. I know why some people want that. Because they are scared of Mexicans. Or they think we are illegals. Meanwhile, some customers hire us because they want to pay us less. I accept that. But what I don't accept is flat out racism like this Duke Ellis is saying."

Rossi considered how out of character Joe Garcia's monologue may have been. Rossi figured him as a man who mostly let his actions speak for him.

Garcia affirmed Rossi's perception. "Sorry. I don't mean to offend anybody here. It's just ... frustrating."

Doc leaned in. "No apologies needed, Joe. I was born and raised here in California. I'm seventy-two years old. I know the history of this place. Of this city. I think we need to say it like it is at this table if we are going to get to a verdict. And that's coming from a fella like me who usually keeps his trap shut."

Again heads nod.

Melanie had been itching to break in. "I agree with you both. But here's the thing we need to remember. No matter how dumb and stupid this Duke Ellis character is—two things: first, as his lawyer said, he has the *right* to say this stuff. And second, he wasn't at the riot. Remember, no witnesses said that he directly told them to go to the Curtis house. So that's why the guy, you know the one in the orange jumpsuit, Frank something-or-other, is in jail. Because he did what he did. *That's* the crime."

Jane cut in. "Frank Templeton is the witness you're referring to, Melanie. He was the Nazi sympathizer. The first witness in the trial."

"Right, that's the guy." Melanie continued to make one last point. "Look, I am not saying anything Ellis said is okay by me. I'm just asking if it is okay by the law ... the Constitution."

Hero decided to clarify: "Good point, Melanie. Remember though, the First Amendment is not absolute. You cannot cry 'fire' in a crowded theater, if I recall, because it can cause injury."

Russ: "Unless there is a fire."

Rossi knew that Russ was trying to lighten the mood. It didn't work.

Hero was composed. "Of course. Yes. But we ... I should say, *our* laws can ban certain speech on television, so we need to ask ourselves if language that promotes hate also damages our culture. And what should be done about that?"

Rossi realized that Hero approached drama in an understated manner. Nevertheless, his words packed a punch.

Lauren: "Well, that's why there are hate crimes, right?"

Jim, in rebuttal: "But those *are* crimes. You know, physical crimes. Ellis didn't physically do anything. The guys who did, they are going to the slammer, getting what they deserve."

Regina cleared her throat, and with that small sound, all heads rotated to her. "I bet you all are wondering what the black woman thinks, huh?" She let that settle. "Well, first, I have to say I was surprised that I even *got* on this jury. I guess sooner or later they couldn't avoid some folks of color getting a seat at *this* table." She tilted her head to Joe, who gave a slight nod.

"Second, I'm a realtor so I know a thing or two about people's intentions, just like Jim. Keep that in mind. And last of all, I want you to know something else about me. I'm a conservative." Again she settled herself before she continued. "That's right. I'm a Republican. Always have been. My father had a hero—Jackie Robinson. My father told me if Jackie is a Republican then so are we. So I wanted to get that off my chest. As for Duke Ellis and what he said, let me tell you, it is not anything I haven't heard over and over in my daily life."

Regina shifted her body forward. "Racism isn't just what I hear. It is what I feel in my bones. What I just know when a client meets me in the office and assumes I'm the receptionist. And then they try to tell me they are not racist, but the assumption they made tells me how they have been led to think. Understand, the color of my skin determines whether or not my client trusts me. It is a fact of life for black Americans. So I guess what I am saying here is this: do you all think that this trial is going to change anything? Really? I wish it would, but one guilty verdict doesn't make anything better for black people. Sometimes it makes things worse."

38

DELIBERATIONS: DAY 1, HOUR 2

Rossi knew that Regina had just flipped the script on what the trial might accomplish. *Is this trial and whatever verdict we deliver—counterproductive?*

Jane sensed this was a moment that needed to breathe. "Regina, I am so glad you are wondering what impact this trial will have. Let's take a little break and grab some coffee or a snack. I, for one, need to use the restroom. Okay?"

Silent concurrence.

Rossi and Regina remained seated. Then Regina surprised him by asking him, "Tony, you taught high school, right?"

"Thirty-two years, Regina. I've got the scars to prove it." Rossi smiled.

She nodded. "I imagine you do. Did you teach in the suburbs or the city?"

"Well, that's a trick question. I taught at a very blue-collar public school in the suburbs. Lots of languages. Some kids had too little and some had too much, if you follow."

"Oh, I follow," she replied.

"Yep. This is a navy town with lots of kids who are Filipino, Asian, Mexican, and African-American. Lately, there are the kids from Eastern Europe—Serbia, Croatia. There were times when I felt I had to teach more English than history because they were all coming to school with different languages and a completely different world view."

"I can see that. That's something I deal with in real estate." She rose. "I'm going to grab some coffee."

"I'll join you. I need to stay awake. Afternoons are my Achilles' heel."

"Oh, you too?" Regina smiled. "Welcome to the club."

Rossi couldn't help but ask himself: *what was her sudden interest in his teaching career?* So he stirred his coffee and made a decision. "Regina, do you have children?"

"Yes, I do. Two boys. They just got into high school. That's why I wondered about you and what you taught. My boys are twins, but I swear they couldn't be more opposite. One's in the band; the other plays football. They get on each other's nerves more lately, trying to out-cool the other brother." She sipped her coffee now that it had cooled. "But they are both good boys. If they aren't, my husband and I will have something to say about that." A knowing smile.

"My three are out in the world. Hopefully, staying out of trouble."

Regina gave him a look that implied, *don't try to be so humble.* "I am quite sure you have done an outstanding job, Tony."

"I have a great wife to thank. She was also a teacher."

"My mother was, too. What grade?"

Rossi noticed others coming back to the table. "Mostly fifth grade."

"Oh, that's a fun age. My boys were inseparable then." She paused and calculated her next question. "Do you mind if I ask you a few questions about how you taught students, later on when we are not in deliberations, Tony? I would appreciate some advice."

"Any time. We retired teachers never really call it quits. I think it is in our blood, being in the 'kid business' as I like to say."

Regina mouthed *thank you* as Jane seemed ready to get the discussion rolling. They took their seats.

———

Adam, the youngest of them, began with a question. "Here is my problem with ... I'll just say it, *a guilty verdict*. See, the thing is that I think he is guilty, but—then I think where this all leads. Like the defense attorney said, you get on a slippery slope ... and who's to say what is hate speech? I don't want to bring up Trump again, but he is always trashing China, and I wonder if that's right. I mean, if I were Chinese, I'd be pissed. And then I think, well, what if some jerk hears what Trump says and trashes a Chinese store or something? Is Trump guilty of inciting this guy?"

Jim: "That's my problem, too. I kinda regret voting for him now. But you have a point."

Lauren: "Well, maybe Trump should think about what he is saying before he shoots his mouth off on Twitter ... Sorry. I know we said we weren't going there."

Hero: "The difference is that Duke Ellis told the men to 'kick the'—sorry—'niggers out of the county, out of the state.' That's a direct call to action to some people. When the President chastises the Chinese trade policy, he is not calling for physical action like you brought up. Instead, he creates political action—trade tariffs."

Melanie: "That's the difference, I think."

Kim: "Okay, but what about the Muslim ban?"

Russ: "What about it?"

Kim: "He told them they couldn't come into our country because he believed they were terrorists."

Russ: "Some of them were ... are. Remember 9-11?"

Adam: "That was a long time ago. Are we ever going to get past that? I mean, prisoners are still in Guantanamo."

Jim: "Yeah, well, some of those extremists think that America is the devil and that it is their holy right to kill Americans. I sure as heck don't want to see that plastered all over the TV."

Lauren: "Isn't that Adam's point though? Where do we stop? Do we censor people because they may be a terrorist because of their religion ... or what they wear or what language they speak?"

Rossi decided now was a time to direct the discussion to something that had been on his mind as soon as he first heard the name *William O. Douglas*, whom he had admired since he was a college student.

"I want to ask Russ to put something else on the whiteboard, because it may help us stay focused. Do you guys remember when ... I think it was the judge who explained that 'inciting a riot' went before the Supreme Court in the *Brandenburg* case?" He paused. All the jury members wore a look that told Rossi, *Well, yes and no.* So he continued, "I wrote down Justice Douglas's definition of incitement. I think I have it down here ... yes." He looked at his notes.

Russ was up in a flash with the black marker. "Tony, go ahead, I'm ready."

Rossi read Douglas's words from his notebook. "Quote, '*whether the words used are of such a nature as to create a clear and present danger that bring about the substantive evils that Congress has a right to prevent.*'"

Rossi then panned both sides of the table. "So did Duke Ellis create a *clear and present danger*? That's one question. Was it *substantive evil*? And should *Congress have the right to prevent* that speech? I think that is what we need to decide."

Russ underlined the words Rossi emphasized.

All eyes were glued to the words that Douglas had called "the test."

Jane: "To be clear, I believe that Brandenburg, who was a Klansman, was saying terribly racist language, but the Supreme Court overturned the lower court's guilty verdict. Right? At least that is what I caught from the judge's explanation. So I think that Justice Douglas was saying that *Brandenburg* was not meeting a test of what incitement is. Am I wrong here?"

Doc: "No, that's correct, as I understand what the judge told us."

Kim: "Yes. But when was that case? I mean, times have changed and the courts change their minds, don't they?"

Rossi knew now was not the time to sit back; after all, he was the one who brought this to the forefront. "I'm pretty sure it was 1969. The Vietnam War was being protested, and the previous year Bobby Kennedy and Dr. King were assassinated. It was a terrible time." Rossi turned to the case in point. "I think that Mr. Brandenburg did not directly incite a particular group. He gave a radio talk, and people wanted to shut him up for being a racist. The trouble was there was no specific riot that occurred based on his speech. At least, that's the impression the judge gave me."

Regina: "There sure were a lot of riots, Tony. In Washington, D.C., and many other segregated cities. I know! My family lived in East St. Louis. It was bad, especially after Dr. King's death. But, I'm sure you know that, Tony."

Hero wanted to weigh in. "Yes, well, if you are a certain age." His knowing smile brought some non-verbal responses, both in agreement and slight surprise. "But, Tony, are you saying that the speech has to *directly* cause the riot? And without that, one does not naturally assume incitement?"

Rossi tried to clarify, "I am not exactly sure of what my position is ... *yet*. But this is what I'm wondering. It's almost fifty years since the *Brandenburg* decision, and racism is still just as damaging and even getting worse in places like Charlottesville. Words like *nigger* are still used to attack. That word and many others are just a trigger for violence. Black and white people are still being killed. Maybe not in this Ellis case, thankfully, but we know it happens. And it keeps happening. So how does it stop and when?"

"Hold on. Wait." Melanie looked to the fluorescent lights above as she tried to figure out what she knew she had to ask. "I think we are getting way, way ahead of ourselves. Are we talking about, what, writing a new law or something? I'm confused. We aren't here to decide how racism can be stopped, are we? I mean ... look, I am not a racist," she put her hands out in the form of two stop signs, "but I don't think we are the language police either. If I had to decide right now if this Ellis guy is guilty, well, I have no problem voting *yes*. But—and this is a big but—based on what you guys are saying, what does *guilty* mean ... or what does it do? It's like Adam said, where does it end?"

Doc scratched his chin. His closely trimmed white beard made him look distinguished. The spectacles hanging precariously on the bridge of his nose bobbed as he spoke. "Melanie, that is a good argument. I am glad you had the guts to make it. And *no*, I don't think you're making a *racist* point." He leaned back. "There's a reason why all manner of news people are out there pounding the courtroom doors. It's the same reason that this case was even brought to a criminal court, instead of a civil one."

He pointed at the television. "For once, the FBI caught someone on tape saying what we all know gets said behind closed doors. Or whispered. Or winked with some damned handshake. So what we need to do here is go back to the questions Tony raised: did Duke Ellis create a *clear and present danger*? If he didn't, then we are done. If he did, then we continue to the next question. We can't worry, yet, where this is taking us. We need to decide what the law says and if Ellis broke it." He took up his coffee. "Anyways, that's my two cents."

Russ, still standing by the whiteboard, said, "So ... this may take a while, huh? Guess, maybe another night at the hotel?" He smiled. Everyone's expressions appeared to acknowledge that the Holiday Inn Express was going to have some extended patronage.

As foreperson, Jane felt it was her duty to give some direction when the ship seemed to list. "Russ. Thanks for keeping us from not getting too on edge. I wouldn't jump to the conclusion about how long this is going to take. So I suggest, unless you all think it unwise, that we take a preliminary vote on the one count of incitement to riot. What does everyone think?"

She took inventory. When all affirmed her decision, she came to the next question. "Should we raise our hands, or have a paper vote without any names on it? I've done it both ways on the juries I've been on."

Lauren piped up. "I appreciate everyone's honesty here. I know this is a heck of a lot more complicated ... and kinda over my head a bit ... but all I am trying to say is that I trust everyone, and however people want to vote is okay with me. But maybe this first time, let's go with paper votes, okay? I know that I may change my vote later—all of us may—but I'll feel better keeping it sorta secret for now."

Jane glanced around. "Paper, okay?" Heads nodded. Henry, the bailiff, had given her several pads of paper, as well as pencils. She did the distribution. "Let's take a short break and come back in fifteen minutes. Just fold your vote and put it in front of my seat. I'll tally it up and see where we stand."

Kim quickly shot a question to Jane. "Can we vote *not sure* instead of *not guilty*? Would that be okay?"

Jane decided that would be fine. With that, the first vote began.

39

DELIBERATIONS: DAY 1, HOUR 3

"Here is how we stand so far: five of us voted *guilty* and the other seven voted *not sure*. No one voted *not guilty* so far. So obviously, Kim made a good point. Most of us need to discuss this before we know exactly how to vote. You don't need to tell us how you voted if you don't wish to yet, but can we start with Doc's suggestion. Doc, you brought up Tony's first question: do we think that Ellis created a clear and present danger?"

Doc: "I think so, but that's just me. I think he knew exactly what he was doing. The problem in my mind is, did he know that they would go to the Curtis house and do all the damage, or did he just know that he wanted them to get out to the voters and get them to not vote for Curtis?"

Hero spoke next. "If the second objective was his intent, then I think he would have told the people to get on the phones and phone bank. I have done that before. Or maybe he would have had them organize neighborhood canvassing. But he didn't say that, at least not on the videotape the FBI has provided."

"Okay, true," Melanie jumped in, "but remember the kids

who were accosted by Bud Temple? Ellis's campaign people were already staking out their turf and ..."

"Right," Adam cut in, "but even then—those guys weren't handing out flyers like the kids were. They were doing the opposite. They were physically intimidating them from doing the right thing, which I admit is bad, but not like trashing Curtis's property!"

Melanie: "All I was trying to say is that I think maybe his campaign was passing out flyers ... I don't know."

Lauren: "It was pretty coincidental that Duke Ellis just happened to be there to supposedly stop harassing those two kids. It was kinda like, shoot—what's that term for it?"

Rossi: "Passive aggressive."

"Exactly, thank you, Tony. I think he intended to scare them. I think that's the whole way he operates. Fear. Like that witnesses said. The whole white supremacy thing is all about putting fear into people. They don't want blacks or other minorities to vote." Lauren's face had reddened.

"*Passive* aggressive, huh?" Regina leaned in. "What's so passive about what's going on at the Curtis home? Passive! Did you hear that man in court, people? Sorry, I don't mean to go off, but he just came right out and said it on the witness stand —whites are superior. Period. What does that mean? It means that I am inferior to him. I am sub-human. That's the whole slavery justification argument. And we are talking about one hundred and fifty years ago since we fought the damn Civil War. What he is saying is *go back to Africa, nigger. This is a white country.* So we can say what we want here, but if that man walks free, then you know what's going to hit the fan. If that's free speech—then I won't be free and neither will anyone else they don't like."

Regina didn't speak often, but when she did, Rossi knew *the rage she was holding in was going to explode.*

Joe: "Regina's right. I voted guilty because in my mind any

reasonable person would hear what he said and know that those are fighting words. The man is a coward. He said what he said, pushed their buttons, and then he headed home for an alibi. Remember, he *thought* he was talking only to his buddies —the guys who would do his dirty work. When the cameras roll, or like here in court, he is all apologetic. I've seen it plenty of times in my life." Joe thumped his thick, calloused finger on the table.

"So you're saying Ellis is lying about incitement, even though he was saying that he wanted political power and not through violence?" Adam's tone sounded more confused than questioning.

Garcia's finger marked his stake in the ground. "That guy hates guys like me. Hates Mexicans." He looked up and for a moment realizing again how out of character this was for him. Then with one breath, he decided to let his suppressed anger spill into the small room. "Look, I am a quiet man. I do my job. I don't make waves. I just shut my mouth and don't do politics. I can't. Why? Because look what happens. Trump gets elected and says that my people are rapists and murderers. That we are drug dealers. That Mexican immigrants, hell, anyone south of the border, are just like Regina said—*sub-human*. Man, he locks kids in cages. He rips them from their parents. It's not the country I want to have." Joe turned his hands up, facing him. "I worked my ass off to make it here. I know that the USA needs a fairer way for my people to come here legally. But that is for another day, another trial. For now, I think people who say what Ellis said must be held accountable."

Rossi understood. *He laid it on the table. It was a challenge. He didn't like doing it, but he had had enough.*

Jane made a bold move. "Can I ask if anyone disagrees with the idea that what Ellis said was *not* a clear and present danger? I know I'm asking you to speak up. I also know that Joe passion- ately feels one way, but I think Joe would want you to feel you should speak. Right, Joe?" She received his affirmation. "Anyone?"

A beat. Then another. The clock ticked. Rossi realized it sounded like the ticking of a bomb.

Finally, Jim spoke up. "Look, Joe. I hear you, man. I've worked for thirty years at Sears. I've worked my ass off, too. I worked with all kinds of people: black, white, gay, straight—whatever. So I know how things work, especially in the corporate world. But I'm no fan of Affirmative Action. I think people need to be treated fairly—no matter their race. I've been screwed sometimes ... I think so ... because I'm white. And that sucks. Okay. So, all I am saying is this: yes, what Ellis said is dangerous. I can say that with a clear conscience. I just want to know, if I vote guilty what does that mean? It's what Tony was saying. What do we do if we think someone is being racist or saying racist stuff? What if the police arrest a black man because they think he *looks* suspicious? Are they automatically considered racist? I mean, help me here."

It was so quiet in the room that Rossi heard the clock's second hand tick to four o'clock. It was late. He looked into the faces of the other eleven. They were at a tipping point. Was now the time to push forward, and if he did, did he know the exact direction to navigate? He turned to the foreperson.

"Jane, I would like to answer Jim, but I am not sure, this late in the day, how everyone feels. I'm sure people want to call home. I know I do. And I'm sure we all want to know if we can reach a verdict today or not. So what I am asking is, do we keep deliberating or call it a day?"

"Let's go with the majority rule here," Jane responded. "If you'd like to call it a day, say so. No judgment. If you want to go another hour until five o'clock, say so. If you want to have dinner here and keep deliberating until, say, eight o'clock, then make your choice for that. Okay? So let's go around the table.

No one wanted to stop just yet, despite their weariness. The overwhelming choice: to work until five o'clock then call it a day. Jane felt that they could start fresh in the morning. She asked Henry to come in the room. And when he did Jane asked about deliberating on a Saturday if they had to. Henry told the jury that he had already spoken to Judge Lewis about the remote possibility.

Henry explained, "The judge said that because you all are sequestered that he would prefer to have you continue on Saturday, but today's only Wednesday. He hoped that you could reach a verdict tomorrow if you can't tonight. That still leaves Friday. Court is usually dark on Fridays, but the judge will do anything he can for you. He appreciates your efforts, and he told me to tell you that if there are any questions, any questions at all, that he will be ready to speak with you. Not to hesitate. Okay?"

There was a slim hope they could reach a verdict. Rossi knew there was an even slimmer hope his sleep would be all that restful.

————

The clock ticked: four-thirty.

During a short break, Rossi thought about the issue of what constitutes racist language. Jim had made a good point. "Jim, I get what you were asking earlier. It's too bad that people have to be so careful with what they say. I am sure guys like Bill Maher will have a field day with language that isn't always *Politically Correct*. But as a teacher, I can tell you this. One thing I prided myself on was presenting history and literature in a truthful manner. I wish that demeaning words like the N-word or any other racial or sexual slurs were no longer an issue. I wish skin color didn't matter. I wish religious beliefs and sexuality were not how we put people down. But that is not the world we live in."

Rossi looked at the faces of the other eleven. As he did in his class, he had to gauge their reactions. They were looking for a direction. "I could stop bad behavior, artificially, in my classroom. But walk out the door, step into the real world, cross the Mason-Dixon Line, or even sit in a press conference with the current administration, and it all comes back."

He decided it was time to move to the second part of the definition of incitement. "So if we answer the second question: *'is it substantially evil?'* I say we need to face it and call it out. If we don't, then another jury will be sitting in these very seats in a month or a year and the stakes will be even higher."

"Wait," Russ said. "So, are you saying that if the President tweets something that some people think is racist, or whatever, that he should be stopped? Is that where this is going?"

Adam blurted, "He does it all the time."

"Twitter and Facebook are private companies with social platforms. Those organizations have the liberty to decide what they wish to do with someone's posting. They can censor what they want to ... and have. But the government has an obligation to decide what 'free speech' is acceptable, because it is not absolute," Rossi explained. "What I'm saying is that if someone posted or tweeted that they were going to hurt someone, that is a different matter. And it becomes *criminal* if they actually do it."

He again measured how his fellow jurors perceived his words. "What we are deciding in the Ellis case is fundamentally different from someone posting a racist message. In this case, I do believe there was intent by Mr. Ellis to call for action and, I think, in this courtroom, he gave the reason why he encouraged that action. He believes he is *entitled* to be superior to people who are black or brown."

Melanie frowned, "But how can you judge his intent?"

Hero spoke up. "I have read that intent is not something you can measure. However, the results that spring from the action are the best way to judge intent."

Regina, sarcastically: "So if the guy is a mediocre racist and doesn't get results, then it's not really incitement?"

"Well, that is an odd way to put it," Hero smiled, "but perhaps it is reasonable. If someone advocated racist or sexist ideas, and no one listened or followed, then the perpetrator is merely a 'fool up on the hill.'"

"Okay," Melanie wanted clarification, "so are we saying the *N-word*, I don't even like saying it, is now a crime? Cause if we are, good luck trying to enforce it."

Kim followed up, "Not only that, but every time we ban something like that, people say it more. I think the witness we heard from New York—you know, the older man who was an agent for Lenny Bruce—that man was making that point, right?"

Joe: "But I don't think this is about banning a word. It is about charging a guy with a crime. In this case, getting people so riled up that they smashed a guy's car and tried to torch his house, not to mention scared the hell out of his family."

Jane interrupted, "I think what we are really hung up on is the impact of our verdict, am I right?"

All quietly affirmed her point.

"So," Jane continued, "is this even what we should be talking about? I'm just asking. Aren't we tasked with deciding whether or not Ellis started a riot?"

Hero answered Jane's query. "Jane is right. The jury is not supposed to consider the impact of the verdict. We can ask the judge about it, but on the juries when I have served that was always made clear to us."

Most members nodded. Some seemed resigned.

Doc coughed. "I'd like to make a point. I know that we think what he said is reprehensible. But people say lots of terrible things to others. Those terrible things may or may not cause an action. I think we need to remember that this is still a First Amendment issue. I'm not saying he had the right to say what he said, but I sure am asking you all—are you prepared to say he does not have the right to *his idea* of free speech?"

Lauren, who kept looking at her watch, chimed in, "Okay, look, it is getting later and later and I am not sure that we are gonna decide for sure if this Ellis guy is guilty or innocent tonight. For me, it is cut and dry. Guilty. He's a jerk, first class. I have no need to listen to his crap. He has a right to say it, but that right is out the door once he gets his goons to do something like what I am damn sure he intended." She gathered herself. "Whew. I had to get that off my chest. So if we wanna talk some more about free speech and all and what it's gonna lead to, fine. But I think we should take another vote and see what is what ... before we call it a night." She paused. "And I really gotta call home and make sure my husband and the kids managed to agree on what the heck to eat."

Smiles. Nodding.

Jane: "I agree, let's vote. Some of us have made it clear what we think, so if it is okay, let's do a show of hands. Who would vote guilty at this point?"

Some hands were thrust up quickly, some slowly. Some hands wavered.

"So, Lauren, Joe, Regina, and Tony all say guilty. Wait ... add Jim to that. Anyone else?"

A few hands fluttered but others remained on the table.

Then Russ stood up and said, "You know what? I think he is guilty. I mean, for cryin' out loud, he knew what he was doing. You mouth off like he did and there's a price to pay. If one of my kids I coach said something even close to what he said—then he is gone. And you know what? He'd probably get suspended, too." Russ was getting angrier by the minute.

"Okay then." Jane looked around one last time. "I guess we are split 6-6." Then she stood and opened the door.

Henry appeared as if by magic and stepped partway into the room. "Well, I hope you folks have had a good talk. No verdict, huh?" He checked with Jane, who gave the thumbs down. "So, I will make arrangements to get you over to the hotel. I'm sure everyone is hungry and pretty tired. It'll take at least ten minutes to get the bus here. We will leave the way we entered, folks." Henry ushered the group into the corridor.

Regina looked at Henry and whispered just loudly enough for Rossi to hear, or maybe she wanted him to know what she was to ask. "People still out there protesting?"

"Yes, ma'am. It seems when the sun goes down, things get a little dicey out there. Don't worry though, we've got it under control."

40

THE PROTEST

Henry's assessment that the protest was "under control" was not exactly how Rossi saw things from his window seat in the mini-bus containing twelve jurors, two bailiffs, and the driver—who was a federal marshal.

As soon as they exited the alleyway leading from the court on to Union Street, they saw the crowd gathered at the corner of Union and Broadway. The police were struggling to keep the traffic flowing through the intersection. The sidewalks were so crowded that people had spilled into the street and the crosswalks had disappeared. There was only a thin path for cars to get through. The crowd poured into the adjacent parking lot, which seemed to be a maze of confusion with cars trying to exit and people filling in the gaps between cars holding signs.

Rossi saw various messages, mostly in support of Congressman Curtis and ridiculing Duke Ellis as a racist. There were "Black Lives Matter" banners stretching four feet being held up by demonstrators.

Russ, sitting next to Rossi, muttered, "Oh, my God. Look at this."

It seemed like people in cars were either honking their

horns in support, or the drivers were furious at being unable to go forward or back up. The jurors' vehicle was only inching up the street.

When Rossi leaned forward to see what was happening across the street, he noticed some type of skirmish in the middle of the parking lot. A cluster of police officers was slicing, single file, into the crowd, pushing their way in an effort to break things up. He spotted a large sign that read "White Power!" People were waiving a Confederate flag and there were several yellow "Don't Tread on Me" Tea Party flags, along with red, white and blue TRUMP/2020 flags.

All the jurors were talking at once. Twilight had settled into the downtown and the police had just started turning their cars into the parking lot with their headlights illuminating the scene. Rossi could tell the traffic on Broadway was stopped for at least three blocks because he could spot the flags of various nations in front of the U.S. Grant Hotel.

Once something like this starts, it is hard to control.

Demonstrators came right up to the bus and chanted, "This is what democracy looks like." Rossi did not feel threatened. On the contrary, his adrenaline was pumping, and he couldn't help but be encouraged that so many people cared about the very issue before him and his companions. Henry told the marshal to just get through the intersection and stay on Union Street. He was speaking into an intercom emphatically asking the police cars nearby to provide an escort to get the mini-bus northbound on Union Street. They inched forward.

As they managed to squeeze through the Broadway/Union intersection, Rossi spotted the media vans. All three local affiliate stations were lined up on the west side of Union, and news crews were filming in front of the Hall of Justice. Several local reporters appeared to be interviewing protesters. The mini-bus's speed picked up as the crowds thinned out when Ash Street emerged. The marshal was told to turn east on Ash

Street to get to the hotel. Rossi looked at his fellow jurors. All looked noticeably, and understandably, affected by what they had witnessed; some were relieved, but others were energized.

So much for sequestering them from the news.

————

Deborah answered her cell on the first ring. "Tony, are you okay?"

Rossi disguised his voice. The last thing he wanted her to think was that he was worked up. *Rattled* would have been just about spot on. "Oh, yeah. I'm fine."

"What do you mean *fine*? I'm watching the news—which I am not supposed to be speaking to you about—and *fine* isn't a word I would use to describe what's going on downtown. Where are you ... and is the trial over?"

"I'm at the hotel now. And the trial is not over yet. It has been a crazy day."

"You're telling me." Deborah's voice was a blend of relief and anxiousness.

"Right. I'm sure you are wondering what is happening so let me tell you what ... well, what I can tell you, okay." Rossi had thought this part out before he called. "So, we are in delibera-tions now. We heard all the closing arguments, and we have been at it since lunch. We are making progress. I can't say if we will be done tomorrow—I hope so."

She was caught off guard. "I-I guess, I just thought that maybe you'd be done."

"It's complicated. But I have to say that the jurors are really a good group, and we are all trying to work together. I can't say any more than that. Anyway, once we got into the bus to go to the hotel, I was blown away by what was going on outside of the courthouse. I mean, sure, I knew groups were protesting in the morning each day, and I noticed that each morning the crowd was getting bigger—but ... then we come out and it was a mob scene."

"Tony, you have no idea. And maybe I shouldn't say too much. But this thing, this trial, I mean, it is getting national attention. I'm going from CNN to local news to the network news and this is one of the top stories." Deborah paused, feeling her way in a conversation that she couldn't believe she was having. "Is there any demonstrating by your hotel?"

"No. We are seven blocks away and it's pretty dead here—thankfully. I just want to ask one question; maybe I shouldn't but the whole sequestering thing is kind of out the door once we hit the streets. Anyway, just tell me if any people have been hurt or anything like that." Rossi winced as the words flowed from his cell to hers. He knew he was in a gray area when it came to the judge's instructions.

"No. Thankfully. Lots of chanting. A little bit of a dust-up with the people walking around with Confederate flags ..."

"Yeah, I saw that."

"... but the police were on that quickly, and it seems, so far, like it isn't going to flare up. Of course, the media is having a day—they are interviewing both sides. Oh, I shouldn't say much, right?"

Rossi relaxed for the first time on the call and leaned back into the one chair the room provided. "Right. The less I know the better. I guess the judge made a good call about us being here though. I'd hate to think what it would have been like if I was trying to go home. That would have been nuts."

Deborah decided to break the tension with her next remark. "So are you drinking yet?"

Laughter.

"I think I am going to break down and have a beer at least. I'm gonna grab a bite to eat after this. Have you heard from our kids?"

"Um, yeah. They know their father is in the thick of the

whole civil rights debate, and then they all called when they turned on the news. So, yeah, I heard from them." She was being sarcastic, but that was her way of covering up for the fact that she was not telling him the truth. Earlier there were a series of arrests when fights broke out. People were sent to the hospital. The media was reporting that when darkness arrives things could escalate quickly. Deborah couldn't help but feel that the media saw this as some bizarre form of entertainment. She recalled a friend in the news business telling her how newsrooms operated. "If it bleeds it leads," he told her. All this she kept to herself.

Rossi jarred her back to the here and now. "Okay. Deb, please call the kids and tell them everything is fine. This isn't some episode of *Law and Order*."

"Oh, no. It's more like *60 Minutes*, Anthony. This ... this is ..."

"Honey. It is what it is. I'm just taking it one step at a time. Our two bailiffs are with us 24/7 and they are terrific. I'm safe and probably we will come to some conclusion tomorrow."

"Let's hope." Deborah sighed. "Call me before you turn in. Oh, and are you sleeping okay? I know you. You get all wound up. Take something if you need to. You need to not stress. Okay?"

"Stressed? I think you've got the wrong guy." Rossi knew she saw right through him. She always did.

41

TEACHER DREAMS

Why couldn't Rossi sleep well? Was it really the cars humming by on the freeway? The unfamiliar surroundings? The air-conditioner bursting into full life in the middle of the night? The pillow too soft or too hard? The loneliness of ending another day without Deborah at his side? Sleep did not come for one nagging reason: he could not *compartmentalize*. That was Deborah's strength. Whatever troubles she faced, she could put each in hibernation until she was awake and could then tackle them in the light of a new day. But Rossi's brain didn't operate like hers. His conscience kept demanding to be released.

The sign above his former classroom's door read:

The Mistakes of the Past Always Repeat
When Ignored in the Present

Deborah had finished her calls to each of her adult children. Peter had been following the case religiously. He thought that it was highly unlikely that Duke Ellis would be convicted. "Mom, it has to be unanimous. Not gonna happen. I don't care how persuasive Dad may be. There will always be some people who will feel that he couldn't incite something that he didn't attend. Maybe if he was there ... and who knows? Maybe he was there —wearing a mask or a hood or whatever those crazies wear. Mom, I wish I was wrong."

Deborah could see his point. That's what worried her. How much would all this take out of her husband? He was competitive. He took things to heart. This was no sport, no game. This was a man's family that was attacked. The trial would set a precedent. One way or another. What if it was a hung jury? What then? Would he compromise his personal moral code for a legal loophole?

Her conversation with her daughter Sophie were less about the verdict but more about why *men* like Duke Ellis are allowed to prey on the innocent. Sophie was angry. "It is an open and shut case. Mom, the man is a racist of the first order. He never quit the Klan! He just says that for political purposes. I read what he said in the *Post* about how the blacks are inferior and need to be back in Africa! He's been posting all over Twitter going back years. If they bring that up in court, then the jury will nail him because he is all about violence. God, I hate him!"

Deborah understood where she was coming from. They raised their children to be inclusive of all people, all religions. She and Tony taught them 'The Golden Rule' and for the most part they felt their children tried their best to be true to that principle. Sophie's weakness could be her stubbornness—she stood her ground and made her parents proud. Sometimes that resolute attitude made her naïve to others motivated by self-interest and greed, particularly in her workplace. Fortunately, Deborah knew her husband Stanley often balanced out her unbending opinions. *The yin and the yang.*

Gina was another story. Her concern was for her father's

well being. When she was on the phone, Gina spoke in complete paragraphs. "Mom, I just know how Dad is. He's not like you. You are calm. You don't get angry. Well, except when I screw up, but that's different. Aren't you worried about him? I mean, seriously, Mom. I saw the protests on CNN. Things got really ugly tonight. I'm glad they have Dad away from all that. But you know Dad—he will wander right down there and see what's going on." She finally took a breath.

Deborah knew Gina was her father's daughter. She thought like he did. She too would let curiosity get the better of her. It had been a challenge to keep her on track and focused so she would graduate in four years. She loved Berkeley and could see herself as a permanent fixture there. "Gina, listen to me. He is fine. And I have been all over him to be careful. I know he understands the gravity of the situation. If he would ask for anything from you guys, it would be that you not worry about him. Trust me."

Deborah left the last conversation spent. At least she knew she had done what she promised. She also knew that she needed to put her worries aside because as much as she had deep concerns for him, she had not slept well since he left.

He was a dreamer. He always remembered his fairly bizarre dreams. Conversely, Deborah would never recall her dreams. Her nightmare was that she couldn't fall asleep. While he tossed, turned and snored, she often worried. If there was a problem with the kids, or at school, or with Tony, sleeping didn't come easy. Of course, her husband was not aware of this. He often marveled at how, in his words, *she compartmentalized* the problems of the day. Truth be told, she was a good actress. *Most mothers are.* Tonight would be another night that would require her to meditate and try to not worry about not falling asleep. *Easier said than done.*

———

Rossi's fitful sleepless nights were the consequence of teaching for more than three decades. History lessons often reappeared in his dreams. He called them *Teacher Dreams.* This night's semi-conscious reverie took him back to James Michener. Michener's work *Kent State: What Happened and Why* ended with a single plea: *"Tolerance, God how we needed it then."*

Michener explained why four innocent young people were shot and killed at Kent State University by the Ohio National Guard in May 1970 during the Vietnam War protests. The question of who was responsible became moot. All that mattered that day was a tragic combination of forces that would not back down: frightened, confused National Guardsmen ready to fire their rifles aimlessly and the angry student protesters who mocked them and everything they represented. Americans had witnessed far too many soldiers coming home from the jungles of Vietnam in coffins only to now realize that the battlefield had come to the Heartland. The anthem "Four Dead in Ohio" kept playing in Rossi's head as he tried to sleep.

A woeful sense of *déjà vu* disturbed his dreams. Ignorance and intolerance still coursed through the veins of American society, a plague for which there was no convenient vaccine. Without compassion and understanding, hate would always reemerge, fueled by institutional systemic bigotry and willful ignorance.

Rossi's mind kept hammering him with poignant lessons he had introduced to his students over the decades: the grainy newsreel images of Hitler and the savagery faced by soldiers Tom Brokaw labeled *The Greatest Generation*; to the authors who revealed injustices they faced at home. Zora Neale Hurston's segregated Harlem. Jeanne Wakatsuk's Japanese internment camp in Manzanar. And perhaps worst of all, Elie Wiesel's horrific survival in Auschwitz. The more he tried to stop recalling each story, each lecture he gave, the more stories began to populate his mind.

———

After finally sleeping for three hours, Rossi awoke to the sounds of a police siren screeching down the street. He rustled himself to the bathroom, thirsty from the dry air of the droning air-conditioner. He sipped some water and stared into the mirror. He checked his watch. It was one-thirty. He tried to clear his mind, but for reasons that perhaps only other teachers could comprehend, his thoughts flashed back to one of the most difficult days in his career.

He remembered the fateful September morning. A freshman sitting in the front row of his first-period class raised her hand and, with unbridled, heartbroken innocence, asked him, "Mr. Rossi, why did those people fly planes into the Twin Towers?" Thirty-five faces pressed him for an answer that made some sense of the wicked world. He told them he could not be sure exactly why, but that he knew it was an act of terrorism. When the students asked why anyone would do such a thing, he tried to answer them as honestly as he could.

"Terrorists believe that their way of life is the only one they can accept. The people who crashed into the buildings have a *singular* point of view. Theirs is the *only* belief that matters. They have only *one* right answer to how others should live their lives."

One is always singular. *Two* is plural.

He remembered struggling to explain what he meant to his students that day as each class came into his room with more questions than answers. By the time he faced the final class of the day he recalled how he put together his thoughts. "The only way to defeat a terrorist is to never give in to the idea that only one way to live is acceptable. That is what *pluralism* means. Tolerance. Open-mindedness. That's what makes America strong."

———

In those ambiguous minutes before one awakens, dreams can be their most vivid. Rossi's final dream found him standing among murky shadows in the crowd that watched a larger than life Klansman seething vitriol. Just as this figure roared his revenge on James Curtis, he ripped his pointy white hood off, and the crimson visage of Duke Ellis burst into view. Suddenly, Rossi awakened from his nightmare and quickly grasped where he was. The sweat had soaked his t-shirt. He knew he could not sleep another minute, so he showered, shaved, and then sat in his room's lonely chair, pondering what this day would mean to him.

He understood that this trial's verdict had implications beyond one politician's infamy. If Duke Ellis was permitted to bellow to the masses that there is only one *singular* race that deserves the privilege of citizenship, that other races are inferior, then Ellis's words would inevitably ignite violence and tragedy. But how does society reconcile its rules of civil behavior and boundless freedom? If only one choice is acceptable, moral, and righteous, what will we become? Will we quash the liberty to speak one's mind, however demented and cruel? Or will we turn away and ignore the violence of words? And in the end, who will decide when the line is crossed? What possible compromise could avoid hypocrisy?

He finished dressing and packed his lightweight suitcase. He hoped that he would spend the next night and all the nights to come far from here. He glanced above the door at the message that explained the checkout time. Then he remembered the message above his classroom door.

The Mistakes of the Past Always Repeat
When Ignored in the Present

42

HENRY AND ROSE

Henry and Rose were having coffee at the cafe around the corner when Rossi entered the small café. Henry looked over and tilted his head in such a manner to indicate that the empty chair was there for him.

"Morning."

"Thanks, Henry. Good morning, Rose. I thought I was the only one who was the way-too-early riser." The fast moving waitress had her coffee decanter in hand and asked if the newest addition to the booth wanted her to fill the extra cup.

"Oh, thank you, please." Rossi smiled up at her. She nodded and pointed to the cream on the table.

"Anything else, sir? Would you like to see a menu?" she asked while she was checking the tables to her left and right.

"Yes. That would be great," Rossi replied. The waitress reached behind her back and like a magician revealed the well-worn menu tucked under her apron's tie strings.

"Thank you, again." Rossi took the menu and tipped a splash of cream into his coffee. He then leaned back and clasped his hands around the warm mug. "As I was saying, I suppose I'm not the only early riser, huh?"

Rose smiled. "No, sir. Sarge and I are always up and about. I hope you slept all right?"

Rossi rolled his eyes. "Well, I got enough, I suppose. Makes one appreciate your own bed. Rose, you called Henry 'Sarge'?"

"Absolutely. Henry is pretty tight-lipped, but he was a sergeant in the police force. He's always been, at least since I've been with the court system, our Sergeant at Arms."

"Now, Rose ..." Henry began.

"Don't worry, Henry. I'm not going to go on embarrassing you with all the awards that I *know* you earned on the force or with the court." Rose then delivered an aside to Rossi. "He's too humble. We all admire him—so does Judge Lewis."

"That is quite enough, Rose. I'm just doing my job. Speaking of which, Tony, you all have quite a day ahead of you. Anything you think you're going to need from us? We are here for you." Henry pivoted on the stool, indicating that he was about to get moving.

"I don't know yet. But I know all of us appreciate both of you." Then he thought for a moment. "Can I ask you one thing?"

They both nodded.

"Could we request the transcript of a witness's testimony? I took notes, but I wondered if that's possible."

Rose said, "Certainly. If you know what you need, Mr. Rossi, have the jury foreperson request to hear the witness testimony or see a transcript. But a written note to the judge is necessary."

Henry added, "You must talk to the foreperson, Jane, first. She is the point person between Rose and me, okay?"

"Sure thing." They both started to leave just as Doc sauntered in.

"Hellos" and "Good mornings" were exchanged. Then Doc took a seat across from Rossi.

Again, the same waitress appeared out of nowhere and the same exchange occurred. With one quick move the used mugs were placed on her tray, and a fresh one placed in front of Doc. She produced the same menu magic trick and both men looked at each other as she retreated to the next booth giving both of them time to look over the somewhat limited offerings on the well worn, slick menus.

Doc blew on his coffee. "Our waitress moves awfully quick. I suppose that's from a lot of experience with folks like us who are up early." He took a sip of coffee. "The older I get, the less sleep I seem to need."

Rossi replied, "Sorry, Doc. I need sleep, but I'm afraid until we finish this trial, I'm not gonna get too much."

Doc's eyes traveled down to the menu. "Indeed."

In a flash, she was back. "So what's it gonna be, fellas?"

43

DELIBERATIONS: DAY 2, HOUR 4

I t took a while to get settled. Jane called the group to order. "Thanks, everyone. Well, let's get started. We left yesterday split pretty evenly, but we agreed to continue discussing the meaning of incitement and whether Mr. Ellis's actions meet the definition. We still have the two definitions on the whiteboard. How do people feel now that we can start fresh this morning? Why don't we first go around the room and find out if people still have the same viewpoints as yesterday?"

Lauren: "Same. Guilty."

Jim: "Still guilty. I think he knew what he was doing."

Kim: "Hmm. I'm still not sure. I definitely need to hear more information."

Russ pointed to the whiteboard: "Like I said last night, when I look at the board and see the judge's instructions and the other definition that the Supreme Court wrote, you know, the test for knowing if there was incitement. Well, I think that Ellis *used* his words and that is the action he wanted ... Oh, I'm fumbling around. It's early. Anyway. Guilty."

Adam: "I'm still hung up on the whole thing about what

this means. What are we saying? Are words, and *just* words, a crime? And since he wasn't there, I'm not sure he is guilty."

Melanie: "I'm with Adam. I don't want people saying the things Ellis said, but I don't know if saying those things is illegal or criminal. So I am still leaning not guilty."

Hero: "I have some questions that I need answered. I'd like to review what certain witnesses said again, especially the FBI agent Howard Matt and Mr. Ellis's testimony. I think that will help me decide."

Doc: "Yep. I think I need to remind myself what they said, too. And also Bud Temple. He seems to me to be the instigator, and I want to know how much he was influenced by Ellis."

Joe: "I know what I need to know. And I have to say, judging from what I saw last night out there in the streets, there are a lot of people who have a pretty good idea what Ellis was all about. Just saying. So I'm voting guilty."

Regina: "Same."

Rossi: "Guilty, but I asked the bailiffs if we can see the written testimony of certain witnesses. And you guys have named the same ones I am interested in: Ellis, the FBI agent Matt, and Bud Temple. I think if we look into what they said, we might just see *intent* more clearly."

Jane: "I talked to Rose, and she is bringing us the transcripts shortly. I, myself, am conflicted. I'm a bit of a history buff, as librarians go. And I know that justice is a long arc, as Dr. King said, but before I know for certain that Ellis's words demanded this *particular* action, I am ... well ... not so sure. I will say I am leaning to changing my vote to guilty. I think it is important to remember that the law is the law. How it is received by the public, whether it is popular or not, shouldn't sway us. I think that is why the judge sequestered us."

General agreement. Even Joe Garcia nodded.

Rose arrived with a stack of stapled papers. "This is the

testimony you asked for, Jane. I have Temple's, Agent Matt's, and the defendant Mr. Ellis's."

Russ helped Rose distribute. Henry asked if there was anything else they needed. When no one responded, he and Rose left promptly, and each of the jurors began sifting through the information. There were at least ten minutes during which each seemed to be reading some portion of the testimony.

Hero was the first to speak. "I was most interested in what Bud Temple had to say when Attorney Peters questioned him, but also the way he reacted. If you look at the second page of his testimony, well, no need. Let me read it. Peters to Temple: 'I submit that it takes very little to incite these men to anger and rage that makes violence inevitable.' As you may remember, Temple was so angry that he literally screamed at her when asked about his racist views. You recall he said that the Jews, Mexicans, and others need to go back where they belong, even the Chinese, which I will overlook. One point I have been considering is that this man can't seriously be considered a 'campaign manager' in the way I would view it. He is not a political adviser. He is a man who seems to me to have a huge chip on his shoulder, and if anything, he came across as ... security personnel. So it seems to me that Mr. Ellis knew exactly who he was targeting and what Bud Temple would do. Attorney Peters also knew which buttons to push when she had Mr. Ellis on the witness stand."

Hero sat back and crossed his hands in front of him. He awaited a rebuttal. His implication of a guilty vote was clear to Rossi.

Lauren slipped in, "He reminded me of a bouncer at a bar. And remember he had all the stuff in the trunk of his car to burn a cross, even the lighter fluid."

Adam started and stopped. "Okay. Okay. He is a jerk and not in any way a real political genius. But he said, straight up, that

Ellis did not tell him to go to the Curtis home. That's direct. Don't we need to have that nailed down?"

"How else do we know intent?" Melanie shook her head. "That's what I asked yesterday."

Rossi calmly reminded everyone, "We can judge intent by the outcome of someone's actions. That's what Hero said yesterday." He then shuffled through papers in front of him and picked up one particular sheet.

"I'm looking at FBI agent Matt's testimony. He said, and I quote, 'He—Ellis—had been fermenting anger and violence. His opinions being voiced publicly and privately were becoming dangerously close to incitement—until he actually achieved his goal. Thus, the government has charged him.'" Rossi looked up. "So, the FBI knew what Ellis was doing, and until the night in question, the FBI did not act because they needed actionable, concrete evidence that Ellis was instructing his men—and almost all of them showed up at the Curtis home —to 'kick' people of color 'out of the county, out of the state.' I think that speaks volumes."

Adam: "But that was the FBI's opinion."

Jane: "But also remember, Judge Lewis told us that this was going to come down to a value judgment. So I think that is what Tony and Hero are saying. It was the opinion of the FBI, and we can be guided by that."

Regina decided to lean into that very point. "Look. I get that some of us are a little unclear when we ask: *did he tell Temple to do what he did.* Look, there are code words and dog whistles that some people use to get across what they want to say without saying the exact words. I am sure you all know what I'm saying. I, for one, know exactly what Ellis means."

She took a breath and decided to push all her chips into the center of the table. Rossi wondered when she would finally call the racial bluff. With her elbows on the table and her fingernail pointed directly on the transcript, she announced, "Ellis means to say that he is better and more valued as a human being than I am simply because of the color of my skin. Look right here, in his testimony. Peters asked him why he said *nigger*. And his answer is," she read sarcastically, "'It's a figure of speech.' And then Peters says, 'Pretty ugly figure.' And Ellis says, smugly, I might add, 'That depends on your point of view.' So my *point of view* is this: I am black. I hear what he says and I hear *a threat*. A serious, deadly threat, and because he is so sneaky, he wants others to do the dirty work. There's a long history of this ... crap. But he knows exactly what he's doing and who he hired. He hired thugs like Bud Temple, and he knew they wouldn't need much of a push to try to scare Mrs. Curtis and maybe get her husband to just quit ..."

She stopped herself. She was so angry that her eyes had a wet glaze, and she did not want anyone to see how much it hurt.

Rossi knew. Most of them did. Few could make eye contact with her.

Quiet.

Jim spoke up. "Look, I served in the Army. I know how things are in a unit. Check out Ellis's military record. Do you know how much of a screw-up you have to be to just get a general discharge? *FUBAR.* You guys know what that means, right?" He waited for all to get the meaning of *FUBAR*. Kim, sitting next to him indicated she was lost. "Effed up beyond all recognition." All then nodded, so he continued. "Actions do speak loud. Ellis fought with the blacks in his unit and look what it says in his record. He called black soldiers 'jungle monkeys.' Heck, his commanding officer, his CO, even heard him. Man, Ellis is lucky he didn't get *his* ass kicked—literally."

Kim finally spoke. "Look, I'm no lawyer, but does all this that you are saying go against the fact we are supposed to see Ellis as presumed innocent? I mean, is what Ellis did in the past mean he's guilty now? That's what I need to know. That's all I am saying."

Frustrated, Lauren glared down the table at Kim. "Okay, fine. Think about what Ellis is saying to us. Two days ago, Ellis, straight up in court, says that if you aren't like him, white and privileged, then you don't deserve to be a real citizen ... or at least he wants you out of our country. Look, I'm not a political person, Kim. And I'm not black or any color other than white. Heck, I am privileged! And I just find him disgusting. He makes me sick." She gathered herself. "Sorry, I'm not judging anyone here. I just think this is cut and dry. Sorry, Kim."

Kim looked at Lauren and mouthed *I understand.* Rossi wondered if she really did, or if she was just feeling pressured to agree.

Joe: "He wants me, and Hero, and Regina out. I don't know if anybody here is Jewish or Muslim, but them, too. Thing is, he has a right to believe that, I guess, but he doesn't have a right to push people to do something like he did against someone."

Melanie: "But he used *words.*"

Joe: "Okay. But words cause actions. What words could he say about you, Melanie? I know what he would say about me. I know *exactly* what he would call me. He'd want me to mow his lawn, and he'd want me to do it cheaper than some white guy. Why? Cause I'm Mexican. And now he wants me out of *his country!* You gotta put yourself in my shoes ... or Regina's, or anybody that he thinks isn't *American* enough."

Rossi knew that Joe's anger had been simmering, but it had reached a boiling point.

Jane stepped up. "Guys, I know this is getting heated, and I know that people are trying to keep things in perspective. So let's not make this personal to each of us ..."

Doc interrupted, but with a soothing voice. "Jane, sorry to cut you off, but I don't think we are getting *too* personal. I think we are being very honest. See, maybe it is time we really speak what we know and how it makes us feel. This man Ellis is digging into the heart of why we have so many problems with each other in this country. We don't always believe, *really believe,* that we are all equal."

Doc placed his hands so that Joe and Hero, beside him, knew he was including them in what he was about to say. "Remember what Ms. Peters said. She told us that we were going to decide not just the rule of law, but also the *spirit* of the law. I think that meant we were going to have to face our own consciences."

At that moment, Rossi understood with a clarity that others may not have, how the wisdom of Doc's experience, being in the Navy and living in the community of what America aspires to be—on a ship that heads out to sea with all of humanity dependent on the goodwill and honest intentions of each other. How that service had shaped his values. Doc was a patient man. He listened. He questioned.

Doc continued, "I know I have to look in the mirror and ask myself—is this man's free speech *excluding* other people's right to life, liberty, and the pursuit of happiness? That's in our Declaration of Independence. I pledged my allegiance for fifty years to those words. Look, I can't say that Ellis's words *didn't* lead to their actions. In the Navy, when someone spouted off the crap that Ellis said, he would see a bunch of sailors staring him in the face ready to knock some sense into him. This guy hasn't a clue what being an American is really all about. And that's why I'm voting guilty."

44

DELIBERATIONS: DAY 2, HOUR 5

Doc's words sucked the air out of the room. Some pages of the witnesses' testimony were shuffled, but otherwise the clock's continuous movement was the only sound that filled the room.

All eyes looked to Jane. Rossi knew she was thinking of calling a vote. Before she could, he made his final pitch.

"The world has changed so much in just the last twenty years. A racist statement can appear in a Facebook post or a tweet and then go viral with almost no effort at all. Someone imitating Ellis can incite others to do harm to someone because of their skin color, their religious views, their nationality. It is personal because Ellis wanted it to be. He isn't even trying to be logical or factual. He's playing with our darkest emotions: fear, jealousy, and greed. I guess what I'm getting at is that words fly out there in the ether, and the damage can be irreparable. So a healthy society ought to realize it and seek to do all it can to *deter* the crime before it happens."

Regina looked at Rossi and pursed her lips. She placed her hand on top of his.

Tick. Tick. Tick.

Russ cracked his knuckles and teed up Jane. "I think we should see how people vote. I don't know if it needs to be by hand or paper but ..."

Melanie interrupted him and looked at Jane. "Jane, you have done a great job. I'm sorry if I have been holding up everything here. Well, I'm not really sorry ... I think that I just didn't ... hmm ... I didn't, or I just haven't been exposed to ... like Doc said, as many people as you have ..."

She was stumbling heroically, Rossi thought.

"... I've probably been the most privileged person here. Except, of course, I'm a woman. And I have had to live with a man, a white man—my husband—who has *the power*. Men like him always do."

Suddenly, her voice cracked as she realized she couldn't stop. She had no other choice but to explain herself, and that required a confession that took everyone but Rossi by surprise. She forced the words up from her heart to her throat with a breath that required her to grit her teeth. "It's hard ... I mean, my husband is just like you described, Joe. He hired a gardener, a Mexican—I think he is, maybe. Or Latino. Anyway, he told me that they were cheap. Cheap labor is what I thought, but he meant cheap *people* ... worth *less*. Like you said, Regina, sub-human. And did I say anything? No. I didn't even think anything was wrong or unfair ... I didn't even think. At all. And then he tells his buddies, in front of me, that these same people should be rounded up and tossed in a truck and sent back where they came from. And I just stood there and ..."

She was quick to wipe a tear that had escaped and was plummeting down her cheek. "And my children went to private schools. I know what we were thinking ... keep them away ... away from ..." She gathered herself. "My husband insisted that even in college they had to be ... and we had the money. I'm just ... living in our own bubble, I guess." Her voice began to shake noticeably. "So I get to live the American dream, you know. And when my husband, when he bothers to be home, talks to me—he makes it sound like it's a war. Like we have to fight each day to keep what we have. All of the ... rich *crap* we have. So much that we don't even think about it. I don't."

No one wanted to say a word.

Hero reached across the table and slid the tissue box to her. She smiled at him. "Thanks. I can't believe I am getting so emotional." She dabbed her eyes. "It's just being here with you. And hearing that man on the videotape ... and right in front of me. And my own husband is saying some of the same things, like you said, Regina, *in code,* and sometimes he doesn't even bother with hiding it. And I just ignore it all because ... because ..."

She knew why.

So did Rossi and it pained him.

Rossi decided her confession deserved absolution. "Melanie, we all hear you. We do. And I, for one, am just as guilty of ignoring too much bigotry or even people's careless-ness. I heard, or read somewhere, that racism is like a fine dust —a pollen—that fills the air. Sometimes it is worse than other times. But it is invisible to most people. But in a certain light, you can see it. And it just chokes us. Nobody is immune. None of us."

Quiet.

Jane softly posed that the group take a short break. General agreement.

Talk of coffee, restrooms, and stretching one's legs filled the void. Joe decided to quietly speak to Melanie. Rossi could spot a gentleman a mile away. Kim offered to go with Melanie to the ladies room after Joe had hugged Melanie.

Regina looked at Rossi. "About that question I had about my boys in high school, can we exchange email addresses? Once this is over, I'd like to contact you. Now's not a good time, you know?"

Rossi agreed.

———

Once everyone was seated, Russ took up the gauntlet again. "A vote, Jane?"

Kim, sitting next to Russ, said, "I'm good with saying how I vote, but if we still want to go with paper, that's fine, too. And I want to add that ..." The words never came to her lips. She merely looked at Melanie. One woman to another. Rossi surmised that they may not share the same tax bracket, but they shared the same personal betrayal. After a beat, she managed to say, "It's okay. I think I'll just deal with it later. But thank you for your ... for what you said, Melanie."

Jane looked at Adam, the only one who had been silent.

He said, "I'm good. Look, guys. I'm just a part-time college student and a full-time bartender and hopeful musician." He smiled. "I learned more during this week, with you all, than I think I've learned in all the classes I've ever taken. I really respect where you guys are coming from and all your experiences. So, I say let's vote."

And so they did.

45

THE VERDICT SPEAKS FOR ITSELF

The *San Diego Union-Tribune* of October 9, 2017, page A1:

"History will record that slavery was planted on America's soil in 1619. The roots grew so deep that despite Lincoln's best intentions, the cultural, economic, and political consequences of subjugating human beings on the basis of the color of their skin were never going to disappear even if one black man was elected the nation's president. A post-racial society is not defined by one person, it must be plural. In the case of Duke Ellis, it required twelve votes."

Deborah Rossi knew that her husband would be sleeping in this morning. She read the article twice. Then she jumped on her laptop and read *The New York Times* editorial claiming that "the decision in the trial of George 'Duke' Ellis in the Southern District of California in the County of San Diego may evolve into a landmark case as it moves up the appeals process, eventually landing on the docket of the United States Supreme Court. The unanimous decision by the twelve jurors to convict Mr. Ellis on one count of inciting a riot carries with it a maximum of five years imprisonment. More significantly, it would make Ellis 'incapable of holding any political office.' Mr. Ellis's attorney James Devlin immediately appealed the decision."

She began a Google search and saw that the Ellis case had grabbed headlines in Chicago, Los Angeles, Boston, and Atlanta. She stopped searching when her phone rang. It was a reporter from Riverside County asking if this was the home of one of the jurors in the Duke Ellis case, and if Anthony Rossi had any comment on the verdict. Deborah told him what her husband had said last evening at dinner to a reporter for the *San Diego Union-Tribune*:

"*The verdict speaks for itself.*"

The reporter asked if she could print that. Deborah just hung up. *Clearly, this reporter didn't get it.* It was the third call they had received. It would not be the last.

Deborah wondered, *How did these people get our phone number?*

She heard a rustling upstairs and knew that the phone call must have gotten her husband out of bed. She couldn't remember the last time Tony had slept to nine o'clock. Exhaustion can do that.

———

Yesterday, Rossi called her at noon to say that they had reached a verdict and that he was not sure how long it would be before they went into the courtroom and then eventually be released. He sounded relieved but anxious, too. He asked if the protests were still going on.

"Yes, Tony. It is still very crowded around the Federal courthouse and down Broadway." She said she was surprised but relieved that the trial was finally over. She did not ask what the verdict was, nor was it offered. She told him to call again as soon as he knew when she should leave to come downtown to pick him up. She toyed with her earring and sighed. "I bet you are drained."

Truer words were never uttered.

Deborah guessed that her husband would not want her to drive downtown and deal with the protesters. "Tony, I *am* coming to get you, no arguing. Okay? Where should I pick you up?"

He had already discussed this with the other jurors and with the bailiffs. All agreed to either make their own way or have a bailiff take them to the hotel's lobby. From there, relatives or friends could take them home, or the court would pay for an Uber. Rose would go with them because Henry needed to be in the courtroom with Judge Lewis.

———

At three o'clock, Deborah pulled into the parking lot of the Holiday Inn Express. She saw her husband sitting on a bench outside the lobby with what she assumed was the bailiff.

"You must be Rose," Deborah greeted her warmly. "Thank you for all you've done for Anthony and the jurors. I know he is very grateful—I am, too." They shook hands.

"You're very welcome, Mrs. Rossi." Rose hesitated for a moment and then smiled at Rossi and shook his hand as well. She told him, "I rarely say much about the trials I work, Mr. Rossi. But I admire you and the rest of the jury. This wasn't easy for you, I know."

Again Rose considered what was "appropriate" to reveal. "My husband is a detective with the police department. He was able to sit in on the trial during some of the most disturbing testimony. He called me an hour ago to tell me how courageous the decision was. He's seen an awful lot of racism and ..." then she whispered as she looked from side to side, "... in his years on the force, racism is a problem there, too. He wanted me to tell you that you jurors will have a positive impact." She shook Rossi's hand again and wished them both well.

Rossi thanked her. His curiosity needled him. "Rose, your husband is a detective. I can only imagine what challenges he faces."

"Yes. Our last name is *Hernandez*. You both must know how many barriers he has had to climb. I am very proud of him." She let the implication settle. Finally, she looked around noting that everyone was gone but the Rossi's. "Well, I need to get back. Drive safely." And then she walked quickly back to the waiting mini-bus.

Deborah held Rossi's hand as they returned to their car. It was at that point she surmised that he was the last juror there. "Have the other jurors all been picked up, Tony?"

"Well, I called you later after they left. They came over with Rose in the minibus. I walked."

Deborah almost dropped her purse as she was digging for the keys. "You what?"

"I walked over. I needed to. I just couldn't sit another minute." He tried to be as nonchalant as possible.

"Wait. You're telling me you walked out of the courthouse, right into the protest?" Deborah found her keys, but before getting behind the wheel she had to compose herself.

"I didn't throw myself into the protesters, Deborah. Henry showed me out the back door. Come on. Let's go get a beer. I'm hungry for some comfort food."

Deborah knew she didn't want to berate him for what she was sure was something totally in his character. His inquisitiveness would have gotten the better of him. She knew he would tell her what he learned in that detour; he had always been the kind of person who didn't shy away from conflict. He would need time to process what the verdict meant to those who stood vigil on Broadway and Union—both for and against George 'Duke' Ellis.

———

During their early dinner, Rossi had gotten Deborah up to speed with the ebb and flow of the trial, and then the debate that followed in deliberations. He spent some time speaking about certain jurors he had become fond of, especially Doc and Regina.

He had complimented Doc for his patience and wisdom. Doc's metaphor was profound- that we all live on the same ship, and although we can't ignore the differences among the crew, by simply being in close quarters, good people can see that pulling together is what creates a force that is stronger than anyone can imagine. Division merely tears the fabric of society. Doc needed to understand the landscape before he passed judgment. Rossi wished more people could take the time to consider how and why people act as they do.

As for Regina, he told Deborah that he had given her his email. She wanted to continue to pick his brain about how she and her husband could guide their twin boys in high school and beyond. One thing Rossi told her struck a chord. "Regina, many parents assume that once they get their children into high school, they can step back and leave them to their own devices." He emphasized this point, "If anything, that's when you really need to be watchful. It's then that some of the biggest mistakes can occur ... and some of the greatest joys experienced."

Deborah wasn't surprised that Rossi dispensed this advice. She knew all too well the truism. *Once a teacher, always a teacher.*

———

"So how are you feeling this morning?"

"Like I need to *really* retire."

They smiled at each other.

"Hungry?"

"Not quite. Coffee, though." He dropped in a splash of milk.

While he stirred his coffee and shook off the night's cobwebs, Deborah read the text messages from their children. Each one congratulated him for his determination to make a difference in their world. As his oldest daughter Sophie remarked, "You went from the classroom to the courtroom, Dad. We couldn't be prouder." Pete texted, "Dad, I should have never bet against you!" And finally Gina's was all heart, "Hey, Dad, please take Mom on a vacation 'cause you guys deserve it, Love you!"

Deborah Rossi could tell that her husband was still absorbed in the events of the last week. She knew how he processed things. He nibbled around an issue, circling around and around until he reached the crux—always talking to her—but to himself, mostly. That was rarely her method of putting an issue to rest. She could quietly take apart the concern and break it down, understanding the challenges as she reached closure. Their marriage worked because, among other reasons, they both arrived at the same destination sooner or later, no matter how delayed the arrival. Deborah thought about how they navigated the decades in rhythm. More often than not, they could find those moments when they were in time—in step with each other. If not, they knew that the other would wait for them to find that spot where their hands would clasp again. So she allowed him to find his stride, and before long, Anthony Rossi voiced what happened in the courtroom when all was said and done.

———

He would describe the faces of those with whom he served ...

Regina's face, righteous and dignified. Joe Garcia's solemn affirmation as Jane read off the verdict in a calm, controlled voice. Adam's wide eyed recognition of the poignancy of the moment. Russell's steely glare at Duke Ellis. Heroyuki's poker face revealing nothing despite knowing everything. Doc's melancholy over his country's unrelenting effort to remove the stubborn stain of racism. Jim's glance at Judge Lewis, hoping for some hint of affirmation. Lauren's impatience to "get this over with." Kim's awareness of the power of her convictions. And Melanie's defiant expression as she finally stepped out of her husband's shadow. With their unanimity, Anthony Rossi's jury came to this reckoning.

Rossi told Deborah of Roberta Curtis's face as she heard the verdict; the restrained smile that flashed momentarily from the revelation that justice would not be delayed or denied.

About Duke Ellis's face as the shock of an unexpected guilty verdict staggered him.

About James Devlin, inscrutable, placing his hand on Ellis's shoulder.

About prosecutor Jean Peters' face, as she fought to conceal that glimmer of triumph, for this may be the first of many battles she and Patrick Rosen could face in the due course of James Devlin's appeals.

About the reaction of Judge Paul Lewis, whose impartial nature remained so, despite a verdict that aroused the court-room's gallery to guarded applause.

About Henry's farewell advice as Rossi walked out the back door: to remember why they were sequestered in the first place. That the important work of a juror is in "that deliberation room, not in front of the cameras."

About how he peered from afar at the cheering mass of people carrying signs and chanting various slogans. About how passionate they were. About how many of them were young, like his former students.

About how some in the crowd who, like him, were relics of a time when protesting about civil rights or Vietnam or the ERA was a lesson in contrast—either black or white. It was only decades later that the answer turned to a shade of gray.

About the angry, defiant ones waving their flags as they stomped away, vowing incredulously: "This isn't over!"

Deborah would listen to her husband in the days to come. And she understood. *There would be no whitewash of justice this time.*

THE ORIGIN OF WHITEWASH

In the summer of 1978, as I traveled through Europe with a backpack and a first-class Eurail train pass, I had several books tucked in the pack: the trial of Ethel and Julius Rosenberg, Lenny Bruce's life story, Bobby Seale and the Chicago Seven, and Daniel Ellsberg's *Pentagon Papers* were part of my train ride reading material for my two-month trip.

Once I got back to the States and began my second year of teaching, I had the idea of writing a Readers Theater that tested the limits of free speech. The KKK had a foothold in Fallbrook, California, just north of where I taught high school in Rancho Penasquitos. Roger Metzger was making some headlines spouting the usual racist drivel that had been delivered from the Grand Dragon, Robert Shelton (seriously, that's what he was called).

During my Christmas break of two weeks, I, along with my colleague Mark McWilliams, penned *Whitewash*. At the time, I coached the Speech and Debate program at Mount Carmel High School, and we needed a fundraiser—and I needed a cast and a theater. We added the 'slides' (pictures of the historical figures in the script that were blown up on the walls of the theater) and a soundtrack to set the scene for the drama that would unfold.

I was twenty-two years old. Mark was nineteen and in college at UC San Diego. We could not have possibly known that the *show*, as we called it, would be so well received by audiences, reviewed by the *San Diego Union,* and repeated over the course of three decades, once directed by one of my alumni, Karen Harkins Slocomb. The Mount Carmel Drama department even staged it as a play. Over the years, I have been encouraged to revisit the script by many of my friends, notably Linda Englund. During the 'Covid Era,' I reread the original script and concluded that the 1979 production was far ahead of its time.

Donald Trump's divisive language encouraged white supremacists, jingoistic nationalism, and was the prologue to the events that horrified the nation on January 6th, 2021 when the United States Capitol was breached by Trump supporters, claiming that the presidential election was 'stolen' from the former president. Trump's language raised the issue of what *incitement* is, as well as the speaker's responsibility for the events that flow from that *free speech*. At that point, I was convinced that *Whitewash* was relevant—now more than ever.

Some historical figures I read about like the Rosenbergs and Bobby Seale did not all make it into the novelization of *Whitewash*, but the protests that surrounded their controversial lives were part and parcel of how I came to conclude that freedom of speech is to be cherished but can also be abused.

That fine line between the two is what should make each American consider what one says, how one says it, and what implications her or his words create. David Brooks, *The New York Times* columnist and author, crystalized my thoughts on the subject on June 26th, 2020: "Words can thus be a form of violence that has to be regulated."

In a world filled with tweets, Facebook posts, news channels that ignore journalistic standards and riddled with conspiracy theories run amok on social media, only an educated and informed citizenry can ascertain fact from fiction. I should add, there is no such thing as alternative facts—just opinions.

One last thing, when I wrote the Readers Theater version of *Whitewash*, there were two endings. A jury of twelve, selected from the audience, determined whether George 'Duke' Ellis was innocent or guilty of 'inciting a riot.' I will not reveal the results, but I will say this: each performance ended with the audience debating the ending. I hope this novelization of my work of forty years ago gives my readers pause to reconsider assumptions they may harbor.

A Preview of Robert Pacilio's *The Restoration*

In 1947, the Village Theater on Coronado Island held a "by invitation only" Grand Opening. The islanders were excited to have the opportunity to see a movie without navigating their way across the bay to downtown San Diego. Gregory Larson's parents sat in the red plush seats of the Village Theater to see the Best Picture of the Year, *Gentleman's Agreement.* The film so moved them that their son, born months later, would be named for the film's lead actor—Gregory Peck.

World War II was over, and the Baby Boom Generation was born. In the decades to follow, Gregory Larson became enamored with UCLA co-ed Raquel Mendez. Meanwhile, on the Jersey shore, Abby DiFranco held hands with her boyfriend, Navy hero Jack Adams. All four lovers were destined to face the sexual and cultural revolution in America, headlined by the mayhem of the Vietnam War, the debilitating post-traumatic stress disorder that ensued, the corruption of America's political leaders, and the insidious breed of terrorism that originated in the Middle East, eventually spreading across the Atlantic Ocean.

To escape these tumultuous times, the two couples turned to the movies, often a source of inspiration, humor, and hope. But soon even their quaint Village Theater fell victim to the ravages of time and profit margins. Consequently, their favorite cinema was boarded up. Its Art Deco design became dilapidated, and its once spectacular murals of the San Diego skyline vanished into faded, grimy walls and torn curtains. The Village Theater's long-time projectionist mused, "Some awfully sad things that happen just change you, I guess."

When does someone find the courage to face his or her tragic past and haunting loneliness? *The Restoration* begins with a gentleman's agreement that binds Jack Adams and Greg

Larson. But it is the women in their lives, Abby DiFranco and Raquel Mendez, who understand that by restoring the Village Theater to its original grandeur, they are actually restoring themselves—heart and soul. In *The Restoration,* it becomes clear that "you have to break down walls to reconfigure, remodel, and renovate ... you have to leave the best memories and create new ones."

A Preview of *Meet Me at Moonlight Beach*

Noelani Keoka and Lewis Bennett sit next to each other in the waiting room of Dr. Amos Adler, an aging African American psychiatrist, whose unconventional wisdom and loyalty to his patients becomes their life preserver. His two final clients are unaware that they are two of a kind, both trusting souls; blind to the betrayals life delivers in one swift, shattering blow.

Noelani, a native Hawaiian aspires to be a professional dancer in Los Angeles, but her future hinges on the power of her legs to propel her and the pressure of men who pursue her. Lewis has a passion for teaching that is threatened by a rare disease and by his wife's ambition for the finer things in life. How does one react when life's inevitable trials reach beyond one's control? What happens when lovers ignore the warning signs of duplicity in those they trust?

In Robert Pacilio's newest novel *Meet Me at Moonlight Beach,* he explores the physical and emotional consequences that come from misfortune and blind faith. This contemporary novel, set in the coastal town of Encinitas, California, a quaint yoga and surfing Mecca, addresses the resilience necessary to face one's fears, acknowledge the need to change, and embrace love once again. *Meet Me at Moonlight Beach* raises the question of how people can recover when their world suddenly goes dark.

ACKNOWLEDGMENTS

I always wanted to be a singer in a band. Seriously. Alas, I have no musical talent, except the ability to sing out of tune while driving my truck. Luckily, I have always had a 'band' of supporters standing right behind me as I hunt and peck my way while I compose my manuscripts.

As an *independent* author, my band has been my background singers, willing to read, create, cajole, and promote my work into something harmonious and meaningful. Most recently Michelle Nguyen has been my advocate with social media, helping me navigate the Virtual Book Clubs and videos I have produced. Then there are the folks who have been following my work for years: Sandy Gonnerman, Joyce Daubert, Linda Englund, Monique Lampshire Tamayoshi, Faye Visconti, Bob Bjorkquist, Christa Tiernan and Robin Blalock Falcone. All have embraced my efforts, and for that I will be forever thankful.

I would not be able to publish my work if not for the superb work of my editor and interior book designer, Michelle Lovi at Odyssey Publishing in New Zealand. I owe so much to her attention to detail. For *Whitewash,* she designed the cover along with Wesley Tingey's photography.

When it came to the issues of legal jurisprudence, I needed the advice of Karen Harkins Slocomb. Karen also agreed to edit the early drafts. I have had the pleasure of collaborating with her many times over the years and I have learned so much from her. She also directed a production of *Whitewash* in 1998. Rafael Bernadino, the former Los Angeles Police Commissioner, also gave me guidance on the criminality of *incitement,* and that was critical to the novel. (Although to be honest, I strayed from one piece of legal advice he gave me. Fortunately, he excused it and told me to just claim *poetic license.*) David Fares kept listening to my thoughts on trial procedures and read through the early drafts of *Whitewash* always encouraging me. If there are errors, they are mine and mine alone. Hopefully, *poetic license* will excuse some of my gaffes.

There is one person, above all, who is responsible for the novelization of *Whitewash*—Mark McWilliams, my longtime collaborator. We have worked together since 1979 on various Readers Theaters I have written, and many that he directed. One day, when he has the time to step away from his laudable efforts to help those who have been challenged with disabilities, I hope Mark will follow my advice and publish his own work. He is a far better writer than I will ever be, and without his wisdom, I could never have written either versions of *Whitewash.*

I learned long ago that nothing I accomplish matters if I do not have family to share it with. I am immensely grateful that my wife Pam read each draft of *Whitewash* and gave me wise counsel regarding the experience of being on a jury, especially as jurors deliberate the fate of the accused. Pam's support and encouragement has been vital in my transition from teacher to writer.

One last note, the film *12 Angry Men* captures the many prejudices of jurors as they try to be fair and impartial. It was a source of inspiration for me. The American system of justice is not perfect and it never will be. It is a *trial* in the truest sense of the word as we strain to find justice for all.

ABOUT THE AUTHOR

Robert Pacilio was born to teach. He taught high school English for 32 years and was awarded San Diego County's "1998 Teacher of the Year." He has been a regular speaker at various teacher conferences, including the California Teachers Association. *Meetings at the Metaphor Café*, his debut novel, was nominated for the California Young Readers Award, and with its sequel *Midnight Comes to the Metaphor Café*, he enjoys returning to classrooms to read excerpts to students, as he transforms himself into the novel's fictional protagonist, Mr. Buscotti. Both books have been adopted in several school districts.

His two most recent novels, *Meet Me at Moonlight Beach* and *The Restoration,* center on the themes of courage and resilience, as his characters must face physical and emotional trauma while they endeavor to restore their faith in themselves and the ones whom they love. *The Restoration* takes place on San Diego's Coronado Island. The Coronado Historical Society, the Coronado Village Theater, and the Coronado Eagle and Journal have enthusiastically supported his novel. *Meet Me at Moonlight*

Beach is set in his home town of Encinitas, California. The *San Diego Union's* columnist Karla Peterson called *Meet Me at Moonlight Beach* "a love letter to Encinitas ... [Mr. Pacilio] still believes in the power of words. He still loves a good redemption arc. And once he's said his piece, he hopes his audience understands a little bit more about themselves and the world around them, and that they will learn to love what they see."

Mr. Pacilio lives in Encinitas, California, with his wife Pam. His adult children are his pride and joy.

He can be reached at robertpacilio@gmail.com.

His website gives information on his speaking engagements. www.robertpacilio.net

Made in the USA
Middletown, DE
21 September 2021

48431702R00166